Mad Max

UNINTENDED
CONSEQUENCES

Betsy Ashton

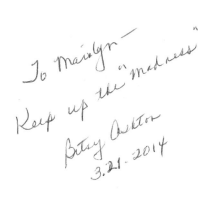

To Marilyn —
Keep up the "madness"
Betsy Ashton
3.21.2014

NEW YORK
VIRGINIA

Mad Max
Unintended Consequences

by Betsy Ashton

© Copyright 2013 by Betsy Ashton

ISBN 9781938467400

Published by
 köehlerbooks™
an imprint of Morgan James Publishing

5 Penn Plaza, 23rd floor
c/o Morgan James Publishing
New York, NY 10001
212-574-7939
www.koehlerbooks.com

Publisher
John Köehler

Executive Editor
Joe Coccaro

 In an effort to support local communities, raise awareness and
funds, Morgan James Publishing donates a percentage of all
book sales for the life of each book to Habitat for Humanity
Peninsula and Greater Williamsburg.
Get involved today, visit www.MorganJamesBuilds.com

Viruses MS2 144
Viscosity 77, 113, 125
—, intrinsic, of protein 110, 113, 115, 135
—, reduced specific 113, 135
Voltage, phototube activating 35

Water, structure 3
Water-alcohol mixtures 139
Water-propanol mixtures 111, 138, 139

Wave length of light 10
Wool 128

Xanthine oxidase 80
Xenon lamps 31—33
X-ray diffraction, analysis 3, 81 ff.
— —, method 5

Yeast alcohol dehydrogenase 100

Molecular Biology, Biochemistry and Biophysics

Volumes published:

Vol. 1 J. H. van't Hoff: Imagination in Science. Translated into English, with Notes and a General Introduction by G. F. Springer. With 1 portrait. VI, 18 pages. 1967. DM 6,60; US $ 2.80

Vol. 2 K. Freudenberg and A. C. Neish: Constitution and Biosynthesis of Lignin. With 10 figures. IX, 129 pages. 1968. DM 28,—; US $ 11.50

Vol. 3 T. Robinson: The Biochemistry of Alkaloids. With 37 figures. X, 149 pages. 1968. DM 39,—; US $ 16.—

Vol. 4 A. S. Spirin and L. P. Gavrilova: The Ribosome. With 26 figures. X, 161 pages. 1969. DM 54,—; US $ 22.20

Vol. 5 B. Jirgensons: Optical Activity of Proteins and Other Macromolecules. 2nd edition. With 71 figures. IX, 199 pages. 1973. DM 59,80; US $ 24.60

Vol. 6 F. Egami and K. Nakamura: Microbial Ribonucleases. With 5 figures. IX, 90 pages. 1969. DM 28,—; US $ 11.50

Vol. 8 Protein Sequence Determination. A Sourcebook of Methods and Techniques. Edited by Saul B. Needleman. With 77 figures. XXI, 345 pages. 1970. DM 84,—; US $ 34.50

Vol. 9 R. Grubb: The Genetic Markers of Human Immunoglobulins. With 8 figures. XII, 152 pages. 1970. DM 42,—; US $ 17.30

Vol. 10 R. J. Lukens: Chemistry of Fungicidal Action. With 8 figures. XIII, 136 pages. 1971. DM 42,—; US $ 17.30

Vol. 11 P. Reeves: The Bacteriocins. With 9 figures. XI, 142 pages. 1972. DM 48,—; US $ 19.70

Vol. 12 T. Ando, M. Yamasaki and K. Suzuki: Protamines: Isolation, Characterization, Structure and Function. With 24 figures. IX, 114 pages. 1973. DM 48,—; US $ 19.70

Vol. 13 P. Jollès and A. Paraf: Chemical and Biological Basis of Adjuvants. With 24 figures. VIII, 153 pages. 1973. DM 48,—; US $ 19.70

Vol. 14 Micromethods in Molecular Biology. Edited by V. Neuhoff. With 275 figures. XV, 428 pages. 1973. DM 98,—; US $ 40.20

Prices are subject to change without notice

Volumes in preparation:

Breuer, H., and K. Dahm: Mode of Action of Estrogens
Burns, R. C., and R. W. F. Hardy: Nitrogen Fixation in Bacteria and Higher Plants
Callan, H. G., and O. Hess: Lampbrush Chromosomes
Chapman, D.: Molecular Biological Aspects of Lipids in Membranes
Haugaard, N., and E. Haugaard: Mechanism of Action of Insulin
Hawkes, F.: Nucleic Acids and Cytology

Volumes in preparation:

JARDETZKY, O., and G. C. K. ROBERTS: High Resolution Nuclear Magnetic Resonance in Molecular Biology

KERSTEN, W., and H. KERSTEN: Antibiotics Inhibiting Nucleic Acid Synthesis

LAUFFER, M. A.: Entropy-Driven Processes in Biology

MATHEWS, M. B.: Molecular Evolution of Connective Tissue

QUASTEL, J. H., and C. S. SUNG: Chemical Regulatory Processes in the Nervous System

SCHANNE, O., and ELENA RUIZ DE CERETTI: Impedance Measurements in Biological Cells

SHULMAN, S.: Tissue Specificity and Autoimmunity

SÖLL, D., and U. L. RAJBHANDARY: Transfer-RNA

VINNIKOV, J. A.: Cytological and Molecular Basis of Sensory Reception

WEISSBLUTH, M.: Hemoglobin: Cooperativity and Electronic Properties

YAGI, K.: Biochemical Aspects of Flavins

Practical Molecular Genetics. Edited by H. MATTHAEI and F. GROS

Acknowledgments

First, to my best friend and husband, Terry Naylor, who read multiple drafts and was always honest in his comments on what I wrote, *Mad Max* is dedicated to you with love.

To my novel "midwives," I thank Sally Roseveare, Susan Coryell, and Becky Mushko for their support in reading early drafts and providing necessary critiques. John Koelsch and Keith Martin read the first fifty pages and gave important guidance. My two writing groups, Lake Writers at Smith Mountain Lake and Valley Writers, the Roanoke chapter of the Virginia Writers Club, encouraged me to read sections of the novel and provided excellent guidance in strengthening key scenes.

To Smith Mountain Arts Council, many thanks for naming an early version of this book its best unpublished novel for 2009.

At Tinker Mountain Writers Workshop, Fred Leebron's group provided critical comments that led to reshaping several main sections of the novel.

To various friends and family who read early drafts and liked the book even then, I hope you'll like it better now. To those friends and family who told me bluntly that I could write better, did I get it right?

Sincere thanks to my agent, Dawn Dowdle at Blue Ridge Literary Agency. Her guidance through multiple edits and one extensive rewrite made this book possible. And to publisher John Koehler, executive editor Joe Coccaro and my patient copy editor, Cheryl Ross, at Koehler Books for believing that *Mad Max* had legs and would appeal to a wide audience.

Had it not been for Abigail Trafford's *My Time: Making the Most of the Bonus Decades after Fifty*, I would never have dared to show what I was writing to anyone outside of a small circle of family and friends. In a sense, Trafford's book gave me permission to enter a new life at the same time as Mad Max enters her own new life.

And last to Chan Preston, whose life experiences provided the impetus to start this story. Some of what happens to Dr. Hunter came from lengthy late night conversations.

CHAPTER ONE

Raney and Eleanor, two of my dearest friends, sat at a small table in Le Bistro in SoHo, gossiping about their grandchildren. I tossed my ankle-length mink trench and fedora atop their coats and slid onto an empty chair. Henri placed a cup of coffee beside me, offered a short list of lunch specials, and vanished into the back.

"Why do we call him 'Henri'?" Raney asked. "His name's Barney."

"Same reason my grandkids call me Mad Max. It fits."

We scanned the menu we all knew by heart. Henri returned, took our orders, and left. Talk returned to our grandchildren. Raney brought me up to date on what her darlings were doing: school dances, track meets, mid-year tests. All the usual stuff.

"My granddaughter's pregnancy is not going as well as it should." Eleanor's perfect, slightly old-fashioned diction revealed her upper-crust British upbringing. "I may go to Phoenix to help."

"Oh, dear," said Raney. "I hope it's not like her first one."

"We will not know for a month or two."

I felt a familiar itch of envy for the easy relationships Eleanor and Raney enjoyed with their daughters. So normal.

"How are your grandkids, Max?" Raney asked.

"Great. Alex can't stop buzzing about his ice hockey team. They're having their first winning season. He's so psyched. Em texts about her next school break. She wants to visit."

I talked to or texted with Alex and Emilie every day since their father, Whip, gave them cell phones for Christmas. I had more fun with my grandkids than I'd had with my own two children. Maybe it was because I had almost no responsibility except to love and spoil them. Maybe it was because I could send them back to their parents when I got tired.

"What about Merry? When was the last time you talked to her?"

"Last week. She complained about how cold January has been."

"She should live in New York." Raney shook her head and laughed.

My daughter and I had an off-again, on-again relationship, which started after her father's death when she was eleven. I wanted us to be more "on" than "off" and worked hard to pick my words so she wouldn't take offense. It didn't take much to set her off at times.

"I was in Richmond over Christmas and spent all my time with the kids. They have their own phones now, so I call them directly. I call Merry just once a week. I don't want to meddle."

"Why do you let her get away with placing such restrictions on your relationship?" Eleanor asked.

"She reminds me grandparents have privileges, not rights. I can't lose contact, so I play by her rules."

Truth be told, I let Merry dictate the terms of our contact with each other, even though I knew I was taking the coward's way out. I'd asked Merry more than once why she seemed distant so much of the time, but she refused to discuss it. I couldn't force her to forgive me for whatever infractions I committed while raising her. All I could do was maintain as calm a demeanor as possible.

"Hey, I scheduled my annual ski trip." I wasn't in the mood for a discussion on something so touchy.

"Changing the subject?" Raney winked at me.

"Sure am."

Henri brought our salads and disappeared. We ate in near silence for a few minutes.

"What do you think about this new artist? He's supposed to be all the rage in Europe."

We always ate at Le Bistro when one of our favorite art galleries had an opening. Otherwise, SoHo was way too far off our beaten path.

"Did you see his catalog?" Raney asked.

"I did. He is too avant-garde for me. I prefer more conventional art where I can actually recognize what the artist painted." Eleanor pulled the catalog from her handbag and flipped it open to a couple of abstract pieces. "Take this one. I do not see 'Forest and Trees' in this swirl of orange, yellow, and red."

"Maybe it's a forest fire." I didn't like the painting because the colors were too vivid. I was, however, interested in a mid-sized portrait of two sisters in more muted colors. I pointed to the painting in the catalog. "I really want this one. So peaceful."

"Where would you hang it? You don't have much wall space left."

Raney was right. I'd hung way too many prints and oils throughout my apartment.

"Probably in my bedroom. I'll move something."

We lingered over lunch and gossip until half an hour after the official opening of the gallery to avoid the crush of patrons pushing to enter.

I milled around wall-to-wall people who sipped wine and talked about the new hot artist having his first New York showing at Primary Colors.

The crowd churned and whirled, groups forming and reforming near the artist holding court in a rear corner. Servers danced around patrons and offered wine and hors d'oeuvres on silver trays. Tiny napkins and toothpicks drifted to the floor in a rain of elegant litter. New guests brought welcome cold air into the room's stuffy heat. It was nearly February. Had the opening been earlier in the winter, expensive perfume would have warred with mothball-protected coats. Mothballs would have won.

Nancy Blair, owner of Primary Colors, worked her way through the crowd and gave me the requisite number of air kisses, two near each cheek. She did the same with Raney and Eleanor, who then moved off to look at the paintings and drawings hanging on matte-white walls. Nancy linked her arm through mine and led me toward the artist.

"Wait till you meet him, Mrs. Davies. He's positively the most amazing painter I've had in the gallery in years." Nancy's breathless delivery was all gush.

As we struggled through the crowd, my cell phone buzzed. I didn't recognize the number, frowned, and flipped up the cover. I shrugged an apology at Nancy.

"Hello."

"Maxine? Is that you?"

"Yes." I pressed a finger against my free ear to block the ambient din.

"It's Bette."

Bette? It took me a second. Right, Merry's mother-in-law. She rarely called.

"What's wrong?"

"It's Merry. She's been in an accident."

Merry? Hurt?

"Come home, Maxine. She may not make it."

I hitched my handbag up on my shoulder, my brain spinning from Bette's message.

"I've got to get out of this noise. I'll call you right back."

I shut the phone, waved at my girlfriends, and pointed toward the coat check.

"I have an emergency," I apologized to Nancy. "I have to leave."

"I'll hold Two Sisters for you."

"Maxine, you look like a ghost crossed your grave. What is wrong?"

Eleanor tipped the coat check girl, and we walked out into the New York winter cold. Crosstown wind made me pull my trench coat tighter around me. Raney stepped off the curb and flagged down a taxi. The skies had dropped since we entered the gallery, and the smell of snow was in the air.

I gave the girls a thumbnail account of Bette's call.

"Could she be overreacting?" Eleanor knew of Bette but not how she might behave in a crisis.

"I don't know. I've never seen her in an emergency."

Before I could press the recall button, a text came through. "Mom's hurt bad. I'm scared. Please come home."

Emilie.

I sent my granddaughter a text and called Bette. "What happened?"

"The police called this morning. Her car ran off the road last night. She's hurt real bad." There was fear in Bette's voice. "The Colonel is at the hospital, but he doesn't know much more than I do. All the police could tell us was that they found her car this morning."

"I don't understand."

"I'll tell you more later. She's in surgery. A herd of specialists are working on her."

"But—"

"Just hurry, please."

"I'll be there as soon as I can." I clamped down on my emotions and tried not to panic. "Where's Whip?"

"He's been in the Middle East for several weeks. He's due home today. We've tried reaching him, but no luck. He's probably in the air. We had the kids overnight and got the call this morning when the Colonel and I were driving them home."

"How did they find you?"

"I don't know. Anyway, the Colonel dropped the children and me at their house and went straight to the hospital. Call me here. Oh, here's the Colonel's cell number."

Bette rattled off a series of numbers. Before I could fumble for a piece of paper, Eleanor held up a small notebook and a silver pen. I repeated the number to be certain I heard it right. Eleanor jotted it down.

"One more thing. The EMTs airlifted Merry to Virginia Commonwealth Medical Center, not County."

"Why?"

"VCU has a better trauma center."

"I see. I'll be in touch. Thanks." I shut the phone.

Eleanor and Raney talked over each other in their efforts to find out what happened. I told them what little I knew. Our cab hit every possible red light as we made our way uptown where shoppers and tourists thronged the sidewalks in spite of the cold wind. Our driver stomped on the brake when a couple stepped into traffic without looking. When we stopped in front of my building on the Upper East Side, my doorman hurried to help. Eleanor asked him to call my car service.

Raney took charge of getting my bag packed. "You find a flight. We'll do the rest."

I worked my phone until I found the last seat on a US Airways flight to Richmond through Washington National. I had just over two hours to pack and get to LaGuardia. I glanced out the window. Oh great. Snow.

"How long do you think you will be gone?" Eleanor moved through my bedroom, selected clothes, folded them, and put them into my roll-aboard suitcase.

"No idea. A week, probably."

I stood helpless near the window and looked across Park Avenue into the snowy park. *Please don't let Merry die.*

With all that was on my mind, I forgot to change out of my standard gallery attire— cashmere sweater, matching wool trousers, scarf, and boots. I'd been channeling Ingrid Bergman, elegant and understated.

I called the hospital but got the runaround. An emergency room nurse told me she couldn't give out patient information; it was against regulations. I wanted to shout "Regulations, my ass! I'm her mother!" but I knew it would do no good.

I called the Colonel. He hadn't seen Merry. When he arrived, a half-dozen doctors were in a curtained-off area at the back of the emergency room. He used his colonel's voice, but the ER nurse was adamant.

"Should've been a drill sergeant."

The Colonel's words made me smile for the first time since Bette called.

I called Emilie next. She was scared and worried about her mother.

"I feel Mom's dying."

"I'm on my way. My flight leaves in a couple of hours. If you find out anything, text. Okay?"

"Okay."

My phone buzzed again with a text from Alex. "I beat Em at Clue last night. Mom wrecked her car."

I held out the phone to Eleanor and Raney. "Trust a ten-year-old to have his priorities straight."

I walked toward my apartment door then stopped and took a detour into a guest bedroom. I rummaged through a drawer until I found a battered toy, which I tucked into my shoulder bag.

Raney opened the door, and we left my apartment. The ten seconds we waited for the elevator seemed like an hour.

"Try and keep things on the 'on' side with Merry." Raney put her arm around my waist. I heard "before it's too late" even though Raney was too diplomatic to say so.

"Make this a wake-up call."

I hugged my friends, promised to call, and stepped into my car.

"I'll do my best. Just hope it's good enough."

Raney blocked the door. "Did you ever think we'd see Maxine Davies have a Mommy two-dot-oh moment, Eleanor?"

"Certainly not."

"Merry'll tell you I wasn't good at Mommy one dot oh."

"Well, now you have a second opportunity."

"Life is giving you a ...," Eleanor fumbled for a word, "doo-wop."

"Do over." Raney laughed.

"You guys are giving me a do over?"

"Don't blow it." Raney shut the car door and stepped back. Both women waved goodbye.

CHAPTER TWO

Less than four hours after I spoke with Bette, I walked down the center aisle of that last plane to National with a connection to Richmond and found my seat. The last one in the middle of the last row. I squeezed between a large woman in the window seat and an even larger man on the aisle. I fetched the toy from my bag and held it in my lap. I closed my eyes and leaned against the back of the upright seat. I couldn't recline an inch since there was a bathroom right behind me. Before I realized what was happening, memories, like an old movie, began their thousandth rerun in my head.

My husband Norm and I returned from a Friday night dinner date. We laughed and talked about stopping at the farm store for ice cream and cones for the kids.

I looked past Norm in the passenger seat. Two pairs of headlights raced toward me. Before I could react, one car slammed into the passenger side and spun us out of control. The second car braked and veered to the right, rolled over in a corn field and exploded in a fireball.

I was pinned to the driver's door, my husband's bleeding body in my arms. The driver of the lead car stared at me out of dead eyes, his body halfway through his windshield. I couldn't see Norm's face, but his blood soaked my lap. I was sure I held a dead man. I screamed and screamed before passing out.

I stopped the movie at the end of the first reel, unable to watch it from beginning to end. I wanted to look out the window, but the woman had pulled down the shade and stuffed her pillow into the recess. I stared at the top of a balding head in the fully-reclined seat in front of me and sighed. I was one second away from pitching a fit and elbowing the people beside me. If either moved a hair, I'd be squished. I wanted to cry and wring my hands, but I couldn't. Not in public. Instead, I stroked the toy, finding solace in its familiar worn spots.

I revived as the fire department cut me free. I thrashed and screamed, "Please. My children. Take me to my children!" My stomach convulsed, and I thought I'd throw up. Instead, I hiccupped.

A doctor set my broken wrist, told me there was nothing he could do for my ribs, and kept me in the hospital overnight to be sure I didn't have a concussion. The next day, my sister-in-law brought fresh clothes and drove me home. I sleepwalked into the house to deal with two distraught kids.

The jet bounced to a landing in Richmond so uncomfortable it threw us against our seat belts and sent loose items racing down the aisle. I might not have been able to move side to side, but nothing stopped me from lurching forward. Had there been any room in the overheads, sure as hell items would have shifted during flight.

I grabbed a cab, phoned the Colonel, and fretted most of the way to VCU. When the taxi pulled up at the emergency room entrance, I put on my I'm-wearing-my-big-girl-panties-and-can-deal-with-anything face and marched through the automatic doors. The Colonel met me, held me in a worried hug, and took charge of my roll-aboard. Door to door, it was less than twelve hours since Bette's call.

"No news."

Please don't let Merry die. I wanted to hold her again.

The molded plastic hospital chair in the ICU waiting room didn't fit my body, so I sat upright, two inches of space between my spine and the chair back. I tried to relax and meditate, but all I could do was chant the same thing over and over: *Please don't let Merry die.* My throat constricted and tears burned the backs of my eyes. I stepped into the bathroom.

When I came back into the waiting room, I sat and dozed. Instead of the bad dream, my mind drifted over happier times with my children. I remembered vacations at the beach, birthday parties, and trips to amusement parks. I even remembered cleaning up Merry's vomit the first, and last, time I took her on a rollercoaster.

I tried not to wring my hands, but the ache in the right one told me I failed. I'd talked to the doctor in charge of her care, a Dr. Jenkins, soon after I arrived, but he knew little more than that her injuries were extensive. They were treating each crisis as it occurred.

"I need authorization for this and other surgeries."

Other surgeries? What other surgeries?

"Is her husband here yet?"

"Not yet," the Colonel said. "We've left messages on his cell."

"We can't wait. What's your relationship to Mrs. Pugh?"

"Father-in-law." Dr. Jenkins shook his head. He looked at me.

"Mother."

"You'll do."

The doctor handed me a form. I scribbled a barely legible signature.

"If she makes it through the next twenty-four hours, she has a chance."

I blocked out all thoughts of Merry dying. I sucked in my stomach and thrust my stubborn chin out.

Across the room, the Colonel dozed, breath burbling with each respiration, chin on his chest. He snorted awake, which startled me out of my reverie. Merry's doctor stood in the doorway. He must have seen fear on our faces, because he held up a hand, palm outward.

"No change. She's still in surgery. She was bleeding into her chest. I'll be back when there's news. Don't worry if I'm gone a while. We've got a lot of work to do. Why don't you get something to eat? The cafeteria hasn't poisoned anyone lately." With that, Dr. Jenkins loped toward the elevators.

The Colonel said he'd stay in the room and wait for Whip if I wanted to get coffee or something to eat.

I walked down seven flights of stairs to the cafeteria. I needed to move and didn't want to be confined in an elevator. After picking up a coffee and sandwich, I caught a glimpse of my reflection in a window. I was a mess. I'd left the fedora at my apartment, but my highlighted hair needed a good combing. I tucked my hair behind my left ear, leaving the right side to graze my chin. I flipped open my phone and punched Raney's number on speed dial.

"Talk to me." Raney was as blunt as it got.

I told her what little I knew.

"So, Merry's in a coma?"

"Yes. The Colonel said no one's been able to talk with her."

"Are you holding up all right?"

"Almost. I tried to doze on the plane, but my mind kept rerunning images of Norm's death. Everything was as vivid as it was the first time. I haven't seen Merry, but I keep imagining what she went through. I want to throw up."

"I shouldn't wonder."

"I called Jack in Oregon. He's stuck in Portland. Both kids have the chicken pox. Neither he nor Merry had them." I rubbed my right temple and played with the sandwich I didn't want. I wished my son lived closer. "Whip should be home soon."

"Good. The sooner the better, huh?" Raney turned down the volume on her CD. *Vivaldi. I love Vivaldi.*

"You know, when you told me to take it easy on Merry before it's too late—"

"I never said that!"

"I realized I don't know how. She's blamed me for her father's death since she was eleven. She's said, more than once, if her father was driving, he'd be alive today."

"That's bullshit."

"I think Merry would be glad if I'd died as long as her daddy was still alive."

"That was so long ago. Surely she doesn't still blame you."

"She does."

As recently as last summer, Merry's off switch flipped. Out of nowhere, she said it was my fault her daddy was dead. I bit my tongue. That wasn't the time to try and talk rationally with her.

"Hostility was Merry's way of coping with the un-cope-able. She did a damned good job pushing me away."

Merry's grief turned into anger when I could no longer be a stay-at-home mom. She and Jack became latchkey kids with Merry in charge of her younger brother when I went back to school and later to work. That was when I began skating on a teeter-totter around her.

"That's not rational."

"Neither is blaming me for something I couldn't prevent. She said I abandoned her when I went back to work."

"Well, you aren't abandoning her now. You're there."

"Will it be enough? I want us to get along."

"You may have to go ninety percent of the way. Can you do that?"

"Absolutely. For my sake, as well as hers."

"You're way too self-controlled for your own good. Let her see how you feel."

Raney was right.

I needed to let more of my emotions show. "Now I have one more thing to work on. Transforming me into someone Merry likes."

"Only if you want to. Catch you a little later."

I tucked my cell into my handbag then pulled it out and sent Raney a text. "Love you. Thx."

I picked up two more coffees and the local newspaper and rode the elevator upstairs. The Colonel took the paper and a coffee.

"Haven't seen the doctor since you left." The Colonel blew across his coffee.

CHAPTER THREE

A couple of hours after midnight, Dr. Jenkins returned with a fistful of X-rays. He led us to an examination room and slapped the film up on light boxes.

"I gotta be honest with you. I'm surprised your daughter's still alive. If it wasn't so cold overnight, she'd have bled to death."

The room swayed, but I kept from fainting by drawing several deep breaths. The best way to prepare for Merry's future was to know the extent of her injuries. The doctor flipped on the light boxes.

The Colonel gestured to a group of X-rays. "What's this?"

"That's Merry's skull and face."

I dug my fingers into the Colonel's arm and clung to him to keep from falling. Dr. Jenkins faced the wall, unaware of the mini-drama playing out behind him.

Norm's death was the first time I fainted at the sight of blood. Before, it never bothered me. My son, Jack, was an adventurous little boy, always splitting a lip or cutting his scalp or stepping on a rusty nail. I swabbed and bandaged and wrapped without a second thought. After being saturated with my husband's blood, however, I couldn't handle the sight or copper smell.

"Her left eye socket was pulverized, but the eye itself is uninjured. Bones heal. Her face can be reconstructed."

"What's that?" I pointed to a dark area behind her forehead.

"A hematoma— a large collection of blood. It's growing, meaning a vessel's leaking somewhere and causing her brain to swell. We have a neurosurgeon standing by. Looks like she hit the windshield. Her head stopped, but her brain bounced around inside her skull. It caused the worst damage."

I was dizzy and disoriented when I awoke. What was I doing in a hospital bed? Why was my head throbbing? Did I have a bandage on my forehead? Why was the room spinning?

The last thing I remembered was heading for a face plant on a tile floor. I lifted my head to a pounding both inside and out. The inside pounding was a raging headache; the outside pounding was a gentle tap at my door.

"Merry's in surgery again. More internal bleeding." The Colonel entered my room.

"What the hell happened?"

"You fainted, but you'll be okay. A few stitches, possible concussion. You'll heal."

"Any news from Whip?"

"Nothing. His flight must have been delayed. Merry had the information in her handbag, so we can't get to it. Em's not worried, though. She says he's all right. Besides, she has enough worrying to do about her mother."

"Nothing new from the police?"

The Colonel shook his head. "They said she ran off the road around ten last night, but her car wasn't found until early yesterday morning. It took them time to figure out who Merry was, find us, and for us to call you."

"I don't understand." Had I fallen down the rabbit hole? If this was Wonderland, there was nothing wonderful about it. "Why did it take them so long?"

"I'm not sure."

"Someone must have seen what happened. Don't the police have any witnesses?"

"None so far."

"It just doesn't make sense."

"Her car was in the river."

"In the river? As in, under water?"

"Nose first in the mud. A fallen snag stopped the car from plunging into the James."

A frightening image emerged of the dark waters luring the car downward. Then a vision of skeletal wooden fingers trapping the car and snatching Merry from death.

"There had to be another driver."

"There was. The cops found an overturned truck off the road. They thought it was a single-car accident because there were no skid marks. Just past dawn a jogger spotted tire marks in the grass leading to the river and looked down the embankment. He saw the car's rear bumper jutting out of the muddy bank and called nine-one-one. Only then did the police realize a second car was involved."

"What did the other driver say?"

"Nothing. He's dead."

CHAPTER FOUR

The Colonel left, and I stared at the ceiling. I wanted to see my daughter, but my doctor wouldn't allow it. Different doctor than Merry's. I might have been able to talk Dr. Jenkins into letting me at least take a wheelchair ride to the ICU. This doctor, whose name I couldn't remember, dismissed my request with a flip of the hand. *Bastard.*

I counted the ceiling tiles yet again. Twenty-four across, sixteen down. I slept until I sensed I was no longer alone. I peeled my good eye open. A relieved-looking Colonel led Whip into my room. I'd never been so happy to see my son-in-law.

"Whip! You're here."

I held out my hand. Whip seized it in a two-handed death grip and leaned over to kiss my cheek.

"Just got in."

"So you haven't seen Merry?"

"Not yet. Down getting an MRI. Right, Pop?"

The Colonel nodded. "Checking on the bleeding in her brain."

"No change, huh?"

"Not really."

"What did the doctor say? Is she going to be all right?"

Whip asked the question each of us had asked so many times. All we knew was Merry was in bad shape.

"Find a wheelchair, Colonel. I'm coming with you."

"Will your doctor—"

I held up a finger. No one was going to stop me, even if I returned to this sterile hospital room later feeling dreadful.

The Colonel rushed me into the elevator and up to ICU. He turned into the waiting room and pointed Whip toward a hard plastic chair. Whip poured a cup of stale coffee and gulped it. His hands trembling, he paced. "Gotta talk to Merry's doctor."

"We've got specialists all over the place, but Dr. Jenkins is in charge. He's been here since the ambulance brought her in."

"Didn't Merry say anything about the wreck?"

A gurney whooshed by, two orderlies guiding it down the corridor. I barely glanced at the heavily bandaged thing on it.

"Nothing. She's unconscious, son."

When the Colonel called Whip "son," he was serious.

"Was that Merry?"

"Yeah."

Before the Colonel could stop him, Whip ran out the door. We chased the gurney and stopped just outside Merry's room. VCU's ICU was state-of-the-art with glass walls facing nurses' stations. Two orderlies lifted Merry into bed, hung intravenous bags on racks, plugged her into monitors, and pulled blankets up over her breasts. Her head and face were covered with bandages with slits for her nose and mouth.

A nurse materialized at Whip's side. "Are you Mr. Pugh?"

Whip couldn't take his eyes off the bandaged face. "Yeah."

"The doctor wants to talk with you."

The nurse's image reflected in the glass separating us from Merry. Didn't nurses used to wear white? This one wore a flowery tunic.

"Dr. Jenkins to ICU. Dr. Jenkins," a disembodied voice came over the intercom.

Six minutes later, a young man in stained surgical scrubs bounded up, pulled off Latex gloves, and tossed them into a trash can.

"Hello, Colonel. Mr. Pugh?" Dr. Jenkins looked from father to son.

"Yes."

"I'm Scott Jenkins."

"Winston Pugh."

They shook hands.

"Mr. Pugh—"

"Call me Whip."

"Whip."

"How's Merry?" Whip scratched the back of his hand.

"We've stabilized her."

"Will she be all right?"

I'd asked if Merry would live, more than once. Listening to Whip ask the same thing wasn't getting us anywhere.

"What are you doing out of bed, Mrs. Davies?" Jenkins frowned. He stalled for time before answering Whip's question.

"Waiting to hear how Merry is. Now, will she be all right?"

"I'll let you stay if you promise not to faint again."

I winced at the headache doing a Ringo Starr impersonation behind my eyelids and gave Dr. Jenkins a thumbs-up.

"Back to your question, I have no idea if Merry will be all right, but I think she'll live."

The three of us stared at the doctor. An honest man who didn't have all the answers? No "It's too soon to tell" or "We're doing all we can" bullshit. I could trust Jenkins because he was as blunt as me.

"It's a good thing she was in the car so long. The cold, her heavy coat, and being unconscious probably saved her life."

"How so?" Whip rubbed tired eyes.

"Her body temp was low enough to slow down blood loss. She was unconscious, so she didn't struggle. Otherwise, she'd have bled out, um, sorry, bled to death, before anyone found her. Merry suffered broken ribs, a punctured lung, and damage to her pelvis. Her face hit the windshield or steering wheel. Parts of her face were shattered too. Left eye socket, the zygomaticomaxillary complex—"

"The what?"

"The cheekbone. Some damage to the upper jaw too. We can put the bones back together over time, but I'm most worried about the swelling in her brain. We still haven't found what's causing it."

"Is the damage permanent?" I asked, hoping not to faint again.

"The damage could be permanent. It might not. I'm not a neurosurgeon." Dr. Jenkins turned to Whip. "I'm sorry about the baby."

"What baby? Merry was pregnant?" Whip shook his head as if trying to clear his thoughts. "I had no idea."

"She was about eight weeks along. Not much more."

Oh shit. She lost another baby.

The Colonel patted my shoulder.

"Can I talk to her?" Whip turned toward the ICU.

"Yes, but she won't respond. We're keeping her in a coma. Maybe she can hear you, maybe not."

CHAPTER FIVE

Back on my floor, an angry orderly pushed the Colonel aside, fussed me back into bed, and warned me not to leave the room again. I was too tired to argue. I lay back and slept.

When I woke up, I pulled a mirror from my makeup bag and finally took a look at the damage I'd done to my face. A bandage at the hairline. Plus a black eye. I'd heal. I combed at my hair. It was hopeless.

A throat cleared.

"Come in, Darla." I started to nod toward a chair but remembered my headache.

Best friends, Merry and Darla were inseparable, so I saw her often when I came to visit. I hadn't been back to Riverbend since Christmas, though. I wished we were meeting under better circumstances.

Darla's eyes were red rimmed. Before I could open my mouth, she burst out with, "It's all my fault! I should never have let her drive." She buried her face in her hands. "It's so sad."

"Yes, it is. You knew she was pregnant?"

"Uh-huh. She couldn't wait to tell Whip. They've tried so hard."

"What did you guys do the day of the accident?"

"Normal stuff. Shopped, gossiped, went to a movie, had dinner." Her smile was watery.

"Merry didn't drink, did she?"

I couldn't imagine her drinking more than a glass of wine even if she weren't pregnant. She'd never drive drunk, not after she accused me of drinking and driving when her father died. I'd had two drinks at dinner that night. Both were iced tea. Unfortunately, Merry never believed me.

"Well, we were celebrating the baby. Only a glass of Merlot. Merry said she wasn't going to lose this baby. She was so happy."

"How do you know about the accident? Has it been on the news?"

"No. We went to Saks's semi-annual shoe and handbag blowout. We were both way bad." This time the smile was sunny. Darla's tears stopped. "I had her purchases in my trunk, so I took them by the house. Bette told me."

I rested on my pillows and relaxed to Darla's prattle about their day.

"Merry was late. Traffic sucked, but we still found some great bargains. I bought a pair of boots to die for. Winter white, above-the-knee, with four-inch heels. Merry warned me I'd break my neck in them, but I don't plan to wear them outside. Those babies will never touch rain or snow. Miracle of miracles, they came in my size."

"Did Merry buy any handbags?" My daughter and I shared a passion for extravagant purses.

"A Prada and a Jimmy Choo. Even at seventy percent off, they were obscenely overpriced. She was lucky there was nothing else she liked. She spent a boatload of money.

"Anyway, we stuffed everything in my car and went off to cry through a chick flick. Then we walked the length of the mall to Charley Brown's for dinner. Just after we settled into our booth, Merry's phone vibrated. Alex asked if he and Em could spend the night with his grandparents. Bette said it was fine, so we didn't have to eat and run."

"Was Merry tired? Her first trimester was always wicked bad."

When she carried Alex, she dragged her butt around the first four months, almost too exhausted to move. She called the baby a welcome little parasite that drained her energy.

I realized Darla didn't know Merry lost the baby. Time enough for that later.

"I think so." Darla walked around my room and twisted the Venetian blinds open.

"The last thing I said was 'drive carefully.' She said she was fine and would call me soon. She'd take the back way. The road was dry, so I didn't worry about her crossing the old trestle bridge. I shouldn't have listened. I should have driven her home. It wouldn't have been that big a deal."

"Well, you didn't. Don't beat yourself up for taking Merry at her word."

Merry met Darla thirteen years earlier in their obstetrician's waiting room when she was pregnant with Emilie and Darla was carrying Molly. Merry joked they must be related because she was born a Livingston and Darla married one. Though they never established kinship, they became sisters by choice. Later Darla became my second daughter.

"Merry's a big girl. She'd have told you if she was too tired. From what little we know, a pickup hit her where the road turns down from that narrow bridge. Threw her car over the edge of the embankment toward the river. She must not have seen it. No skid marks. It was an accident, pure and simple."

Darla seemed unconvinced. If anyone could sell tickets for a guilt trip, she could.

CHAPTER SIX

I was trapped in my hospital room, waiting for my doctor to get around to releasing me. I hadn't seen him yet and wondered how he could assess my physical status from afar. If he didn't show up within an hour, I was checking myself out. When my phone rang, I sat up way too fast and paid a terrible price.

"Hello."

"Max? It's Raney. How's Merry?"

"No change."

I tried to tuck my cell under my chin, but that made my head hurt worse. I sucked in a deep breath and regretted it. I hated the smell of hospitals. Too much antiseptic, alcohol, and other disinfectants. I sneezed.

"Oh dear."

"She keeps bleeding into her brain."

"You don't sound so good yourself. Are you all right?"

"Stupid me. You know how I love the sight of blood."

"All too well. Eleanor and I've picked you up off the floor more than once." Raney laughed. "Don't tell me you fainted."

"That's too genteel. The Colonel said I did a major-league face plant when I saw the X-rays of Merry's face and skull."

"Are you all right?"

"Do you remember the dancing hippos in *Fantasia*?"

"Okay, you've lost your mind."

"Nothing so melodramatic. Six stitches and a headache that feels like those damned hippos in a conga line."

"That's an image I won't forget, thank you very much. Seriously, do you think Merry's going to be all right?"

I pushed at my pillows and twitched the less-than-attractive hospital gown higher on my shoulders.

"Seriously, I have no flipping clue. Whip's with her and the Colonel's been running himself ragged bringing me news. I went up to ICU to see for myself but got busted back to jail."

"Good one. You hate people telling you what to do."

"You've got that right. The doctor's worried she may have brain damage. She was pregnant, too, and lost the baby."

"Oh dear. Do you need me?" Raney would be on the next flight if I asked.

"Not yet. Every hour she lives gives me hope. We'll cope with what comes next, later." I wiped tears from my cheeks. "Don't look for me to come home soon, though. I can't leave until Merry's out of danger."

If she's out of danger. Unbidden, the awful thought ducked out from behind a hippo. Get back there.

"What will Merry say when she wakes up and sees you?"

"She'll accuse me of butting in. As usual." I willed the pain to stop, but it ignored me.

"Let me know if you need anything."

We said our goodbyes and hung up. I didn't hear Whip until he sat next to my bed.

"You look like death eating a cracker."

"Back atcha, Max."

"Thanks. I resemble that. How's Merry?"

"Back in recovery. Stopped the bleeding. For now." Whip leaned forward, elbows on his knees. "Really glad you're here."

"What does Dr. Jenkins say?"

"If there are no more major complications, they'll try to wake her up in two days."

"Oh dear." I reached out and took Whip's hand. "How're you holding up?"

"Not as good as I look." Whip knuckled bloodshot eyes. "Gotta stay with Merry until she's conscious, at least. Haven't thought about what happens afterward."

"So, are your parents going to stay with the kids?"

"Can't ask them. Mom's got her hands full taking care of Pop. You've seen how bad he is."

I had.

"It's his heart. Keeps postponing an angioplasty. Mom thinks he has a blockage."

Whip's eyes looked even sadder than they did a few minutes earlier. He stared through the half-closed blinds beyond my bed at yet another gray wintery day. Pages for doctors whispered through the partly-closed door.

"Can't leave Merry," he said.

In between naps and bouts of fear, I thought about a promise I made to myself when I left Richmond, when I put bad memories behind me. After I married my second husband, I relocated to New York City and settled in. I created my own mantra: I'm never living in the South again, and I'm through raising children. Merry's accident blew that mantra out of the water.

"Send the Colonel and Bette home. I'll take care of Alex and Em for a few days. Okay with you?"

"Thanks." The relieved look on Whip's haggard face was all the answer I needed.

"Leave the kids to me." Not the time to talk about the length of my involvement.

There was a tap at the door. A uniformed policeman, belt weighed down with the tools of his trade, beckoned to Whip.

"Come on in, Jerry." Whip met him halfway. They slapped each other on the back.

"The Colonel told me where to find you." Jerry rolled bowlegged into my room.

"Max, this is my friend Jerry Skelton. We shoot together at the range. Jerry, meet Merry's mother, Maxine Davies."

"I've heard a lot about you, Mrs. Davies." Jerry nodded and shook my hand.

"Unless you have bail bond receipts, it's all lies." I laughed and winced. Will I ever learn?

"I heard about Merry and wanted to stop by."

"Thanks."

"I talked to the cop who found the truck."

"Let me guess: drunk driver." It was the only answer that made sense.

"Yes, ma'am. Blood alcohol count three times the legal limit."

Whip clenched his fists. "Dead?"

"At the scene."

"Any other details?"

"He was a regular at your neighborhood bar, Buddy's."

"Buddy's? Go there all the time with Merry. A regular, huh?" Whip frowned. "Wonder if we knew him."

Jerry pulled out his notebook and flipped pages. "Name's Herbert Griffith."

"The guy from the GE plant? Never known him to get drunk. Couple of beers, a game of pool or two, some bullshit stories. Nice enough guy. Shit, even shot pool with him a few times."

What are the odds of Merry being injured by someone she and Whip know?

CHAPTER SEVEN

My doctor released me with orders to take it easy. I signed the forms and went back to the ICU waiting area, steeled against the possibility of bad news. I peeked into Merry's room and saw she was plugged into a wall of devices with beepers and moving lines. I flashed back to the TV series *The Bionic Woman*. *Please don't let this be her future.*

Whip held Merry's hand and told her about his trip to Abu Dhabi. I stood in the doorway as if watching a tableau. Whip was in such obvious pain that my heart thudded loudly. I remembered better times just after they met.

Every summer ended with the Battle of the Bands at Riverside Park. The year after she graduated from high school, Merry went to the concert with several girlfriends and was still giddy the next day over this cute drummer she met. I overheard her talking on the phone to a girlfriend who was home sick with a bad cold.

"He's totally gorgeous. No, they didn't win, but I actually went up and introduced myself."

Merry paused.

"Tall, tanned, dark hair."

Another pause.

"No, really short hair. I wish it were longer, but it'll grow out."

Pause.

"He invited me out for a beer."

A beer? Merry doesn't drink.

"Of course I went. What do you think, I'm stupid? Yes, I even drank part of a beer."

She did?

"Yes, he asked for my number. We're going out next week before he goes back to college."

College? How old is this guy anyway?

"His parents live in town, but he goes to the Colorado School of Mines."

Oh well, this could be a short summer romance.

"He's going to be an engineer."

Passenger train or freight?

"I'm going to marry him."

You are?

Whip and Merry lived a cliché. They fell in love that day at the rock concert. Now, seventeen plus years later, Merry and Whip were still happily married, wrapped up in each other and the kids.

Whip stepped out of the room.

"Any response?" I gazed around him at the mummy.

"None."

The Colonel snorted awake and dry washed his face with his hands.

"Can you take me home, Colonel?"

Home? Home was New York City. Where the hell did that slip come from? Thank you very much, Dr. Freud!

I whispered, "I love you," kissed Merry's bandaged forehead, and promised to be back soon. I avoided the indignity of being "driven" to the hospital door in a wheelchair by going up to see Merry. Arm in arm with the Colonel, I marched out the same way I entered—on my feet and on my own terms.

The sun had come out, but its brightness did nothing to lighten my mood. I chatted with the Colonel for a few minutes, but my mind whirled with everything I'd have to do to change my life, even for a few weeks.

While my gut knew Merry's recovery would be lengthy, if at all, I could only see myself helping until Whip got his head around raising the kids. I pulled my BlackBerry out and scanned my upcoming meetings, marking those I could move, those I could do by conference call, and those I'd have to go back to New York to attend.

The Colonel and I completed the drive to the suburbs in silence. I stared at the winter-shrouded yards when we turned into Riverbend, long one of the most desirable suburbs near Richmond. Bare limbed specimen trees accented each front yard, as precise as Buckingham Palace guards. Bushes displayed end-of-season haircuts; some were wrapped in burlap to prevent frostbite. This region got frost and snow. Why grow plants not rated for your hardiness zone?

I looked at Merry's street through a different lens. Up until that moment, I'd seen the street for what it was—an upscale suburban enclave on the outskirts of a medium-sized Virginia city. Now I looked at it as a place where I might live for a few weeks. The focus shifted. The view made me uncomfortable.

Whip and Merry lived at the end of a cul-de-sac, the only whitewashed brick in a cluster of redbrick colonials. At least the white showed a modicum of originality. The black shutters and red door were the approved decorating treatment for every two-story house in the neighborhood, no matter the outside color.

Dear God, Merry's raising Alex and Emilie in a Hallmark Hall of Fame suburb. I bet everyone baked the same cookies on the same day. I shuddered. I left this lifestyle behind so long ago. Can I really return to it, even for a short period of time? I'd be happier taking the kids to New York. My apartment had more than enough room.

Bette met us at the door. She appeared worried about the Colonel. Truth be told, so was I. He looked ready to collapse. His heart must be worse than Whip knew. Then she saw my face.

"The Colonel told me you fell. Are you all right?"

"Looks worse than it is. Besides, Alex is going to love teasing me about my black eye." I looked around the entryway. "Are the kids home yet?"

It was early afternoon.

"Not until four."

Bette led us into the kitchen and ground coffee for a fresh pot. I inhaled with a sigh of gratitude and turned half an ear toward the Colonel's latest recap. Merry's house was a stark contrast to my formal apartment. I looked around and recoiled from the fake country motif. Everything had a rooster or chicken on it.

Wasn't this cows and sheep at Christmas? When did she switch to chickens? Too much junk on the countertops made them unuseable.

"Maxine? Earth to Maxine. Cups?"

"Sorry." I searched for and found cups, sugar and cream, and spoons. Bette put some cookies on a plate, and we sat at the round pine table.

"We've talked about taking the kids home with us, but we live too far away to get them to and from school every day." Bette stirred sugar into her coffee and picked up an Oreo. "It would be different if it were summer vacation."

"Well, it isn't. It's out of the question. You'd spend all day shuttling the kids around."

I tried to remember where their house was. I'd been there a time or two, but all I remembered was it was way out on the east side of Richmond, beyond the farm community where I grew up.

"We can take Em and Alex on some weekends. Will that help?"

"Absolutely."

Keeping control of my emotions was practiced conditioning that started not long after I became a single mother. Perhaps it was a way of protecting myself. Perhaps it was necessary to keep my family moving forward. I never could decide which it was, but it didn't matter. Being in control kicked in whenever there was a crisis.

"Now, Colonel, don't pull that face. No arguing. You both need some rest. We'll work through this together. Okay?"

The Colonel looked at Bette and then smiled.

An hour before the first bus was due, Bette bundled the Colonel into the car and drove away. I used the time to snoop into every room in the house. Emilie's bedroom was neat and organized. Alex's belonged to a ten-year-old boy. The only organized place was his desk. The master bedroom was littered with Whip's dirty clothes and shopping bags of handbags Merry bought the day of the accident. I peeked in the bags and decided I wanted to borrow the yellow Prada.

I moved into the fourth bedroom with its private bath. Even though it was the least decorated room, too many things covered every flat surface. I tucked the clutter out of sight, unpacked, and tried to relax. I propped the battered toy in the middle of the bed. I sent Jack a text with a quick update on Merry's status.

I missed hearing the bus but not the cry from the foyer. "Gramma, Grampop, I'm home."

Emilie.

"I'm upstairs."

"Mad Max? Oh my God, is that you?"

"'Tis indeed."

Emilie nicknamed me Mad Max following an argument with my daughter years back. Merry wanted the kids to call me "Grandma." I wanted them to call me "Max." Merry said it wasn't polite and nixed the idea. I got angry. I said I had the right to choose what my grandkids called me.

"Don't be mad," Emilie said.

"How about Mad Max?"

Emilie grinned.

I liked the alliteration, plus the mad part fit my rougher edges. I liked the old *Thunderdome* movies too. Even though Mel Gibson played Mad Max, I thought I might get some mileage out of Tina Turner's role somewhere down the road. I had been Mad Max ever since.

Emilie ran upstairs and into my arms. She squeezed the breath out of me. Not until she released me did she see my black eye and bandage. Before she could get upset, I assured her everything would heal.

"Nothing hurts except for a headache. Don't worry."

Emilie picked her way around the guest room before pouncing on the toy. "What's this?"

"That, dear child, is Puss 'n Boots."

"Where did he come from?"

"My grandmother, your great grandmother, made it for your mom for her first Christmas."

"I've never seen it before."

"When Mom outgrew her toys, I tucked it away."

"May I have it?"

"Not yet. I'm going to hang onto it for a little longer."

"You're here. Mom must be a lot worse than anyone will tell me. All Alex and I know is she was in an accident." Emilie perched on the side of the bed and fiddled with the old toy. "I mean, I know it's bad—I feel it—but Gramma and Grampop treat me like a baby. Will you tell me the truth?"

I looked into a very serious, very scared face. I told her what the doctors said, how her mother was bandaged, and what treatments she was getting. Unvarnished truth tempered by the reality of talking to a twelve-year-old.

"They won't let me see her."

"I'll speak with your dad. You and Alex should see her. She doesn't respond right now, though."

"How long can you stay?"

"Until Mom's better."

Emilie paled, beads of sweat popping out on her upper lip. Her eyes glazed over. I waited. She shook herself and rose on unsteady legs.

"Don't plan on leaving soon. We're going to need you. Mom's never going to be the same."

Before I could respond, the counterpoint of two doors sounded— Emilie's bedroom door closing softly and the front door banging open. Alex was home.

I went downstairs to hug my grandson, who was full of news about his day. He spotted the uneaten Oreos, poured some milk, and sat at the table. I sat opposite, picked up an Oreo, and twisted it apart. I leaned over and dunked my cookie into his milk before licking the sweet icing and crunching the cookie. Alex chattered about what went on in school before asking about his mother. I gave him an even more sanitized version of what I told Emilie. When I was done, he smiled a chocolaty smile.

"You look like a pirate." Alex bit into his third Oreo.

"Avast, matey." I winked my good eye.

CHAPTER EIGHT

Before I left the hospital, I asked Whip about the kids' routines, but he didn't know. After all, he'd been on the road most of their lives. Even when he was home, Merry made the everyday decisions. Well, I needed doctors appointments, key school dates, after-school activities, clubs, sports, and private lessons. I sighed.

I was so out of practice. It'd been more than two decades since I thought about any of this stuff. I was good at it then, even if Merry disagreed.

I stared at the calendar on the refrigerator. A couple of doctor and dentist appointments, but nothing about daily and weekly routines. Merry must have kept all this in her head. Well, I couldn't do that. If I didn't write it down, I'd miss something. I had my own hectic schedule in New York where I balanced charitable events with board meetings and social outings with Raney, Eleanor, and my other friends, the rest of the Great Dames.

I went right to the source. Or sources. The kids. After dinner on my first day in charge, I kept them in the kitchen. Whip was at the hospital.

"So, how long are you going to be babysitting us, Mad Max?" Alex carried a large bowl of chocolate ice cream to the table.

"Is that what I'm doing? Babysitting?" Where did Alex get such ideas?

"I didn't mean it like that, but I'm almost eleven. I don't need a babysitter." Alex stumbled over his tongue.

"I know you don't, but can you drive yourself around?"

"No ..."

"He means, how long can you stay?" Emilie glared at her brother.

"I promised your dad I'd help for a while."

I kept my commitment vague. I didn't want the kids to think I'd returned to Richmond permanently. I leaned over and ruffled Alex's hair, even though I broke the gel he put on it to make it stand up straight. I knew full well he hated it. Tough. I liked doing it.

"A while is going to be a long time, like I said." Emilie grabbed an apple from the bowl on the counter.

"Perhaps. Tell me everything you do. Don't want to miss anything."

Emilie refocused on the task at hand.

I laid the calendar on the table, and together we began filling in activities, times, and dates. Emilie had swim league on Saturdays and soccer three afternoons after school. She also took tennis lessons once a week.

"I'm in a creative writing group after school twice a month. My English teacher leads it. We have lots of fun. We meet on the second and fourth Tuesdays after school. I need a ride, 'cause I miss the last bus."

Creative writing? We didn't have courses like that when I was in junior high or middle school or whatever they called it today. Then again, what some students turned in for homework must look like creative writing.

"Okay, Alex. You're next." I turned to my ice cream-smeared grandson.

"Ice hockey on Tuesdays, Thursdays, and Saturdays. We finish at the end of March. I'm in the computer club. We meet twice a month on Wednesdays after school. I miss the last bus too."

"First and third Wednesdays?" Life as a soccer mom equaled chauffeur. I was going to need a car. Merry's was totaled. I'd have to rent one.

"Yup."

Alex started to wipe his mouth on his sleeve. He looked up, probably to see if I was watching. I was. I raised a single eyebrow. Alex fetched a napkin.

"Next, test dates and vacation schedules. Anything else that's important."

I filled in one month's activities and was shocked at how complicated a kid's life had become.

How could Merry allow the kids to fill up their lives with classes and meetings? Or was this the normal life of a child today? What happened to being kids, doing kid things? Playing, reading, going to movies, lying around daydreaming, studying? The kids needed a PalmPilot. I'd have to teach them to be kids before I left.

"What about you?" Emilie stared at the page of squares filling the center of the table.

"Board meetings in New York, the occasional doctor's appointment, and a ski trip to Aspen."

"Cool. I want to learn to ski. Can I come too?"

"Not this time, Alex. It's all old ladies like me."

"Rats."

"When are you going?" Emilie picked at a bit of spilled food on the placemat.

"Next month."

"Oh, I forgot. I get to sleep over at Andy's or Ben's every Friday and play video games all day on Sunday." Alex kept his eyes on the table.

"Nice try."

We'd concentrated so hard on the calendar, none of us heard Whip come in. "You know better than that."

"Phooey."

"How's Mom?" Emilie glanced at her father.

Whip looked like his nickname. He sat vigil day and night at the hospital while he waited for any bit of good news.

"No change. Want to go see her tomorrow?"

Alex and Emilie nodded.

"Can we go for ice cream afterward?" Alex asked, ever the bottomless pit.

"Use your indoor voice."

Ah yes, that old programmed response. I developed it when Jack was Alex's age. I hadn't forgotten everything about child rearing.

"Sure. Want to come along, Max?" Whip asked.

"I don't think so. I'll see you when you get back."

"She's coming." Emilie glared at me, daring me to say "No."

Guess I'm going to see Merry and eat ice cream.

CHAPTER NINE

Less than two weeks after I overloaded the monthly calendar, a chirpy weatherman announced Richmond was going to get two inches of snow the next day. As the school closures crawled across the bottom of the screen, I couldn't believe every school district threw up its hands and canceled classes.

"We don't have a lot of plows." Emilie grinned. "We get a day off whenever it snows."

"Two inches? In New York, we have to get a foot or more before we even delay the start of the school day."

"This isn't New York," Alex said. "Besides, now we get to sleep in tomorrow."

With nothing I could do about a lost day of classes, I went to bed. When I looked out the window the next morning, I was surprised to see more than a foot of snow lying like a sheet across the driveway and lawn. Then I chuckled.

I tiptoed downstairs and returned immediately. I rapped on Emilie's door until she opened it. I hit her with a snowball. Her yells woke Alex, who suffered the same fate.

"Get dressed. We're going to make a snowman."

"You're crazy."

Alex fled to his room. The sound of drawers being opened and shut told me he was looking for his warm clothes.

"Hey, you guys named me Mad Max."

Emilie scooped a dab of slush off the floor and rubbed it on my face.

By the time both kids were downstairs and out the garage door, I was flopped on my back in the driveway, making a snow angel.

"Come on. It's fun."

Emilie lay next to me. Before long, Alex laughed and threw snow at his sister and me. We had a rousing snowball fight before we built a snowman. We must have made enough noise to wake the neighborhood, because soon doors banged open up and down the street. Kids' shrieks filled what little space there was between snowflakes.

I sent Alex rooting in the garage for a snow shovel, but he returned empty-handed.

"How do you clear the driveway?"

"Snow removal is spring. We just wait until it melts."

I waved both hands at the kids and went inside to make hot chocolate and breakfast.

After the doctors reduced Merry's medications, I expected her to wake up and start talking immediately. That didn't happen. Even out of the medically-induced coma, she was often unable to speak. A deep chill settled into my bones.

Dr. Jenkins handed us off to the neurologist, Dr. Maloney, who would be in charge of Merry's care for the next stage. Whip and I met with him several times while she was in the hospital.

"I want you both to understand Merry's recovery will be slow. She's conscious, medically speaking, but she's nonverbal."

"Meaning she can't talk," Whip said.

"That's right. She's following basic verbal and physical commands, so we know some of her cognitive function is returning, but she hasn't spoken."

"When'll that happen?" Whip ran his hand across his chin, palm rasping on whiskers, eyes clouded with worry.

"I don't know. We're continually monitoring her brain function. We see progress." Dr. Maloney referred to Merry's chart. "She sustained a great deal of damage to her pre-frontal cortex."

"English, please."

I had no clue what part of the brain he meant, although pre-frontal indicated it was probably at the front of her skull.

Dr. Maloney pointed to a model of the human brain. "Here. When she hit the windshield, she sustained injuries to this section."

"What does it control?" I clamped down on my jaw, but I forgot to tighten my diaphragm. I stifled a hiccup.

"Her analytic abilities." The doctor turned the model around to face us. "Merry's brain was injured here and here. Some areas control speech; others control physical abilities—walking, balance. Still others control emotions."

"She could be so damaged she won't come back the way she was?"

"That's possible. Once we move Merry to the rehab center, we'll put her through a battery of physical, occupational, and speech therapies. We'll monitor her progress. In a few weeks, we'll have a better idea of how much permanent impairment she'll have."

A few weeks? Damn.

"She has a traumatic brain injury, what we call TBI."

"Thought that only occurred in military accidents," Whip said.

"Any brain injury can be characterized as traumatic, so no, they're not limited to war injuries."

"Merry may never be normal again?" Whip's face grew paler.

"I'm saying she may return to near normal, or she may suffer from some kind of disability. Regardless, Merry has a long road ahead of her. You need to be prepared."

"Prepared for what?" Whip bore down.

"Merry may have permanent problems with balance and other physical movement."

"We can manage that."

"She may have speech impairments."

"Okay." Whip relaxed a little.

"She may exhibit changes in her personality."

"Like what?" Whip leaned forward, elbows on his khaki-covered knees.

"Irrational fears. Taking no interest in what she used to like. Verbal abuse. Substance abuse. We just don't know."

Whip stood, shook the doctor's hand, and opened the door.

"Where are you going?" I didn't like Whip's expression or the dejected set of his shoulders.

"Out."

Whip returned home late that evening. The kids and I ate at our regular time, and I waited in the family room until his key clicked in the door. I met him in the center hallway.

"We have to talk." I turned on my heel and marched back to the rear of the house. Whip followed and slumped into his chair. I poured drinks and sat opposite him.

"What are you thinking?"

I still hadn't had time to talk with him about my limited role in the family. No time like right now to lay it out.

"Guess Merry's going to be in rehab for weeks, huh?" Tired blue eyes met mine. "She may not recover."

"She may not. We can pray for total recovery, but we should plan for the worst." Like it or not, we had to address our fears. "What are you going to do if she doesn't get better?"

"What do you mean?" Whip looked like he'd finally heard what I said.

"How are you going to raise the kids?"

"Me?"

"Yes, Dad, you. If Merry can't be their mother, you have to take over the day-to-day responsibilities."

Anger rose and my cheeks heated. I never could prevent my face from flushing when I got angry. Whip either didn't notice or didn't know the warning signs. At any rate, I was pissed off. How could he be so dense? Someone had to be there for his kids. It should be him.

"Aren't you going to help?"

"Help, yes, for a short period of time. It's not my job to raise them. It's yours. You'll need to change your life."

"I travel too much."

"Then hire a nanny or a caretaker. You can't expect me or your folks to do this permanently. We've raised our kids. Now it's your turn."

Whip looked as if he'd never considered having to take care of the kids. Alone.

I squeezed his shoulder when I left the family room. He'd never looked so forlorn, but he couldn't dump his duties on me. Not unless I wanted to be the dumpee. I didn't.

I bade Emilie a tearful farewell and headed back to New York to get ready for a long-awaited skiing trip to Aspen. I promised to call and text her daily.

"I'm so worried, Mad Max," Emilie said on my last night at the house. "I don't feel Mom very much."

"What do you mean, you don't feel her?" Once again Emilie left me thumbing a lift on Mr. Toad's Wild Ride.

"She doesn't feel like Mom. I mean, sometimes it's like Mom is trying to break through. Other times it's like a stranger is in Mom's body."

I kind of got what she meant. I, too, watched Merry struggle to find a word or pick up a cup or walk between parallel bars, but Emilie's assessment went to the core of my fears. What would I do if Merry didn't come back?

"Give it some more time." I zipped my roll-aboard and set it on the floor. "Now, what do you want me to bring from Aspen?"

"You. To stay."

CHAPTER TEN

I landed at LaGuardia at rush hour. I should have been relaxed from skiing with my girlfriends, but Emilie's daily updates kept dragging me back to Richmond.

Merry used a cane or walker most of the time. Those sections of the brain weren't permanently damaged. Her speech was more intelligible, but she suffered bouts where she forgot words or mangled them. I looked up "brain trauma." Aphasia, thinking you're saying a word correctly but you really weren't, was a symptom.

I spent another week in New York, doing whatever I wanted. An extended vacation. I continued to withdraw from the day-to-day rearing of the children. I returned the first week of April to check things out. Since my conversation with Whip, he'd hired a series of high school girls to watch the kids after school. Most didn't work out, because either they didn't drive, and therefore couldn't pick the kids up after school, or they were too interested in boyfriends to monitor homework. I heard all of this in detail from Emilie, with occasional crowing updates from Alex.

"Richmond has plenty of colleges. Have you tried an older girl? Or a boy?"

I was frustrated with Whip's failures. Was he making bad decisions? Was he programming the efforts for failure so I would come back and stay?

"I've tried. Not having much success. Can't find anyone I trust to stay overnight."

Overnight? My gut sank.

"You're planning to go back on the road? Merry's not even home."

"That's what I do. I supervise work crews all over the world."

"To the potential detriment of your children. Send someone else. You don't have to be everywhere." Everywhere but home, I wanted to shout but didn't.

I'd learned it didn't do any good. Whip could be as stubborn as I was, and I redefined "mulish" when I dug in my heels.

I began a schedule of two weeks on, two weeks off, not always contiguous. Still, I was able to spend half my time at home in New York and half my time messing around with the kids. I couldn't think of a worse situation. No one was satisfied. I got more and more resentful. Why couldn't Whip see he was shirking his responsibilities?

No matter how I tried to convince myself I didn't need to live in Richmond, Emilie and I grew closer with each call and text message. I helped her with her homework; I encouraged her to break out and be a child; I listened to her fears. Alex's grades plummeted, and he became more irascible. Daily, I grew more concerned because what Whip was doing wasn't working.

I hopped on my now familiar US Airways regional jet through National to Richmond. Whip called and asked me to meet him at his favorite diner for coffee. I picked up my rental car and headed for the diner. I listened to what was on his mind. Turned out to be plenty, but it all boiled down to one thing: He wanted me to come back full-time until Merry could take care of the children.

"Losing ground faster than I can imagine. I'm a fuckup at the house and at the office. I need help, Max. Don't have anyone else to turn to."

I didn't believe that, but Whip did. I knew from talking with Bette that the Colonel faced a double bypass—"at least, I think it's only a double," she said—in the next couple of weeks. I knew Emilie was stressed out and Alex was basically running wild. What I couldn't figure out was how this family collapsed in the months since Merry's accident.

I closed my eyes and felt my cheeks grow hot. I wanted to shout, "Grow up. Crack down on Alex. Make him do his homework. Be there for Em. Be there for your wife." I doubted it would help the situation. So now it was up to me.

"I'll come back but do not, under any circumstances, think this is permanent."

"I understand."

"No, you don't. When Merry comes home, I'll reassess my role. As soon as she can take over, I'll transition everything to her. If she can't, you'll have to hire live-in help. I love all of you very much, but I will not be the one responsible for your household." I waved for a refill for my coffee. "Is that clear?"

"Got it. Max, I'm so scared. I visit Merry every day I'm here. She's getting around better, but she's so different. I can't touch her or hold her, or anything. She's not my wife."

This jibed with what Emilie said she felt; her mother had changed to the point she was almost a stranger. I felt my mushy side taking over. Before I could stop myself, I blurted, "We'll get through this together."

When would I learn to control my tongue and avoid getting myself into such predicaments?

"Dad said the rehab center wants to send Mom home, but she's not ready." Emilie started crying.

We sat on my bed long after she should be asleep. After all, the next day was a school day. Here it was after midnight. She was too tense to tunnel into the pile of pillows I bought to match my bedroom at home.

"Neither are you, dear child."

"I can't do it without you."

In May, after months in the hospital and then a physical therapy center, Whip brought Merry home. I helped Emilie and Alex plan a surprise party with all the neighbors bringing covered dishes. Alex was too excited to sit; Emilie retreated to the quiet of her bedroom.

I tapped on her door and waited until she invited me in. She lay on her bed, book propped on her stomach. She hadn't been reading it, though; it was upside down.

I took the book and set it on the table. Emilie had the saddest expression on her face.

"What's the matter?"

"Mom doesn't want to come home. She's scared. She's angry too. The party's a big mistake." Emilie sat up. I put my arm around her shoulders and hugged her. "You feel this?"

I still didn't understand how she felt what she said she felt. It was real to her, and I was learning to give it proper respect.

"Yes."

Whip had called when they left the therapy center. They were due any minute. We rose together when the doorbell rang. Neighbors slipped in, put food in the kitchen, and gathered in the family room.

We lost Merry at "Surprise!" She didn't speak. She didn't smile. Whip helped her into the family room where her friends came to welcome her, one by one. Merry barely responded. She even ignored Darla and her daughter, Molly.

Whip made a big deal about presenting Merry with keys to a new Infiniti. "A belated anniversary gift." He leaned over and kissed her on the cheek.

She flinched and pulled away, the keys lying unacknowledged in her lap.

I fed everyone and let people escape as soon as they wanted. Within an hour, the house was empty, save for immediate family.

"I want to go to bed."

Whip brought her cane and helped her to her feet. He followed her into the kitchen.

"I knew you'd change everything." Merry had discovered my counter-decluttering meddling.

"When you're ready to cook, I'll put it back just like it was."

"Yeah, right." Merry left the kitchen and tapped her way upstairs.

"How will you do that?" Alex asked.

I held up my cell. "Easy. I took pictures."

Emilie went up to her room after the master bedroom door clicked shut. Alex wandered around like a lost puppy. I shut myself on the patio and called Raney.

"How was the party? Was Merry surprised?" Raney knew what the kids had planned.

"Try horrified." I filled Raney in with minute details.

"Oh dear."

CHAPTER ELEVEN

Merry's return should have been the first step toward Emilie and Alex getting back to normal. No flipping way. Merry might have been back in the house, but she was far from normal. She needed physical therapy three times a week, wasn't allowed to drive, and suffered memory loss, not to mention mood swings and an occasional bout of aphasia.

Three weeks after the disastrous party, I told Whip I needed to go to New York for a weekend.

I caught the last flight on Thursday to be ready for my monthly board meeting the next morning. Given how much help Merry needed, flitting between New York and Richmond would be my norm for the foreseeable future. I couldn't sit around the house all day waiting to activate Max's Taxi Service to pick up the kids or take Merry to therapy. I couldn't replicate my New York cultural activities, but I could bring some of my exercise gear back with me. First thing would be my rollerblades. I loved skating in Central Park. I'd already found several bike paths in Richmond that would be decent substitutes. Between pickups and drop offs, I could at least stay fit.

After a full day at the office, I unlocked the door to my apartment, flipped on the lights, and dropped my briefcase on the tiled floor of the foyer. I crossed the living room to the kitchen and poured a glass of Pinot Noir.

Raney called to remind me of our dinner reservations at Gustavo's at seven.

"I'll be there."

With an hour to shower and change, I carried my wine into the bedroom, stripped, and took the hottest shower I could stand, washing away the fatigue of the day. Wish I could wash away the worry too.

The oil painting of the two sisters in my bedroom represented the last moments of my carefree lifestyle "before the accident." While I dressed, I lost myself in its quiet beauty. Then Emilie called.

Alex was at Ben's house down the street, and Whip wasn't home from work yet. Emilie was supposed to go to dinner with her mom and dad, but her mom made some lame excuse and canceled.

"She yelled at me. She swore too." Hurt and tears clogged her voice.

"She yelled at you?"

"Yes. She does it a lot. Especially when I try to talk to her about me. She pushes me away like she doesn't care. She never did that before the accident."

"What about the swearing?"

I'd never heard Merry swear at the kids. Come to think about it, I hadn't seen much of any interaction between them. Merry spent most of her time hiding in her bedroom.

"She calls both me and Alex—"

"Alex and me."

"She calls Alex and me bad names, words she never lets Dad use. She's not Mom."

Emilie rattled on for several minutes. A picture emerged of Merry becoming more disconnected from her children, more irritable if not downright nasty and pushing them away. Merry's neurologist warned us about personality changes. This must be what he meant. Merry was ill-tempered around me, but I assumed our old friction was reemerging in spades. I hadn't seen her take her bad moods out on the children, though.

"Have you told your dad?"

"No. I wanted to talk to you first."

"Tell him when he gets home. Or maybe over dinner. Make him take you out. Promise?"

"Okay."

Emilie had added another worry to my pile. If Merry, who'd been the quintessential soccer mom before the accident, now avoided her children, I had to break through her self-absorbed fog.

"When are you coming home?"

"Sunday, but I'm coming back here again next month. Would you like to come with me?"

"You bet."

"We'll plan a weekend for goofing off. Sound okay?"

"Yes. See you. Love you."

"I love you, too, Em."

CHAPTER TWELVE

Raney was in Gustavo's when I arrived. We hugged, and she waved at the bartender. "Our table will be ready soon."

I perched on a stool.

"Martini, Mrs. Davies?" the bartender asked.

"Please."

Raney and I became regulars at Gustavo's as soon as it opened. Though new, the restaurant was old-school. Most of the newer places were brass-and-fern bars rather than lush with dark mahogany. Gustavo's felt more like a private club than the trendy place it was.

"Good board meeting?"

The bartender placed a dirty martini with three olives in front of me.

"We've had a terrific breakthrough." I was the chairman of Davies Enterprises, my late husband's company. "We've been testing a new type of engine. It doesn't use gasoline."

"Really? This could be in a car I'd buy?"

I sipped my martini before eating the first green olive. "It could. If we manufacture it, I'll have every oil company in the world putting a hit out on me. No need for gasoline. Period."

"Your table's ready, ladies. If you'll follow me ..."

Gustavo's *maître d'* led us to a quiet table at the side of the main dining room. We stopped talking while we listened to the daily specials, looked over the menus, and ordered our meals and a bottle of Cabernet.

We were well into our first course when the conversation turned serious again. "What's the latest on Merry?"

"She's home." I put my fork down. "She's walking and talking almost normally."

"It isn't enough, is it?"

"No. She's so different. The kids don't understand. To be honest, I don't either."

"Different? How?" Raney looked at the seafood risotto the waiter set before her.

"Her personality's changed. Part of the time she's out of it, disconnected from the world around her. A lot of what she says doesn't make sense. She treats the kids like crap."

I told Raney about the phone call from Emilie. "She acts one hundred eighty degrees different from the way she was before the accident. The brain injury is much worse than I thought."

"Shouldn't she be glad to get back into her routine?"

"You'd think. Before the accident, the kids and Whip were enough. Now, they're not. Her doctor put her on antidepressants and about a dozen other pills."

"Like that helps. Is she seeing a shrink?"

Raney had gone through enough therapy to appreciate the power of psychiatry. Her husband, her childhood sweetheart, was kidnapped years earlier in Syria. Released after seventeen months, he was never the same. She knew firsthand Merry wouldn't get better until she asked for help.

"No. I want her to go. So does Whip. She insists she's fine." I finished the last drop of wine. "Fine, my ass."

"So you've tried to talk to her?"

I picked up a stray peppercorn on the white tablecloth. "Oh, yes. Many times. If I ask her what's wrong, she shuts down. She won't talk to me or anyone else."

"She's leaning on you now, because she can."

"Of course."

"What if you weren't there?"

"I've been chewing over this a lot. Half of me says I should leave. Merry would snap out of it. Half of me says she won't snap out of it. In that case, she'll need more than a shrink to help. Half of me says she could spiral out of control in either case. If she gets too bad, it'll mean institutionalization. Any option screws the kids up."

"You do know that's three halves." Raney twirled the dregs of her wine.

"Never was good with numbers. I want to come home, but I can't. I may have to hogtie and drag Merry to a therapist. She's got to come around. If not, I'll have three children on my hands, instead of two."

"Have you thought about bringing Merry to New York? Lord knows, we have more shrinks than any other city."

"Bring Merry here?"

Raney nodded.

I'd never thought about that. Would getting Merry completely away from her family do the trick? I had to consider it.

"If that won't work, you have a fourth half. You could stay in Riverbend."

"I know. I don't want to stay. Every time I think about leaving, I go on a major league guilt trip. I can't abandon Em and Alex. Whip won't let me bring them to New York for any extended period, so if I'm going to take care of them, I have to be in Richmond."

"Didn't you say Merry was moody as a child?" Raney reached for her latte.

"I thought she was a normal teen. With perfect hindsight, I'm not so sure. Anyway, I took her to a therapist after her dad died. He didn't find anything wrong. She was grieving. He gave her Valium."

"Which was the magic panacea at the time. Take the pill, and everything will be all right."

Raney stirred sugar into her cup. "You know, some of that early hostility could be coming back. Maybe some mental block broke loose. Maybe she no longer has control over what she says."

"Em said the same thing. Now that I look back, Merry was self-destructive in junior high." I half-closed my eyes against the memories. "She used to bite her hands and arms. Said the neighbor's dog did it."

"Really?"

"It didn't last long, though. I forgot about it." I sat in thoughtful silence looking back at Merry's childhood. "In high school she got hooked on diet pills."

"My girls did too. They wanted to be rail thin, so they went for the pills."

"Better than today's bulimia or anorexia. Maybe if I'd paid closer attention, I could have figured out her behavior and gotten her help."

"Maybe if her doctor asked better questions, he could have discovered her problem." Raney's eyes clouded. "You're not a psychiatrist. Nothing in the common literature of the day would have told you what her behavior meant."

"I'm so damned scared. Merry drinks in secret. She's addicted to drugs too. She has piles of prescriptions. Always sucking down a pill or two."

"Sounds like she needs drug rehab more than physical therapy. Can't you get her into a clinic so the doctors can put her through detox and teach her coping skills? Therapy only helps if Merry's ready to admit she has problems, though." Raney sighed. "Listen to me. The new queen of pop culture psychobabble."

"Watch out, Dr. Phil. Dr. Raney's ready for prime time." Raney made me feel better. I still needed a Dr. Phil.

"I hope it works out. I'm selfish. I want you to come home. I miss our weekly dinners and bridge games."

"I miss you too. I want my life back." I didn't feel the least bit guilty admitting it. "I'm way more concerned about Em than Merry. She says such odd things. Like knowing her mother's not doing well. Knowing she's thinking crazy, mixed-up thoughts. Knowing she's not the same."

"Is she trying to get attention?"

"I thought so at first. No, when she tells me something about her mother, she goes very pale. Breaks out in a cold sweat and trembles. She apparently knew the exact moment Merry was injured." I blew on my latte.

"That's not possible." Raney frowned.

"Bette confirmed Em went ashen just after ten the night of Merry's accident. She was distracted the rest of the evening. And she was winning at Clue."

"I wish I could help, but I'd be in over my head." Raney reached out and took my hand.

"Jeez, me too. I haven't a clue what to do next."

"Do you think Em's psychic?"

"I don't know. Maybe. Whip doesn't remember anything like this happening before. Bette and the Colonel don't either. Alex has said Em acts weird sometimes. I thought he was making up stories.

Now I don't think so."

Raney waved for the check. It was her turn to treat.

"I don't know how to help both her and Merry. They need such different things."

"They both need shrinks?"

"Merry does definitely. Haven't the foggiest idea of what kind of shrink Em might need."

"What do you mean?"

"I mean, I can't call the American Psychiatric Association and ask for a New Age shrink who specializes in psychic teens and just happens to live in or around Richmond."

"Why not? You never know who might surface."

"I'll sound like an idiot."

"Do you care?"

"I don't give a rat's patoot. I'll try."

It didn't much matter if I sounded like an idiot or not. If I could find someone to work with Emilie, that would take half the problem off my shoulders.

"You have too much to handle. Just take baby steps. No 'but firsts.'"

"'But firsts'?"

"You know, I need to clean the kitchen, but first I have to reread *War and Peace*."

"Okay, no 'but firsts.'"

We gathered our handbags and pushed away from the table.

We nodded to Gustavo's *maître d'*, assured him dinner was excellent as always and walked out onto the sidewalk where the Friday crowds were queuing up at the hot restaurants.

"I'm coming back next month with Em. Maybe a break and distance from her mother will help."

"Be here on the twenty-sixth. I'll get tickets to Yo-Yo Ma at the Lincoln Center."

"Isn't it sold out?"

"Not if you know the right people." Raney was on the board at the Lincoln Center.

"That would be wonderful. Em'd love it. I'll bring Alex another time. Plan something a boy would enjoy."

The spring night air was soft and warm. We stopped in front of

Raney's building to hug our goodbyes.

"You know, Max, Merry may never come around. She may never be like she was."

I shuddered. I didn't want to think what the most negative outcome could be.

"Remember what Eleanor told you when you left the day of Merry's accident?" Raney kept her hands on my shoulders.

"You mean, about my doo-wop? Because I didn't get it right with Merry the first time around, I have a chance to get it right with Alex and Em?"

"Merry thinks you didn't get it right. Make the most of every day with her and with the kids."

"I know. I know."

Raney shook me slightly. "Don't blow it."

CHAPTER THIRTEEN

I had no sooner landed in Richmond than my phone buzzed. Caller ID showed Darla's number.

"Hey, lady. I just got in."

"Welcome back, I think."

"You think? What's happened?"

This didn't sound good, but I'd heard so much from Emilie over the past couple of days I was prepared for almost anything.

"Can you come by my house? I just made some iced tea, and Em and Molly are at the movies."

"As soon as I can get through traffic."

I worried my way around Richmond and into Darla's suburb. She met me at the door, a strained look on her face.

"Wait'll I tell you about lunch with Merry yesterday."

"She went out?"

If that were true, it would be the first time my daughter went to something other than a doctor's appointment or a therapy session with me driving.

"Not hardly. I took lunch to the house. We sat out on the patio like we used to."

"Let me guess. Nothing you hoped for."

"Not even close."

Darla and Merry were alone for the first time since the night of the accident. Darla served lunch and settled down to eat. That is,

Darla ate; Merry barely picked at the chicken salad.

"It felt so strange being alone with her."

"I know what you mean."

Merry could shut down when she didn't want to interact with someone. I was surprised she'd cut out her best friend, though. I thought it was only the kids and me.

"I told her I missed her. I might as well as have been reading the stock column from the paper. When she deigned to speak, it was to complain about everything." Darla looked sad.

"Starting with me, I bet."

"And about the kids. And about Whip. And about the way she looks."

"Ah, the laundry list of what's wrong in Merry's world."

"In spades. She started in on you, how she wants you to leave, and in the next breath how you need to stay because she needs help."

"I've heard that too. Makes for a schizophrenic existence." My conversation the evening before with Raney echoed through my overwrought brain. "I feel like a daisy: She wants me to leave, she wants me to stay. Either way, I disappoint half of what my daughter wants."

"It's a lose-lose situation. Whether Merry likes it or not, Em's ecstatic you're here."

"I know." I loved being around Emilie, but she was becoming more dependent on me every day.

"Em talks about you all the time. You're lots more fun than her mother. When I told Merry, she yelled at me. I tried to get her to understand both kids need their mother. They need you too."

"They need her more. I get it. I just wish Merry did." I swirled the ice cubes in my tea.

"She claims you're at each other's throats all the time. Nothing she does is good enough."

"That's partially true. I try not to be critical, but I can't change my stripes to plaid overnight. She carries a grudge like she did when she was a teen. I'm convinced it's part of her brain injury."

"She said her face would never be the same. She feels hideous."

"But she's not." I couldn't understand my daughter's continuing belief that her face was horrible.

"It's how she feels, though. Right now, she's not the prettiest thing in Riverbend, but she will be again. I didn't recognize her right after the accident, but she's almost back to normal now. She feels like a freak, like everyone stares at her. She dared me to contradict her."

"Everyone stares? Other than the family, her doctors and you, she hasn't seen anyone." Where did Merry get that idea?

"It got worse. Merry thinks she's out doing normal things, like shopping, going for groceries, getting her hair done."

"Only if I drive her. She hasn't been out of the house once without Whip or me. She doesn't drive."

I had had no idea how deep Merry's hatred of her looks was. Whip could tackle that. Maybe if she had a bit more tweaking done to her face, she'd snap out of the doldrums. Or maybe not. Still, it was worth a try. "Thanks, Darla. I'm so grateful for the update." I stood. "I have to talk with Whip."

I pounced on Whip as soon as the kids went upstairs. I poured nightcaps and pointed to a chair.

"Sit."

Whip took his drink and sat. "What's up?"

"My situation. Merry. The kids. Your role as their father." I sipped my drink. "Where do you want to start?"

Whip waved a hand, which I took to mean "You choose."

I pretty much dumped a load of options on the carpet between us. To give Whip credit, he listened without interrupting. When I took a breath, he ticked off the same four options Raney and I came up with.

"There are two more. Five, you could put Merry into drug rehab. Six, I could take her home. I guarantee she'd be in rehab in a New York minute."

"Other than you staying, my life changes completely." Whip rubbed his bristly chin.

"Earth to Whip. Your life changed the night of Merry's accident."

Whip frowned. "It did?"

"It sure did. If I hadn't rushed back to Richmond, your new roles would be full-time caregiver and full-time father."

"Already was a full-time father."

"Bullshit. More to being a father than being a terrific provider. You've always been that. You've never been around all the time, though."

"Guess I don't get your point."

I forced myself to stay calm. Could Whip really be this obtuse?

"Go back to options one and two. I came here to take care of the kids until Merry came home. She's home. If I leave, and if Merry can't or won't snap out of it, you'll have to pick up the kids after school, cook and shop, help them with homework. That's being a full-time father."

"That's what Merry does."

"Wrong, pal. That's what Merry did. What she does now is lie in bed, drunk and stoned, feeling sorry for herself."

Whip leaned back and closed his eyes.

I waited.

"What are you going to do?"

"Don't you dare shove your responsibilities on me. I'm not your wife." My cheeks grew hot. "The question is, what are you going to do?"

"I don't know."

"You have two weeks to come up with something we can all live with."

I left Whip alone in the family room. He looked more forlorn than he had when Merry was in a coma. I was on the verge of sleep hours later when a wave of warmth, followed by an almost unconscious "Please don't leave" swept over me.

CHAPTER FOURTEEN

After a restless night, I rose early and set out breakfast. Sundays were unscheduled, so those who were hungry wandered in at their leisure. I took my journal outdoors and spent an hour writing about my conversation with Whip.

No matter what Whip thought, the decision really was mine. Nothing short of him becoming a full-time, on-the-premises father relieved me of the responsibility of taking care of the kids. I was so not letting him off the hook without a fight. He needed to squirm and acknowledge what he was asking.

I went over the ideas Raney and I had kicked around and made up my mind. I had to provoke some kind of response, anything, to get Merry's attention. I planned to try the first of the halves: I'd tell Merry I was returning to New York. Permanently. If I could get her to understand she had to take charge, maybe I could also get her to admit she needed psychiatric help. That would be huge and just might put her on the road to recovery and me on the road home. I crossed my fingers and hoped tough love would work.

I returned to the kitchen to find an empty coffeepot. Breakfast dishes cluttered the sink. Someone had eaten. Several someones from the number of plates and bowls. I called up the stairs. Silence. Curious, I looked into the garage. Whip's truck was gone. Not again. Had he gone back to work instead of doing something with his kids? Then I saw the note on the kitchen table.

"Mad Max, Dad's taking us out for the day. I don't know where we're going, but I need to get away from Mom. Love you, Em."

No sooner had I finished cleaning the kitchen than Merry struggled down the stairs. She was still in her nightgown, her hair uncombed, her eyes unfocused. She reeked of last night's booze. While I didn't think she drank this early, I was positive she was stoned on her morning breakfast of painkillers.

"What the hell do you think you're doing here?" The words were a slurred assault.

I struggled to keep calm and not round back on her with my usual stinging rebuke. "Making coffee."

"I said, what the fuck are you doing?" Merry leaned against the doorjamb, one hand holding onto the knob.

"With that attitude, I won't tell you. When you're civil, we can talk. If not, you figure it out." I set out two cups, cream and sugar, spoons and bagels on the countertop. I was starving, so I popped a bagel into the toaster.

Merry sniffed the toasting bagel. "Aren't you going to make me something to eat?"

"No. Have whatever you want." I poured coffee and carried both cups to the table.

Merry wobbled across the kitchen and sat. She cradled the cup in both hands and raised it to her lips. Her hands trembled so much I was afraid she'd spill it.

Steady, old girl. Don't give in. "Now, what did you want to know?"

I kept my voice neutral, as I spread cream cheese and jam on half of my bagel and took a bite.

Merry watched my every move. "I want to know what you're doing."

"Eating breakfast."

After realizing I didn't fix her breakfast, Merry wrestled a bagel out of the bag and tried to slice it. I hoped she wouldn't cut a finger off. She mangled the bagel into two pieces small enough to fit into the toaster.

"I mean here in my house. What are you doing here?"

"I've been here for weeks taking care of you and the kids." I finished my bagel and pushed the empty plate aside.

"Why don't you get out of my house?"

"Now that you bring it up, I will. I'm moving back to New York."

"Wha-at?"

"You heard me. I'm going home. Time for you to take care of your family."

"But, but I can't!"

"You tell me all the time you don't want me meddling. I'm taking you at your word." I kept my head down and glanced at Merry's face through my eyelashes. She was deathly pale.

"I need help!"

"Not as much as you think. The therapist said you can drive. Go to the doctor. See what meds you can cut out. Take over the care of your children. Their entire schedule is on the calendar." I waved at the bulletin board, which had long ago replaced the front of the refrigerator.

"I already do that. I take them wherever they want to go."

Was she so spaced out she actually believed she was back to normal? This tracked with what Darla told me.

"What car are you driving?"

"You're so stupid. My Lincoln, of course." Merry carried her half-burnt bagel to the table and reached for the cream cheese.

"Merry, you wrecked the Lincoln. Whip bought you the Infiniti you've always wanted." I turned aside and blinked tears away.

"He did?"

"It's in the garage. Go look. Start cooking and helping the kids with their homework."

Merry chewed, swallowed, and said nothing. Her brow furrowed.

"It's time you went back to being a wife and mother. Stop lying in bed all day drunk and stoned on drugs."

Merry stared at the table.

Did she even understand?

Her voice rose, and she shouted I couldn't leave.

"You're not making sense. You want me to leave. Then, you don't. You can't have it both ways."

"You're trying to control me. Just like always."

I ignored her. "I'll talk to Whip about finding a caretaker."

"I won't have some stupid stranger in my house."

"Then take care of yourself, dammit. And your children. And your husband." I put my dishes in the dishwasher and poured a refill of coffee to take upstairs.

Merry shouted after me. "Don't you dare leave, you bitch!"

Strike one. Threatening to leave didn't work. Time to think about the second half: a shrink.

I felt like howling when I called Raney.

"So, it's too much to expect Merry to take care of herself and her children."

"Yes."

"Well, what are you going to do about it?'

CHAPTER FIFTEEN

My two-week deadline still had more than a week left when Whip came into the family room after dinner and threw himself into his favorite chair. He had the telltale signs of getting ready to go away for a while.

"Okay, when are you going where?"

Whip jumped and had the decency to look guilty. Well, slightly guilty. "You remember Johnny Medina?"

"Of course. He's scared to death of me."

I met Johnny years earlier. A partner in Whip's construction firm, I liked his solid common sense attitude toward life. He was funny too.

"He's got a fucked up job in Central America. Behind schedule. Thefts. Bureaucratic graft. Sabotage."

"Only you can save the world, huh, John Wayne?"

"Something like that."

"You're running away. Just say so." I was angry enough to call Whip's bluff.

"And you don't?"

"Well, I want to run away too. How long this time?"

"About a week."

"Okay. When you get back, it's decision time."

Whip shied away from talking about Merry.

"I'll make you a deal. You go to Central America. Get some R and R. I'll take the kids to New York. We'll both get away from the problem."

"What about Merry?"

"What about her? I'll leave plenty of food. She'll survive a few days alone. Think of it as a trial run. See if she can handle responsibility."

Whip grinned. "Deal."

"Don't get too comfortable. Think about putting Merry into rehab." I rose and moved toward the door. "Think about treatment. You may have to commit her."

And don't even think about staying in Central America forever. I'll find you. You won't like the consequences of getting stomped by Maxine Davies.

Once I told the kids I was taking them to New York, Alex wanted to leave immediately. Like, the next day. I had to be sure Merry had everything she needed first. I invited her to come with us, knowing full well she wouldn't go. Still, I made a feeble attempt at getting her out of her drunken, drug-befogged existence.

"Leave me alone."

I took her at her word.

Alex sprang a list of everything he wanted to see and do on us at breakfast the day before we were to leave.

I bit back a laugh. "Hand it over. Hmm, Central Park. Can do. The Statue of Liberty. Can do. The Intrepid Aircraft Carrier. We'll see. Ground Zero. Let me think about that."

"I really want to go to Ground Zero. It'd be so cool to look at the hole in the ground."

"I'm not sure I want to go." Emilie stared off into the distance. "So many people died."

"It's been three years since the attack. Please, Mad Max, say we can go."

"Maybe." I didn't like turning what was left of the World Trade Center into a tourist attraction. "Back to your list. The White House and Air and Space. Can't do."

"Why not?"

"They're in Washington, D.C., you idiot." Emilie rolled her eyes.

"No name calling. He's not an idiot. You need to study geography, Alex. We'll start in Central Park with the zoo and the merry-go-round. We can take the subway to Battery Park and ride the Staten

Island Ferry. Then we'll go to the Statue of Liberty and Ellis Island."

I checked off a couple of items.

"What about you, Em? What do you want to do?"

"MoMA. The Natural History Museum. Maybe a Broadway play. A carriage ride."

"Yuck."

"Whoa, Alex. Em's going where you want. You can do the same. Besides, think of it as a vacation with a twist."

"What twist?"

"You'll learn something."

"Double yuck."

CHAPTER SIXTEEN

After trying to see and do everything on Alex's and Emilie's lists, we packed to return to Richmond. We had knocked all but the Intrepid off the lists. I ran out of energy to hike through an aircraft carrier-turned museum. I did relent, though, and took the kids to Ground Zero. We ate lunch in the Davies Enterprises cafeteria two blocks away.

"Wow! You can see everything from here." Alex bolted from window to window. He pointed to places we'd visited. "Even the hole in the ground."

"Were you here on September Eleventh?" These were the first words Emilie spoke since we arrived at Ground Zero.

"I was."

Emilie threw her arms around my waist and buried her face in my shirt.

I decided to drive back to Richmond rather than fly. I wanted my car so I didn't have to rent one all the time. Alex pouted when I told him I didn't have a DVD player in my Jag sedan. I reminded him he had his iPod and several books.

"You can always look at the scenery, you know."

"That's boring."

"Could be, but we're going to drive."

Emilie was happy. "It'll take more time for us to get home, won't it?"

"Sure will."

Our vacation away from Merry had been a godsend. We called every day, but she never answered. Emilie said her mother was "fine." At least we tried.

We hadn't been back two nights when cries came from Merry's room.

I climbed out of bed, my heart pounding, my mouth dry as a fart in a mitten. Was Merry having another nightmare? They'd become more frequent of late, just like they had after her father died. In a rare moment, she told me she suffered two recurring nightmares. In one, bright lights headed straight at her, blinding her, but she couldn't get out of the way. In the other, she looked everywhere for something she'd lost. She called and called, but no one answered. Which one was it tonight?

I walked into an empty, darkened hallway. I listened first at Merry's tightly shut door. Nothing. Maybe she went back to sleep. I peeked into Alex's room. He snored slightly, bathed in the blue glow of his computer screensaver.

I eased Emilie's door open. She was curled in a ball, her oldest teddy bear clutched in her arms. Why was the room so much brighter than usual? Emilie had left a small lamp burning on her chest of drawers. As a toddler, Emilie was afraid of the dark after she got up one night and fell down the stairs. When had she started sleeping with a nightlight and her old teddy bear again?

I backed out of the bedroom and bumped into something solid. I gasped, my heart thumping. Merry stood right behind me.

"You scared the hell out of me." I raised an eyebrow and held a finger to my lips. "Come downstairs. We're awake. The kids are asleep. Time to talk. I'll make some chamomile tea."

I was pretty sure Merry didn't want to spend the rest of the night listening to me. When I walked down the stairs, though, I expected her to follow. She did.

I filled a kettle, measured tea into a pot, and set out mugs. While I cut a couple of slices of chocolate cake, Merry went to the liquor cabinet, brought the brandy and two snifters back to the kitchen, and poured healthy slugs. After the water came to a boil, I carried mugs of steaming tea and slices of leftover cake to the table.

Time for a mother-daughter talk. I planted myself across from

Merry. Maybe I could break through the shell she'd built up.

She rolled her eyes.

"When you do that, you look just like Em when she says, 'whatev-ah.'"

Merry shrugged and sipped her brandy. No response.

Of late, Merry shied away from talking about anything but herself. That suited me fine; tonight was all about Merry. Her rigid face told me to hurry up and get on with it. Like it or not, she'd sit here until I'd said what I wanted.

I could be relentless. I forced Merry and her younger brother, Jack, to interact with me. They wished I was like other mothers who chewed you out and waited for a "yes, Mom." If Merry's friends looked contrite, they were off the hook.

"Why doesn't Em call you 'Mom' anymore?"

Apparently I'd caught Merry off guard. I didn't know where I was headed. I was winging it.

"She does too."

"No, she doesn't. She doesn't call you anything. When we're talking, Em refers to you as 'she.'"

"She's going through a phase."

"It's more than that. She avoids you." I sipped my tea and ignored the snifter.

Merry reached into the pocket of her old bathrobe and pulled out a small bottle. She shook a couple of pills into her hand and washed them down with the rest of the brandy before refilling her glass.

"What did you just take?"

"Pain pills."

When Merry lied, her face gave her away every time.

"Em doesn't want to have anything to do with you."

"That's not true! Where'd you get such a stupid idea?" Merry's face reddened.

"From Em. You won't listen to her. You yell and curse at her."

I pulled an imaginary arrow out of my quiver and shot it across the table. It hit Merry dead between the eyes.

"I do not!"

"Is she lying?"

"Goddamn it, I don't curse." Merry's voice rose.

"You should be involved with your children like you were before the accident."

"Are you accusing me of being a bad mother?"

I stared at my daughter until she looked away. "No, but you're not behaving like you used to. Do you care about anyone except yourself?"

That got through to her. She looked like she wanted to yell—"How dare you?"—but didn't.

"When was the last time you talked with either child? Really talked and listened to them? Spent any time with them?"

"I ... I don't remember."

Merry's voice was slurred from a combination of pills and brandy. "Last week, I think, when I took them to the mall."

"You took them to the mall? So not likely." I gripped my hands in my lap. "I spend more time with the kids than you do."

"So you're a better mother than me? Since bloody when?" The words were bad breath between us.

"Since the accident. You told me I wasn't the mother you wanted when you were young. I did what I had to do. I kept you and your brother safe and alive after Daddy died. I provided more than the basics and less than you wanted. I gave you both a chance to go to college, so you could earn a living and stand on your own two feet." I rose and turned the gas on under the kettle. "Stand on them now."

Merry cursed and accused me of meddling. Called me insensitive. A bitch. Everything and anything.

I didn't miss a beat. "Take responsibility for your family."

"I can't," Merry whined. "I'm too tired."

"If you'd stop putting that stuff in your body, you'd have more energy."

"What stuff?"

Before Merry could move, I reached into her pocket and emptied the pill bottle on the table.

"This. Look at you. My daughter, the junkie." I felt guilty attacking her, but it was part of my tough love plan. Would it work? "What is all this?"

"Oxycontin, Zanax, Ambien."

"What else?"

"Valium and Zoloft," Merry whispered.

"No wonder you can't function." I swept the pills off the table.

My daughter crawled around the floor in a panic. It made me

sick to see how far she'd fallen. Merry retrieved the last of the pills and swallowed another one before she sat back in her chair.

"How much are you drinking?"

"Not so much." Merry reached for the brandy but stopped.

Had she heard a little of what I said? "You lie in bed all day, stoned and drunk."

"What right do you have to criticize me? I nearly died. My baby did."

"But you didn't." I reached for her hand, but she snatched it away. "Neither did Emilie. Nor Alex. Nor Whip. Nor me. We're alive. When are you coming back to us?"

Merry's mouth hung open. "You can't imagine what it's like." She picked at a hangnail.

"You're right. I can't."

"I don't feel anything."

"Oh, I doubt that. I doubt that very much. I think you feel a lot. You feel anger at the drunk. Grief and loss over the baby. Pity about your scars."

"That's not fair." Merry began to cry. She said I'd never understand.

I was sure she felt it wouldn't do any good to explain it to me.

"I want things to be the way things were before the accident."

"Don't we all? Wishing won't make it so. Losing the baby was unfair. What you're doing to your family is worse. You say you want things to go back to the way they were. Run this household."

Merry rubbed her nose with the back of her hand. "Huh? What do you mean?"

"Before the accident, you were a full-time wife and mother. You were involved with Em and Alex, a loving wife to Whip. Now you're an invalid. Stop drinking and get off the drugs."

"I can't."

"Drive the kids to soccer and swim club."

"I can't. I don't want anyone to see me. I'm a freak."

"Is that why you won't go out? You don't like the way you look?" Merry nodded.

"Want me to talk with Whip about finding another plastic surgeon?"

Merry nodded again.

"Okay, but you have to promise to see a psychiatrist. Something's wrong. If you're honest with yourself, you'll admit it. Promise you'll cooperate. You'll go if I make the appointment?"

Merry nodded one last time. All of a sudden, her ears were full. No more of my words would go in. Her face disappeared in a huge yawn.

I shook my head. Mommy would take care of everything. Keep her safe like I did when she was little.

Merry staggered off to bed.

I sat alone in the kitchen for a long time. I reached for the abandoned brandy and took my first sip. I thought about what Merry said. More, I thought about what she didn't say, what I observed. My daughter was in deeper trouble than I imagined. Between the booze and drugs, she couldn't function. The physical therapy center taught Merry the mechanics of living, but not the essence of living. She was relying on too many crutches. Drugs. Booze. Me.

CHAPTER SEVENTEEN

With my mind churning over my middle-of-the-night conversation, I lay in bed in the predawn darkness. One by one, I thought about the problems as I understood them. I formulated a series of baby steps to save my daughter. If one worked, I could go back to New York. When dawn was little more than a fingernail of light, I rose, took a quick shower, and went downstairs.

I was in bed less than four hours and asleep perhaps one. I'd have dark circles under my brown eyes, but I couldn't worry about them. Besides, worry produces wrinkles.

While the coffee brewed, I rooted through the kitchen desk for the list of psychiatrists Merry got at the therapy center. Three were affiliated with VCU and one with County: All were accessible. It was too early to call, so I puttered around the kitchen. I set breakfast on the table. The kids wouldn't be down for at least an hour and who knew when or if Merry would show up.

I carried my first cup of coffee out to the patio. Time to call Raney, who was a dawn riser like me.

Raney picked up on the second ring. After the usual round of pleasantries, Raney got to the point. "You talked with Merry, or you wouldn't be calling me before the garbage trucks finish their morning deliveries."

A New Yorker's joke: Garbage trucks made deliveries rather than pick-ups because piles of trash were stacked on curbs some place in the city every day. I was so homesick. Birds chirping in the backyard seemed insipid to someone who'd grown accustomed to the hubbub of a big city.

"I did. Didn't do a bit of good." By habit, I gave Raney the blow-by-blow of what happened. "You can scratch off one of the halves."

"Tough love, huh?"

"I didn't actually threaten to leave, but I told her she has to behave like she did before the accident." I sipped more coffee.

"The result was?"

"A freaking failure. She's as obtuse as the proverbial brick wall."

A cacophony of horns violated the quiet-zone ordinance where Raney lived. She must have the sliding glass door open onto Park Avenue.

"I'm a crutch, but leaving could damage Merry more than I can live with. I gnawed that bone all night. All I came away with was the urgent need to get her into therapy." I stared at the bottom of my cup and flip-flopped my way back into the kitchen for a refill.

"I agree. So your next step is a psychiatrist?"

"I have a list in my hot little hand. I'll start calling at nine."

"Call between seven and eight. Psychiatrists see their first patient at nine. The earlier you call, the more likely they'll answer the phone."

"Good idea."

"What about commitment?"

"I don't know how to go about it."

"The psychiatrist will."

"Merry promised she'd go if I find her another plastic surgeon." I reminded Raney about Merry's obsession over her face.

"Do you think she'll remember?"

"Doesn't matter. I will. Whip can deal with the plastic surgeon. I'm more worried about what's going on inside her head."

"All the plastic surgery in the world won't help if she continues drinking too much and downing pills like M&M's."

"Let me know what happens."

"Thanks. I'll call you soon. Hugs to the rest of the Great Dames."

Footsteps padded down the stairs. I turned. Emilie rubbed sleep from her eyes. She was getting up earlier and earlier. I suspected she was sleeping as little as I was.

"I heard you fighting with Mom last night."

"I tried to be quiet, but she kept yelling."

Emilie shook her head. "You were both so miserable, I couldn't tune you out."

"I'm sorry, dear child."

Once again, Emilie slipped into a space that excluded me, yet I understood what she meant.

"Mom needs you to help her, not argue with her."

"She needs more help than I can give her." I held up the coffeepot.

"She needs her mommy, just like I do." Emilie stirred cream into the brew in her cup.

Merry needed her "mommy"? I hadn't thought of it that way. I treated my daughter like an adult. Maybe, just maybe, Emilie was right. Maybe I needed to go back to being Merry's mother. Except, Merry, too, often told me how I sucked in that role.

"I mean, she needs someone to understand her. Can't you back off and not poke her all the time?"

"Is that what you think I'm doing?"

"Isn't it?"

I did poke. Well, poking wasn't working. I'd try being nicer to my poor, lost daughter.

"Treat her like you do Alex and me. You don't poke us. You aren't critical with us all the time."

"You're still children. You need guidance, not poking. Support, not criticism."

"In a way, Mom is more like a child than I am. She needs the same thing I do."

"Got the message. Help me stay on track, okay?"

Emilie put her cup down and gave me a bear hug. She nodded against my chest.

I hit paydirt on the second call when Dr. David Silberman answered. I told him everything I could think of about Merry and asked for his help. As luck would have it, he had a slot open on Mondays and Thursdays at ten when Mad Max's Taxi Service was available.

I made the appointment and picked up my rollerblades. I needed to move, and move a lot, to work off my anxiety. Between Whip's squishiness on what to do about his wife and Merry's decline into drugs and booze, I was barely holding it together. The more I exercised, the better off I'd be. I needed a better sense of balance to keep my promise to Emilie about not poking her mother.

Merry denied promising to go into therapy. I told her I wouldn't do a thing about her face until we found out what was going on inside her head. Call it blackmail. Call it coercion.

Merry argued and yelled the night before the first appointment, calling me any variety of names. She was creative in the way she put words together. I kept at her until I wore her down.

Two weeks later, I sat in the waiting room and mulled over an incident from the previous week.

On Wednesday afternoon, I read in my room after my Pilates workout. Emilie was home with a cold, and Merry was holed up in her bedroom. No early warning siren sounded before a battle erupted in the hallway outside my closed door.

"Why do you always shut me out?"

"I don't shut you out."

"You do. You never ask about me, about what I'm doing. You don't care."

"I do."

"Why can't you just be my mother? Why are you such a bitch?"

An open palm met a cheek.

"Don't call me a bitch! I'm your mother. I deserve respect."

"Not when you don't act like my mother. Why can't you just go to the swim league awards dinner? You always went in the past." Emilie's voice was thick, the result of her cold and I suspected also of choking tears. "Or are you going to spend the day drunk again?"

"I won't go. Have your grandmother take you."

"I hate you!" Emilie slammed the door to her room. Merry's door followed a second later.

I'd first heard the "I hate you" accusation right after Norm died. I couldn't let Emilie think she hated her mother. Maybe I could help her understand before things got any worse.

I set my book on the bedspread and went to Emilie's door. I tapped and opened it before she could tell me to go away. She lay face down on her bed, sobbing into her pillow. I sat on the edge and pulled her into my arms.

"I hate her! She's so mean. She hates me too." Emilie's pain poured out with each fresh batch of tears.

"I don't think you hate your mother, Em. You don't like how she treats you, do you?"

"Oh, Grams, she slapped me. She's never slapped me before. Don't you hate her?"

Emilie only called me Grams in moments of extreme duress. I considered her question.

Her sobs quieted.

"No, I don't. I don't like her right now, but I haven't stopped loving her. It's hard to explain, but she's my daughter. I can't turn my back on her."

Emilie snuffled against my T-shirt. I reached for a tissue and handed it to her. She blew a juicy amount into the first one. Two more followed. Her sobs subsided to little more than hiccups.

"Do you know how to help her?"

"Haven't a clue. She's going to a doctor who might be able to, though."

"A shrink?" Emilie sat up and wiped her face. "Do you think it'll work?"

Merry's fingerprints were vivid on Emilie's cheek. My anger rose. If Merry stood in front of me, God help me, I'd slap her as hard as she struck her daughter.

"Let's hope." I left my granddaughter to rest.

For the remainder of the day, I worried over the mess we were in. The longer I was around Merry, the more I wanted to get away from her. I wanted to take the kids to New York permanently. Being in this household did none of us any good. I wondered what Whip was thinking about.

Now, half an hour into the fourth session with Dr. Silberman, raised voices came through the door. Rather, Merry's voice came through. I didn't hear Dr. Silberman's. A couple of heavy thumps inside his office preceded Merry flinging the door open.

"You're a fucking quack."

Merry tried to slam the door, but Dr. Silberman caught it. "Sit down, Merry. I want to talk with Mrs. Davies."

That didn't bode well. I shot a look of pity at my daughter and went into the office. Dr. Silberman set a table back on its legs. A clock and box of tissues were on the floor.

"I have bad news, Mrs. Davies."

Dr. Silberman sat behind his desk and steepled his fingers, looking exactly like Sigmund Freud. "Merry won't work with me. She's hostile and antagonistic, as well as delusional. She doesn't see anything wrong in her behavior."

Merry maintained everything was normal at home. She was running the house, doing the errands, everything. She couldn't understand why I was still getting in her way. I should leave. She was very involved with her children's lives, until Dr. Silberman asked some questions. Then she flew into a rage. She denied feeling angry and said she was taking Ambien to help her sleep and Zoloft for depression. No, she wasn't taking any other drugs.

"Merry said you're interfering in her life, but when I asked if she wanted you to leave, she became agitated. That's when she overturned the table and stalked out."

"Will it help if she sticks with therapy?"

"At this time? No. Merry's uncooperative. Until she asks for help, this is a waste of your money and my time."

"Do you think she'll ever function normally?"

"I don't know."

A door slammed on my hopes of going back home for good. "What if I left?"

"It would do irreparable harm. More, it would put the children in jeopardy. If you left, I think she'd spin completely out of control. Are you planning to return to New York?"

"I want to, but I can't abandon Alex and Em. Or Merry."

Dr. Silberman rose and shook my hand. "I'm sorry."

"Would it be possible to get her into a rehab center to get her off the drugs and booze?"

"It would have to be a voluntary commitment. She could check herself out."

"Could Whip commit her?"

"Involuntarily? No. She's not a threat to herself or anyone else."

Merry sat stiff and defiant, arms crossed under her breasts, when I returned to the waiting room. I walked past her and headed out to the car. We made the short ride home in strained silence. Merry took off upstairs; I took off for the patio.

I hadn't been in the kitchen more than ten minutes fixing lunch when I was subjected to a stealth waist hug. Emilie.

"What brought this on?"

"You're all pinky orange again."

"That means exactly what?"

"You've decided to stay."

"For a little longer."

"No, you're going to stay."

With that, Emilie squeezed me again and danced out of the room, spinning her way down the hallway toward the front door.

At least one of us was happy with the decision.

CHAPTER EIGHTEEN

Twenty four hours after the debacle at Dr. Silberman's, Whip called to say he'd be home the next day. "I'm going to stop at the office on the way from the airport."

"See you after you unwind. Be home for dinner."

I knew the transition from a man's world on a construction site to domesticity could be disconcerting. When I came back from New York, I had to come down from a high of being with my friends. I was never certain what I'd find.

I was in the kitchen, deep in thought, when Whip appeared at my side. He leaned over and kissed my cheek. "Where's Merry?"

I wiped up a spill on the stove. "Upstairs. Napping."

"She been out of the house by herself?"

I shook my head and rinsed the sponge.

"Still sleeping all the time?"

"Yes."

Whip took the stairs two at a time, only to return within a few minutes, thunder in his eyes. "She's taking a shower and will be down for dinner."

"She's been like this every afternoon since you left."

"My fault. I shouldn't have gone."

"You're right. You shouldn't have gone, but you did. Now, we have to deal with it. Merry's sinking deeper into booze and drugs every day."

"Crap. Johnny and I tied one on last night in camp, but I don't get drunk as a daily habit. Got to get her sobered up. Just don't know how."

"Me neither." I'd told Whip about my bargain with Merry, shrink for a plastic surgeon, when he called home. I'd told him to think about committing her too. "Even though the shrink was a dismal failure, maybe a new surgeon will be the magic decoder ring."

"Get on it in the morning." Whip scrubbed his fists through his messed-up hair.

"Any thoughts about residential rehab?"

"Can't do it."

"Can't or won't?" I thrust my jaw out. "What *can* you do?"

Dinner was strained. Merry had washed her hair and tried to look presentable but began drinking even before we sat down. Emilie picked at her food and answered in monosyllables; Alex wolfed his food like a starving peasant. I filled some of the silence with polite, if desultory, conversation. Merry drank. Whip looked mad and scared.

Whip called Dr. Rosenberg, Merry's first plastic surgeon, about her obsession over her looks and asked for a referral for a second opinion.

After much searching and getting nowhere, Dr. Rosenberg found a renowned plastic surgeon who accepted a one year teaching fellowship at Chaminade. That hospital wasn't as convenient as VCU, but it claimed this doctor's credentials were impeccable.

"Mr. Pugh, Dr. Hunter will see you now."

Whip tossed aside a month-old copy of *National Geographic,* and we followed the nurse down a long corridor to a private office toward the back of the clinic. Whip had talked me into going with him to meet the surgeon. I'd agreed to stay through what I hoped would be the final stages of Merry's recovery: her facial reconstruction. If I was going to be responsible for transportation, I wanted to know what to expect.

"Dr. Hunter."

"Mr. Pugh." Dr. Andrew Hunter leaned over his desk to shake Whip's hand.

"And you are?"

"Mrs. Davies, Merry's mother." I, too, shook the doctor's hand.

It was soft and damp.

"I don't need you here." Dr. Hunter sat behind his desk.

"I asked her." Whip crossed his arms across his chest.

"Suit yourself." Hunter held out his hand.

"I brought Merry's records."

The doctor took the large manila envelope, which he set in the exact center of his empty desk. He leaned forward on his elbows.

The sterile office contained the requisite framed diplomas and board certifications, along with a color photograph of a racing sloop on a bookshelf. The photo was like the one you got when you bought a frame. Very professional. Very impersonal. Very not-the-doctor's boat. Nothing in the office reflected his personality. No family pictures. No awards. Just medical texts. Maybe he hadn't fully settled in. He'd just arrived, after all.

We were as nervous as the night Whip asked me for Merry's hand. We both wanted something: He wanted his wife; I wanted my daughter. If Merry would go through the pain, we'd go through the wait.

"Dr. Rosenberg said you're one of the best around. I sure hope so, because we need you to help Merry."

"I *am* the best."

Whip raised an eyebrow, but the doctor wasn't looking at him.

Dr. Hunter opened the thick envelope. He shoved the color photographs aside, jammed the X-rays up on light boxes, and peered at them through half-glasses. He nodded, shook his head, and muttered as he poured over each in turn.

"Hmm, her zygomaticomaxillary complex was pulverized, the eye socket fractured, her nose crushed. Look here. She hit the steering wheel with incredible force. She should have been wearing her seat belt."

"How do you know she wasn't?"

"She wouldn't need me if she'd been buckled in. The air bag didn't deploy either." The doctor peered over the tops of his glasses. "I can tell from her injuries."

Dr. Hunter talked through the changes in the X-rays in turn. By the time he reached the end of the tour, I knew nearly as much about Merry's skull as the surgeon did. I wished I knew as much about what was going on inside her brain.

"Can you help?"

"Of course. Don't get me wrong. Rosenberg's a good technician and did a decent enough job putting the bones back together. I'm an artist. I can bring her back to what she was or where she should be. Rosenberg can't."

Where she should be? She should be Merry.

Dr. Hunter turned to the stack of color photographs.

"Rosenberg did a better job than I thought. What a mess! Where's the 'after' shot? Okay, not bad, but too many scars and her left eye's still all wrong. Do you have a recent photo from before the wreck?"

Whip pointed to the family portrait from last Christmas.

Dr. Hunter stared at Merry's smiling face. "Funny, I thought she'd be blonde."

After getting assurances Dr. Hunter could reconstruct Merry's face, we agreed to bring her in. We shook hands. Whip waited until he was in the corridor to wipe his hand on his pant leg.

"To quote Alex, yuck." I wiped my hand too.

"I hate men with clammy handshakes. Something vaguely amphibian about them."

When Whip told Merry about his consultation with the plastic surgeon, she wanted to go the next day, but Dr. Hunter had no openings for more than two weeks.

"Doesn't he know how important this is to me?" She ranted and raged to no effect.

"He's busy."

On the appointed day, Whip and I took Merry to Chaminade.

We weren't going to have a repeat of the fiasco with the psychiatrist. Whip would decide what work Merry was going to have done, and I would drive her to her appointments. If Merry rejected Dr. Hunter, we had no backup. It was Hunter or nothing. Nothing wasn't an option.

Merry swallowed a couple of extra pills in the car to settle her nerves. Even so, she fidgeted in the waiting room until Whip snapped, "For God's sake, sit still. They'll call you when it's your turn."

"How can he keep me waiting?" In spite of the drugs, Merry became edgier by the second.

"Mrs. Pugh, Dr. Hunter was delayed in surgery. He'll see you now." The nurse led the way.

"About goddamned time," Merry grumbled.

Dr. Hunter stood behind his desk and smiled. "Merry, may I call you Merry?"

He didn't wait for an answer. He didn't acknowledge Whip or me. We didn't exist.

"Sit down. I'll go over your medical history with you first. Then I'll examine your face to see how much work I have left to do."

Dr. Hunter held up the Christmas photo and said it would be the baseline so he'd know where to start. He showed Merry a series of pictures taken in the hospital right after she arrived. She'd never seen them.

"That can't be me!" Her face looked like hamburger.

"You've come a long way, but you're not where you want to be yet. You agree, don't you?" Dr. Hunter smiled at Merry.

Whip growled. When I asked a couple of questions, they fell to the floor unanswered and were kicked aside under the doctor's desk.

"I asked Mr. Pugh if you wanted your old face back or a new and improved one."

Merry sat in silence. Emotions flittered across her face.

When she didn't respond, Whip did. "We want Merry's left eye to look normal. Fix her nose. Refinish the surface of her skin to take away the scars. I'll be happy when you're back to where you were before the accident."

Dr. Hunter frowned. "Will that be enough for you, Merry?"

CHAPTER NINETEEN

Summer crowded in on the Fourth of July. What happened to "I'll probably be gone a week or two" back in February? Every step toward going home came with two steps backward, keeping me in Riverbend.

Merry's first surgery, the major one where her eye socket and cheekbones would be restructured, was scheduled for the Wednesday after the Fourth. Merry, Whip, and I would be alone that critical period before surgery, because both kids were leaving for summer camp on Friday the second.

Alex was going to a two-week computer camp at Penn State University, where he'd stay in a dorm. "I'll be just like a real college student."

Emilie had chosen a yoga camp in the Great Smoky Mountains. "I want something spiritual, Mad Max, some place where I can get away and meditate a lot."

The more she could learn to handle whatever gift she had through exercise and meditation, the better off she'd be. Whip didn't understand all this woo-hoo stuff; Merry didn't care as long as nothing got in the way of her operation.

On the first of the month, Whip came home for dinner. I met him in the hallway and stared at his empty hands.

"Weren't you supposed to bring home Chinese?" I'd overheard him talking with Merry earlier in the day.

"Crap. Merry promised to order dinner, and I was supposed to pick it up, wasn't I?"

Whip turned on his heel and bolted for the Imperial Palace. He called a few minutes later to tell me he had to wait for the order. Merry hadn't called after all.

Merry seemed to be coming around since she met Dr. Hunter. Was I wrong? I watched her closely, but all I saw was her becoming happier with her initial surgery less than a week away.

Merry was on her first public vodka and tonic in the family room when Whip returned. He put the food down in the kitchen, but she didn't move.

"Get up and set the table."

I wasn't prepared for Whip's anger when he pulled Merry to her feet and pushed her toward the kitchen. He'd had time to work up a bellyful of steam while our food cooked. Whip went to the bottom of the stairs and called the kids.

Alex blasted out of his room, shouting, "I beat Mad Max three times at LAPD today."

"You guys made enough noise for the whole neighborhood to know." Emilie grouched.

"Hey ... Chinese. Cool." Alex grabbed a goldfish box and spooned General Tso's Chicken onto his plate. He added rice and Ants in the Trees, a fancy name for broccoli with black beans.

"You forgot extra egg rolls," Merry complained.

Was that all she thought about?

"If you'd called in the goddamned order like you said you would, you'd have egg rolls."

"You always forget egg rolls, Dad." Emilie, ever the peacemaker, tried to soothe the open wound that was her father's heart.

Whip drew in a deep breath and forced a tight smile. "I guess I do."

We ate in silence, except for Alex's exuberant chomping. I had so much more work to do with him. We were halfway through our meal when Whip said he'd be doing a lot of traveling again. He and his longtime partner, Zach "Tops" Zimmerman, spent the afternoon pouring over staffing assignments.

"Tops and I have several huge projects lined up. I'll supervise at least one of them. We're just about out of skilled people. Only one can keep projects running right."

Baloney. Whip wanted to get away from Merry, if only for a few days at a time. I did too. Each trip home was an escape from my disintegrating daughter.

"You're running away." Emilie set her chopsticks beside her plate and crossed her arms.

I laughed.

"I'm sorry, but you look just like your mother. And me."

Merry turned blurry eyes at Emilie. "Yeah, you look like your grandmother."

She probably meant to hurt me, but I refused to get riled.

"You're running away." Emilie hung onto her thought with the tenacity of a Rottweiler. "Mom, make him stay."

"I don't care if he goes or not. It's all the same to me." With that, Merry got up, refilled her wineglass, and went upstairs, leaving her plate on the table.

"Crap." Whip half-rose then sank back in his chair. "Hey, I'm not leaving tomorrow. My first trip will be while you guys are at camp. You'll never know I'm gone."

I, too, leaned back and crossed my arms under my breasts—metaphorically, since I didn't want to be seen sitting in judgment over my son-in-law. Not in front of Emilie and Alex. Whip and I needed to present a united front, even when it wasn't true.

Whip would never be satisfied in a nine-to-five job, home every night for dinner, weekends doing chores, and taking his wife to dinner on Saturdays. He was only truly happy with the dust of a job site on his boots and one of his guns strapped to his hip. That didn't jibe with being a father.

Alex finished a second helping and began a third while his father talked about several contracts his company won recently: another huge job in the Middle East, repair work on I-95 north of Richmond, something in northern Kentucky, and a tricky tunnel-and-highway project in the Peruvian Andes.

"Not another Middle East assignment, Dad," Emilie said. "The last time ended in this mess we're in."

"It's not fair to blame the area of the world."

"I don't care. I don't want you going to the Middle East. Period."

"You mentioned two jobs in the States, one here at home, one in Kentucky." Before I could go any further, Emilie turned pale and sweaty.

"Dad doesn't want either one. He's going to Peru." Emilie's words were distant, yet distinct.

"How do you know?" Whip had never seen Emilie go to her secret place before.

"When you think about going to Peru, your colors change inside. It's complicated. I'll explain it some other time." She waved a hand in dismissal.

"Peru? I want to go too." Alex turned up the volume to his outdoor-voice level.

"Alex." I held up a finger.

"Sorry."

"I'm right. You're going to Peru." Emilie was close to tears.

"It's a huge job. I don't have anyone else I can trust." Whip lost the battle of wills.

"Hadn't you better find people you can trust?" She carried her plate into the kitchen and returned to the breakfast area. "I thought you trusted Uncle Johnny," she said, then she left.

"Does she mean Johnny Medina?" I'd never heard her refer to anyone by that name.

"Yes."

"Why can't he take Peru?" I was ready to fight even a losing battle if it would keep Whip focused on his parental role.

"He just can't. Wife wants a divorce. Has to be here."

"You don't? Your wife needs you, Whip. Here. Think about her."

"Hey, anyone want the rest of the chicken?"

I shoved the half-empty box across the table. Alex dug in with his chopsticks, apparently too intent on claiming the bits inside to bother putting it on his plate.

"I have to think about this." If Whip was planning to disappear into South America, where did that leave me?

"How long is this project?'

"At least six months."

Whip was manipulating me, and I hated it. He didn't even ask if I could stay.

Alex finished the chicken and went upstairs.

"You can't just tell me you're going away for half a year and expect me to drop everything. I have a life too. It's in New York. Adjust your schedule to take care of your children when I go on vacation this summer."

"I have to work."

I clenched my jaw. "You could work closer to home."

"I don't want to."

"Finally, you've admitted it. You're happier away from home. Well, John Wayne, here's my schedule. Plan around it."

I pulled a paper from the corkboard and plunked it on the table: First two weeks of July—Richmond, taking care of Merry after her operation. The kids would be at camp. Second two weeks of July— the Hamptons on Long Island with Raney and Grace, another of the Great Dames who owned a summer cottage on the shore.

"You have to be home those two weeks. I won't miss my annual summer escape with my girlfriends. I can take the kids to the Outer Banks or Myrtle Beach for the first couple of weeks of August."

Long after we'd retired to our respective rooms, I lay propped in bed, my book unread on my lap. Unusual for me, because the book, the latest FBI Agent Pendergast installment from Douglas Preston and Lincoln Child, couldn't hold my interest.

My thoughts tumbled like wet socks in a runaway dryer.

What do I do about Merry? Was her coldness toward Whip at dinner another example of her changed personality? Is it a different manifestation of her self-absorption?

What if Whip takes the kids with him to Peru for six months? Shit, that won't work. I can't see Whip home schooling Alex, let alone Emilie. What if I demand to take the kids to New York? I could make that work.

With the kids with me in New York, I'd be home, but if Whip left Merry for several months, I didn't think his marriage would survive. Even worse, I didn't think Merry would survive. He'd be choosing his job over his wife. He already had. Had he always been like this?

CHAPTER TWENTY

I drove Merry to her final appointment with Dr. Hunter before her surgery because Whip was busy preparing for Peru. We picked Emilie up after swim class and headed to Chaminade.

When the nurse called Merry's name, we all got up. Merry introduced Emilie to Dr. Hunter. I frowned when he blocked the door.

"Mrs. Davis, wait in the outer office."

"It's Mrs. Davies."

"Yeah. Whatever. I'll speak to your daughter. Alone."

"Why?" I thrust my chin outward.

"Because you two will be in my way. Besides, you have no say in Merry's decisions."

"I thought everything was decided. At least that's what Whip told me."

"It's up to Merry. Go back to the waiting room."

I didn't like the way Dr. Hunter touched Emilie's face before he slammed the door. We returned to the waiting room to, well, wait.

Emilie wrinkled her nose. "What a creep. I thought doctors were supposed to be nice. I didn't like the way he looked at me."

She pulled a novel from her backpack and settled down to read. "Neither did I."

Almost an hour later, Merry emerged with a computer printout in one hand. She smiled up at the doctor and walked into the waiting room.

"Well? What did he say?" I tossed last month's *National Geographic* aside.

"He can make me look twenty-one again, instead of thirty-five."

I was stunned. If what Merry said was true, she'd look like a different person.

"Is this what you and Whip agreed on? That you'd look fifteen years younger? Since when did that matter?" I headed toward the elevator. My blood pressure rose.

"Dr. Hunter said he could change the shape of my eyes too. I'll look younger, more exotic, no longer the run-of-the-mill Riverbend Junior Leaguer."

"What's wrong with the way you used to look? You were beautiful, Mom." Emilie leaned against me.

"Now I'll be better." Merry folded the printout, but Emilie snatched it.

"Who's that?"

"The new me."

I looked over Emilie's shoulder.

"The new you? What about the old you? The you we all love? The you Whip married?" I became more and more upset. My cheeks burned.

"Dr. Hunter's going to make some small changes here and there. I'll be almost the way I was, just better."

"These aren't small changes; it's a total transformation. Whip won't like it. Nor will Alex." I returned the paper.

Merry folded it in quarters and tucked it into her purse.

"Em's already cast her vote."

"You'll look like a stranger." Emilie turned her back on her mother.

"You'd better have a long talk with Whip. You guys should decide this together."

"It's my face. I can do with it as I please. Besides, Dr. Hunter said Whip will love the new me."

"How does he know? Is he clairvoyant? He met Whip, what, twice? Does he know him well enough to make such a statement?"

"Get off my goddamned back." Merry climbed into the passenger seat of the Infiniti. I looked at Emilie in the rearview mirror; she just rolled her eyes and shrugged. I noticed a bead of sweat on her upper lip.

I maneuvered onto I-95 and headed home. It'd take us almost an hour to reach Riverbend without traffic, but we'd been in the doctor's office so long we hit an early rush hour backup. I swore under my breath. The cars ahead of us were at a virtual dead stop.

Since we had time on our hands and Merry was captive, I grilled her. The more questions I asked, the vaguer her answers became. When she said it was up to Dr. Hunter to decide what to do and when, I lost it.

"Why are you so mad?"

"Because you don't know what all he's going to do. You don't know in what order. You don't know how long you'll have to recuperate between procedures." More accusations stuck to the roof of my mouth. I honked when a Lexus cut me off. "You have no idea how long it's going to take from beginning to end."

"It's none of your business."

"That's not true. Until I go home, it's very much my business. Talk to Whip. You're going against his wishes."

"I will. Just shut up."

I didn't know who I wanted to flip off more, Merry or the stupid man in the silver Lexus. He was talking on his cell and holding a cigarette. Does he have a third hand?

"I want to look perfect. I'm going to be perfect. Nothing you say will make me change my mind." Merry stared out the window.

"I don't like him," Emilie chimed in. "He's fangy and creeps me out."

Merry slipped a pill into her mouth. She closed her eyes and leaned her head back against the seat. I'd lost her again.

I delivered Alex to the bus for computer camp on the first and spent over twelve hours driving Emilie to yoga camp outside of Asheville, North Carolina. On the way home, I couldn't get Merry's desire to look twenty-one again out of my mind. Lord knew, that was all she talked about.

Now the three of us sat in chairs along the James, waiting for the annual fireworks show to begin.

"I don't want to come home and find a stranger. I want to come home to my wife."

Merry turned away from Whip. "I want to be twenty-one again."

Be? Not look? Where had that come from?

CHAPTER TWENTY-ONE

One night, about two weeks after Merry's first surgery, I lay in bed engrossed in a hair-raising Michael Connelly murder mystery when someone tapped on my bedroom door.

"Yes?"

"It's me," Emilie whispered. "Sorry to interrupt your reading."

"Come in, dear child." I shifted my pillows higher and motioned for her to climb in on the other side of the bed. "Why are you awake so late?"

Emilie pushed and plumped pillows until she found the right mix. She wriggled into the pile and pulled the coverlet up.

"I don't feel right."

I placed a hand on her forehead. Cool. No fever. "Do you feel ill?"

"No. It's Mom. She's all wrong inside."

"How?"

"Well, since Mom woke up from the coma, she's been all wrong."

I knew both kids resented being shut out.

"Help me understand. You 'feel' things I don't. Tell me what it's like so I can get it."

I put an arm around Emilie and tried to snuggle, but her shoulders were rigid. I massaged her neck to see if I could get her to relax. It didn't work.

"I'll try." She took a deep, calming breath, something she learned at her yoga retreat. "Okay, before the accident, Mom was like all happy and bright from the inside out. Now, she's dark. Since she met that creepy guy and had her operation, she's started to get bright again."

"Creepy guy?"

"You know, the yucky surgeon."

I had no flipping clue what Emilie meant. I was in the farthest reaches of the twilight zone. One thing I got, though. Whatever it was, it was very, very real to her.

"How long has this been going on, Em?" I hugged her for strength. For me as much as for her.

"Kinda like my whole life. It's getting stronger as I get older."

My thumbs tried to make a dent in her shoulders. "Have you always been able to feel your mom's moods?"

Emilie rolled her eyes.

"Du-uh. I feel everybody's moods. Not just Mom's."

"You feel mine?"

"It's not mind reading or anything like that."

Didn't she just read my mind? "What's it like, then?"

"Well, some people can see auras around people, but I don't. I feel colors inside people." Emilie pushed herself up and propped both elbows on her knees. "It's like this. Mom's old center color was yellow."

"Yellow's good?" Nothing like drowning in the unknown.

"Yes." She waved her hands like I was an annoying gnat. To Emilie, the answers must be obvious. "Yellow's happy. When things happen, the outside edge colors change, depending on someone's mood. Darker colors mean mad or scared, lighter mean happy or comfortable."

"Does Mom have a different color now?"

"Kinda. It's still yellow but it's like so much darker. She's no longer happy. She's scared. Do you get it now?"

Oddly enough, I did. "What about your dad?"

"Dad's blue, very calm and controlled."

"That's funny. I've always thought your dad was like Paul Newman in *Cool Hand Luke*."

Emilie giggled. "That's, like, so perfect."

"What about me?" In for a minute, in for a mile. Might as well know what she thought of me.

"Pinky-orange."

"That's a different happy from the way Mom was?"

"You bet. You're more like Julia Roberts in *Pretty Woman*—goofy but super nice."

Julia Roberts? No way. Lauren Bacall in *To Have and Have Not* maybe. This child needed exposure to the classic films. It'd be fun to see if she liked *Casablanca*.

"So that's what you meant the other day when you said I was pinky-orange again."

"Yup."

"And Alex?"

Emilie giggled again. "What's that thing called? You know, that old-fashioned tube you look into and turn?"

"A kaleidoscope?" Alex as a toy with ever-shifting colors was perfect.

"That's it. Alex's center is blue like Dad's, but his outer colors constantly change. He bounces all over the place."

"Back to your mom. She's not getting better, is she?"

"No." Emilie leaned against my shoulder. A tear fell on my pajama top. "She's kinda scared, unhappy. She's not warm and bright anymore."

She wiped her eyes on the back of her hand. "She's only happy when she thinks about her face. I wish she'd be happy when she thinks about me. I miss Mom."

"So do I, dear child. So do I."

I wanted my daughter back so badly I could spit. I even missed fighting with her. Was this the way it was going to be, just drifting along? Or would we work through this and emerge in a better place? I didn't want to say it, but I had serious doubts about healing my relationship with my daughter. I was scared shitless she wouldn't get back anywhere close to where she was before the accident.

I had to do better with Emilie. It was part of my doo-wop.

"Mom'll never be what she was. Even when she's bright, it doesn't include Alex and me anymore." More tears. "She doesn't love us. We're like leftovers."

"She's been through a difficult time."

"So have we, but she's never ignored a birthday. Alex turns eleven in two weeks. I thought she'd plan something."

I'd asked Merry about Alex's birthday, but she had "plans." Those plans, which should have focused on her son, didn't include him.

"If your mom won't come, we'll have a great party without her.

I'll make sure Dad's home. We'll have a pool party."

"It won't be the same." Emilie sniffed and wiped her nose on the tissue I offered.

"You're right. It won't." I wouldn't fill her head with false hope.

"I don't know how else to say it, but it's like Mom's not there any longer. She's turning into someone else."

I bit my lip. I wanted to cry and laugh at the same time. Cry because my daughter was causing her daughter so much pain. Laugh because I saw aliens stealing her personality.

"Don't worry. There are no pods growing in the backyard." I hugged her until she grunted.

"I know. I looked. No *Invasion of the Body Snatchers,* but something or someone has snatched her."

"Indeed."

"Don't leave us, Mad Max." Emilie pulled away to stare at me. "We need you so much."

"I'm not going anywhere until we get your mom back."

"She's not coming back," Emilie whispered as she burrowed into the stack of pillows.

As I feared, Merry was a no-show at Alex's birthday party. I plopped in a chaise by the pool and sipped a gin and tonic, light on the gin, heavy on the tonic and ice. The party was over, and I stared at its detritus. Alex invited a dozen boys and girls to the pool party. For once, the weather cooperated.

My head pounded from the shrieks that echoed around the pool all afternoon. The kids had water fights, a water polo match, and swim races, and played blindfolded Marco Polo and dunk-the-girls-off-the-raft contests. I ordered pizza and sub sandwiches. Adults lounged around the edge of the pool or on the covered patio, each keeping a sharp eye on the high jinks. Too much roughhousing earned a kid a time-out.

After four hours in the sun, the party wound down. We ate cake. Alex opened his gifts and, with some prompting from Whip, thanked everyone for coming. The guests drifted away. Alex and Whip went upstairs to try out a couple of new PlayStation games. Emilie was off to her girlfriend Molly's house for a sleepover. As for Merry, she had buried herself in her room with a bottle of vodka before the party began, and never came out.

CHAPTER TWENTY-TWO

"Why don't you send Johnny to Peru?"

"I can't. If I don't get away for a while, I'll lose my mind."

"You're a damned coward, Whip Pugh. Em was right. You're running away."

"I'm all torn up about this, Max. Know I should stay with Merry and the kids, but I can't. Can't watch her deteriorate."

"We've been over this before. Merry needs you."

"Maybe my being away will snap her back to where she was before the accident."

"Maybe pigs really do fly." I didn't see a single chance in hell of either happening.

Whip spent two days with Alex and Emilie before leaving. They went to Kings Dominion where they rode rollercoasters until they were sick to their stomachs. After a day at the theme park, they went to Morton's Steakhouse for dinner. Emilie told me later her dad asked a lot of questions about their mother. Even when he was in town, he wasn't in the house much. He didn't see firsthand how troubled their lives were.

"I unloaded on him. He knows about how much Mom's pushed us out of her life."

"I'm glad you did. Your father needs to hear from you guys, not just from me."

"So after that, me and Alex—"

"Alex and I."

"Alex and I gave Dad a list of stuff we wanted." Emilie handed me a piece of paper. I read it and tried not to laugh. I also tried not to cry. When did these kids get so wise?

Mad Max has to stay until we say she can leave.

Dad has to set up a schedule for when he'll come home and for how long he'll stay.

Dad has to call home every other night and talk with each of them.

Emilie can go out on supervised group dates and have her curfew set at 11 instead of 10 on a weekend.

Alex can continue with soccer, basketball and computer club.

Emilie can continue with swim league, field hockey, and her writing club.

Alex can play video games for a minimum of two hours each weekday and as much as he wants on the weekends.

Emilie can do whatever she wants with her hair.

At least once, Emilie and Alex want to visit Dad in Peru.

Not one mentioned Merry.

"Only nine?"

"Well, there are two more. We told Dad he shouldn't tell Alex to be the man of the house or me to take care of Mom."

I got it. Alex, a newly-minted eleven, needed to be the kid of the house. I could get down with that.

"Why shouldn't Dad ask you to take care of Mom?"

"I do enough of it already, and I want to do less. She's supposed to be taking care of me. I don't want to be a parent. I want to be a teenager."

"I get it. Dad accepted your ultimatums?"

"Not completely. Here's his list."

It's okay with him for Mad Max to stay, but Mad Max has to agree.

He will set up a schedule for coming home as soon as he is settled in Peru.

He will call home every other night and talk with each of them, if they are home.

Emilie can go out on supervised group dates, if she keeps her grades up once school starts.

It's okay for Alex to continue with soccer, basketball, and computer club.

Ditto for Emilie with swim league, field hockey, and her writing club.

Emilie can do whatever she wants with her hair, but absolutely no tattoos or body piercing.

At least once, Emilie and Alex are to visit Dad in Peru, if the worksite is safe and has room for them.

"Dad added three of his own." Emilie pointed to the last bullets.

You'll do whatever Mad Max says. She's in charge.

Alex, you'll bring your grades back to a B+ range. I know you can do it.

You'll both be respectful to your mother.

"And then we did a 'pinky swear.'"

We'd been doing pinky swears as long as I could remember. It was a promise that couldn't be broken.

Emilie held out a crooked little finger. I hooked mine around hers.

"Pinky swear," Emilie said.

"Pinky swear," I promised.

CHAPTER TWENTY-THREE

Whip left on a flood of tears from Emilie, shouts of "take me with you" from Alex, and a hug and kiss on the cheek from me. Nothing from Merry. She didn't even bother to come downstairs to see him off.

With Whip going back to Peru, I could no longer battle with him on a daily basis about Merry. I hoped that would take some of the toxicity out of the house. Maybe I could talk some sense into my daughter.

On the first Thursday after Whip left, I dragged Merry to dinner at Jonathan's Inn to try to restore a normal relationship. I coerced her, because she didn't want to go anywhere with me except to her creepy doctor. Since she'd come through her first major reconstruction with good results, I forced her to celebrate her new-old face.

Jonathan's Inn was old-school, with dim lighting, sound-dampening flooring and widely-spaced tables. Even with a retirement party of over twenty guests celebrating at the other end of the restaurant, our table was tucked into a quiet alcove. I liked the restaurant for its ambience and its filets. It also had the best wine cellar in greater Richmond.

I hoped dinner would tear down some barriers between us and let us chat about trivial things the way we used to. Merry was in a bizarre mood when we left the house. She refused to speak in the car, an obvious hostage to the situation. When we were seated, the waiter poured wine.

"A toast to the return of your beautiful face." I raised my glass.

"Not yet." Merry refused to touch rims.

I sipped around the lump in my throat.

"Give it time. Dr. Hunter said it would take one or two big operations and a few smaller ones."

"I told you, this isn't where I want to be." Merry looked over my shoulder at her reflection in the floor-to-ceiling windows. Darkness blocked the view of the river and created a perfect mirror.

I avoided saying anything about her crazy plan to look twenty-one again. I'd promised Emilie I wouldn't poke her. Mute Merry pushed her lobster around her plate. I ate, not because I was hungry, but because I wasn't going to get suckered into whatever game she played. "What's the matter?"

"Nothing."

"You avoid me. You hardly speak. I want to help, but I don't know how." I pushed my half-empty plate aside and poured more wine. Merry held out her glass.

"I still hate the way I look."

"We've been over this before." Too many times to count. "You're almost back to where you were before your accident."

"It's not enough."

"It's enough for Whip and your children. It's enough for me." Tears threatened to choke me. "I wish it were enough for you."

"I won't feel good until I look the way I did before I got married."

"What?" Where did that come from?

"Or better. Dr. Hunter says I'll look even better when he's done." Merry smiled a private smile whenever she mentioned Hunter's name.

"I'll look twenty-one again."

Whip was excluded from the decision.

"I'll be a whole new me."

"I don't want a whole new you. I want you." I crossed my arms under my breasts. I didn't care if I looked combative. I felt combative.

"I don't care. I want to be perfect."

"Your family doesn't want you to be perfect. We want you to be Merry." Fingers of worry dug into my neck. The muscles knotted, and a headache throbbed at the base of my skull.

"Well, Dr. Hunter says he can make me twenty-one again."

Again, the smile only included Merry and her doctor.

"Who cares what Dr. Hunter wants?" I tried to draw a line between a poke and speaking my mind.

"I do. I'm going to do whatever he says. He knows best." Merry turned away.

"Why do you want to look twenty-one again?"

A riot of sound erupted from the retirement party. "For He's A Jolly Good Fellow" led into a round of applause. I almost missed Merry's next words.

"Because that was before I had kids."

CHAPTER TWENTY-FOUR

Merry disappeared upstairs as soon as we got home. I went into the empty family room to think. So, she wanted to return to a life before kids. When I thought about it objectively, I'd heard her say variations of the same thing since she came home. It finally added up to a whole lot of crap.

What kind of hold did this creepy doctor have over her? Whenever I tried to discuss her upcoming surgical schedule, I couldn't get a straight answer. Her next was three weeks out, another fairly large reconstruction that would keep her in the hospital overnight at least. I remembered the nose and the final restructuring of the cheekbones coming next, but who knew? Hunter may have changed the order of what he was going to do. In fact, he may have changed *what* he was going to do.

I couldn't figure out what "being" twenty-one meant. Did it mean she was getting ready to bolt and dump the kids on me permanently? Well, she did that months ago, so I couldn't see how rolling back the clock would free her of obligations she'd already abdicated. Did she want to end her marriage? What Whip provided of late was room and board. He was an infrequent father and nonexistent husband. I was the center of the family, with Emilie trying to be a close second.

This was a night of "for onces." For once, I was glad Whip was gone. For once, I was glad Emilie and Alex were both at sleepovers.

For once, I was glad Merry was tucked into whatever substance she wanted to abuse. For once, I didn't call Raney.

So, Merry found being a mother inconvenient. Well, she should have thought about that fourteen years ago. Wait, that wasn't fair. Since the accident and the brain injury, Merry had changed. I now believed Emilie. She wasn't coming back.

I sent a silent message to Emilie. "We'll get through this. I promise."

I felt a warmth flow over me.

I called Dr. Silberman and asked him to work me in as soon as possible.

He met me after hours on Friday. He took one look at my face. "Something's happened with Mrs. Pugh."

Boy, did I open up and dump everything on him. I talked for nearly an hour before he brought me a bottle of cold water. I gulped, unaware until that moment how parched my throat was.

"So, Merry's unwilling to be a mother."

"Yes." I sipped from the icy bottle.

"From what Emilie has told me—she's given me permission to tell you what we discuss, by the way—her mother has no interest in her or anyone else." Dr. Silberman pulled a file from his desk, removed a couple of pages and set them aside. "You don't have many options."

"I didn't think I did."

"And Mr. Pugh is still traveling all the time, isn't he?"

"He won't stay home. I won't leave the kids, so we have a standoff. Merry's not doing anything and Whip's off in Peru, happy as a pig in shit."

I walked over to the window and peered out at the gathering dusk. A storm was building. Lightning flashed far off. I needed a knock-down storm to clear the air and my head.

"Have you told Mr. Pugh what Mrs. Pugh said?"

I shook my head. "Not yet. I'll send him an e-mail tonight."

"Call him. You don't want him to read this. He'll need to talk it out."

"You're right. I was being a chicken."

"Mrs. Davies, you had only two decisions: Go or stay. You decided to stay. All the other decisions are Mr. Pugh's."

"I figured."

"Your staying provides stability for Emilie and Alex. Mr. Pugh also has limited options." He tapped his forefinger on his desk. "I'll give you something for him to read. I urge him to retain legal counsel as soon as he can."

"Can you really change your mind about being a parent?"

Dr. Silberman smiled. "Sad but true. Not everyone wants to be a parent, Mrs. Davies. Some decide before they have children; others realize it after. If they decide early, children can be turned over to the courts for adoption, or placed with another family member. Mr. Pugh might be able to gain custody, since you're in the house."

"What grounds would Whip have?"

"There are several: parental disinterest, neglect, mental illness, drug or alcohol abuse. Mr. Pugh would have to stand up in court and swear to his wife's inability to continue being a parent. It would be easier were Mrs. Pugh to agree."

"Either way, Merry and Whip lose."

"Yes, Mrs. Davies, but the children win."

I shook his hand and left. Late that night, I called Whip.

I kept my promise to take Merry to Chaminade for her second major operation. According to Dr. Hunter, he would do two in the hospital; everything else would be outpatient.

Merry was pissed off when I told her I couldn't bring her home. After I'd talked with Whip, I booked flights to Peru for the kids and me. I timed the departure to coincide with Merry's surgery. Darla promised to drive her home, even though the two argued over the radical changes Merry was making. Call me cold, but it was time Merry started driving. I told her I'd no longer drive her to and from Chaminade for every doctor's appointment.

After what passed for dinner, I talked at Merry until the soft chime signaling the end of visiting hours sounded through the wards.

"I can't wait. I've worked with Dr. Hunter on all the computer simulations. He's made so many suggestions to improve my whole face, to make it perfect." Merry looked at me for the first time since the orderly removed the dinner tray. "What?"

"Is this really what you want?" I examined my nails, my face burning.

"Of course. Dr. Hunter says I won't recognize myself."

"This sounds like what Dr. Hunter wants. Is it what Whip wants? Is it what you want?"

"Who cares what Whip wants. Besides, Dr. Hunter—"

"Hello, Merry." Dr. Hunter appeared in the doorway. "Ready?"

"Absolutely. Make me perfect."

Dr. Hunter smiled. "I didn't say I could make you perfect. I said I could make your face perfect. Now, get a good night's sleep. I have a lot of work to do tomorrow."

He glanced at me. "Leave. I've ordered a sedative. Merry's going to sleep soon."

I gave Dr. Hunter a "You arrogant ass!" look. The glare bounced off his back. I gathered my things and walked to the door but stopped just outside the room where I could still see my daughter. I wondered what the doctor would do next.

A nurse came in and gave Merry a shot. She was groggy when Dr. Hunter muttered something about almond-shaped eyes and high cheekbones.

That can't be right. They'd agreed on rounder eyes. Had I forgotten the original computer printout? Nothing on it showed those kinds of changes.

"I'll make everything right this time, Kiki. I promise," Dr. Hunter whispered.

Kiki? Who the hell's Kiki? I was creeped out. I watched with horror when Dr. Hunter kissed my daughter's forehead. What was going on?

CHAPTER TWENTY-FIVE

The day after Merry's operation, Emilie, Alex, and I left for Peru. Darla, who'd promised to bring Merry home, called during a layover in Miami. Merry was home, but we wouldn't recognize her. Hunter had made major structural changes. I worried through the rest of the flight before deciding I could do nothing to change whatever damage was done. I chalked it up to tough love.

I felt cramped and cranky by the time the plane landed in Lima. I'd read and listened to my iPod and despaired about Merry's deterioration. I was more than ready to deplane. I hoped, given enough time and distance, I'd be able to find a way to put things right with Merry. When we walked out of the customs area into baggage claim, Whip stood next to a freckled redhead who barely came to his shoulder. This must be Charlie Lopez-Garcia, Whip's boss.

"Not what you expected, huh?" Charlie grasped my hand with a firm, work-hardened grip.

"Not even close."

"Mom's as Irish as the day is long. Dad's Mexican from Vera Cruz. Lots of blonds and redheads on both sides of the family."

I introduced Emilie and Alex. Emilie had a curious expression on her face; Alex gawked. We fetched our baggage and walked out to the truck that would take us into the Andes the next day.

We pulled away from the hotel just before dawn.

"You'll soon see why I don't drive this at night," Charlie said.

Ten miles out of town, I understood what she meant. When we pulled off the main highway to the interior, the road became little more than a lane-and-a-half dirt track with washouts and potholes large enough to rip the undercarriage out of any truck if the driver hit them too hard. No guardrails. We switched back and forth up the mountain.

Toward the end of the day, we caught our first glimpse of the site when we crested a pass and suddenly, a settlement of sorts amid high mountain pastures came into view. Brown grazers on the slopes were juxtaposed with raw earth, trailers, and all kinds of outbuildings.

"Way cool. Are those horses?" Alex pointed to the grazers.

"No, Alex, they're llamas." Charlie pointed to a couple of trailers and some metal buildings off to one side. "Max, you and the kids will be in the larger trailer. You're looking at our luxury suite. When Whip and the rest of the guys got here, they had tents. Not much else."

"And I loved it." Whip took off his hat and wiped his forehead. "Better now with the trailers and permanent buildings, though."

"I'm going to love this place." I looked around at the raw beauty of the mountains surrounding the work site.

"Kinda grows on you." Whip carried our bags into the trailer.

"The kids can see what you do." I tossed my handbag on one of the bunks. *Looks like I'm sharing a "room" with Emilie.* "Take charge of them for a while too."

"Me?"

"Yes, Dad. You. I'm on vacation."

Alex nearly got himself blown up on the third day when he wandered too close to the blasting zone. I heard an explosion and a thud and ran out of the trailer. Alex lay on his back, covered in dust. He squirmed and coughed.

"Are you all right?" I propped him up and felt for broken bones.

Whip roared up in a truck and leaped out before it came to a halt. Charlie bolted out of the office trailer, yelling for the cook whom, it seemed, had some rudimentary first aid training.

"He's okay." I held up a dirty hand. "Scared, but not hurt."

"What the hell happened?" Whip's fear came out like a bark.

"I got too close to the blasting site." Alex cried as much from his scare as in anticipation of what his dad was going to do to him.

"Follow me, Captain Chaos."

"Captain Chaos, huh," Charlie said. "That fits."

I agreed.

Alex ended up with a lot of bruises and the loss of all privileges for a day. When his dad let him out of purgatory, the kids and I flew to Cusco and rode the bus to Machu Picchu.

"Read this before we get there." I handed copies of a guidebook on the famous Inca city.

Our book said seeing the city at sunrise was an absolute must. We followed a guide up a hiking trail in the pre-dawn blackness. We came to a teeth-chattering halt fifteen minutes before sunrise. When the rays of the sun slid over the surrounding peaks, I understood the special nature of this place. Emilie and Alex snapped picture after picture and walked all around the city, oohing and ahhing over its wonderful state of preservation.

After a picnic lunch, Emilie found a place in an old town square, folded her hands, and closed her eyes to meditate. Alex scrambled over walls and ran down ancient streets, shouting about everything he saw.

I hated to leave, but the guide hustled us back down the trail late in the afternoon even though there was still plenty of sunlight.

"You want to stay longer? Come in summer. Days are longer."

Having climbed up the trail in the dark, I could see why he wanted to return in the daylight. We made it with little more than a twisted ankle. It took one step and not watching where I put my boot to find a rock. I spent the rest of the trip wrapped in an Ace bandage.

Ten days passed before we knew it. We packed to leave when Whip told us he was coming too. Alex and Emilie didn't want to leave. Something was bothering them. Time to find out.

"Okay, spill. What's going on?" I plunked myself down on the side of a cot.

"We haven't heard much from Mom," Emilie started. "She's only answered the phone twice since her operation."

"And then she said we wouldn't recognize her," Alex said.

"But I want to recognize her." Emilie shifted from foot to foot.

"How does she feel?" In a spooky way, her gift was an early warning system into Merry's frame of mind.

"She's happy." Emilie filled the two words with foreboding.

Both children finished packing in silence. I called Merry one last time to tell her when we were arriving, but she didn't answer. I sent a text message, telling her when to meet us at the airport.

Emilie and I were first through the door into the arrival area, my granddaughter chattering a mile a minute as usual. Alex followed right behind, fussing with a loose strap on his backpack. Emilie stopped so quickly, her brother slammed into her. She elbowed me and pointed to where Merry stood near the bottom of the escalator in baggage claim.

Even though she wore huge sunglasses, they couldn't hide the dramatic changes in my daughter's face. Her cheekbones stuck out like blades where before they used to be soft little apples. Her nose was shorter and tipped upward like Michael Jackson's. I ran down the escalator and whipped off her glasses. She looked grotesque. Her eyes were narrow, not round like they used to be. She'd covered the yellowing bruises with makeup, but not even war paint applied with a spatula could hide the structural changes.

"What in God's name did you do?"

So much for being supportive. So much for not poking. I was too angry to tap dance on eggshells as I'd been doing since I promised Emilie I'd be more understanding. Well, screw that. I was damned pissed and didn't see any reason to hide it. Besides I was positive my face had red blotches, a warning sign my daughter had seen far too often lately. Merry no longer looked like the child I'd bore.

Emilie shot Alex a sibling-only look. She grew pallid under her Peruvian tan and blinked away tears.

"Jeez, Mom, what happened?" Alex blurted. "You look awful."

Merry must have misunderstood, because she said the bruising was temporary.

"That's not what I meant. You're a freak." Alex shrugged his overstuffed backpack onto his shoulders and stomped to the baggage carousel.

"We wanted you back, Mom." Tears slid down Emilie's face. "This isn't what we meant. Why'd you do it?" Emilie turned her back and followed her brother.

"We changed our minds because we thought a different eye

would go better with the new cheekbones." Merry's voice rose. Old habits die hard.

"What's with this 'we' shit? You and Dr. Hunter? You and Whip agreed to return you to you." I, too, walked away.

"You leave him out of this. I like my face, and I don't care if you approve or not." Merry's voice grew shrill when we challenged her happiness. We rained on her parade.

"Just wait 'til Whip sees you. Boy, is he going to be pissed!" I couldn't help myself. Time to pound some sense into my daughter's addled brain.

"I don't care." Merry pouted.

"Don't care about what, Merry?" Whip walked up behind her.

Merry whirled around. "What the hell are you doing here?"

"Quite the welcome." Whip kept his voice even. He didn't mention Merry's face, but he took her arm and steered her toward the baggage carousel.

"I meant, I'm surprised to see you. I thought you'd be gone for a while longer. That's all."

The tightening of Whip's lips said he didn't believe her. He wasn't going to take Merry's transformation without comment, but baggage claim wasn't the place for war.

I put my arm around Emilie, and we shared another of those shut-out-Mom looks. Shutting out Merry was an engrained habit. I wanted to blame her for shutting us out, too, but that would have let me off the "I'm the grown-up" hook.

Whip drove home in silence. Merry went straight to her bedroom, where I suspected she washed down a pill with a stiff slug of vodka. Whip followed her upstairs after a few minutes.

CHAPTER TWENTY-SIX

Alex ran down the street to show his friends the treasures he bought in Peru. Emilie and I raided the fridge for cold drinks and wandered out to the patio. I wanted Whip to have some privacy when he confronted Merry; Emilie said she wanted to listen to what he said.

"Eavesdropping, huh?"

"You got that right." She didn't have to wait long before her dad's voice thundered through the open bedroom window.

"What the hell were you thinking? Huh? You went behind my back and changed everything. Not a word in advance? Did you think I wouldn't notice?"

"I didn't th-th-think" Merry stammered.

"You're damned right you didn't think. Was this your idea or his?"

"Dad's using his outdoor voice indoors," Emilie whispered.

"Brat." I put my finger to my lips.

"We talked it over. Dr. Hunter made so many good suggestions. I liked them." Merry's voice trembled.

"Does he have a book?"

"A book? What do you mean, a book?"

"Like books of hairstyles in your beauty parlor. Does he have a similar one for faces? You can pick one from column A and two from column B?"

"Don't be stupid."

"Oops, wrong thing to say." I shut my eyes and wished I could be a fly on the wall in the bedroom instead of an ear on the patio.

"You're the one who's being stupid. Looks like you're picking someone else's body parts. Eyes like Lucy Liu. Cheekbones from Audrey Hepburn."

"Katharine."

"Katharine?"

"The cheekbones are like Katharine Hepburn's, not Audrey's." Merry's voice quavered.

"What's next? Madonna's chin? JLo's lips? Lassie's nose?"

Emilie giggled. "Can you imagine Mom with Lassie's nose?"

"Hush." I pinched her arm.

"What the hell are you talking about?"

"I'm talking about my wife. You, in case you forgot. I'm talking about you making changes because a stranger wants to transform your face into someone else's."

"He's not a stranger."

"He's not family!" Whip's roar would have done Thor proud. "You value his opinion over mine, don't you?"

"I wondered when Dad would come to that conclusion."

"Me too." I'd long ago decided Hunter wielded way too much control over my daughter.

"No ... but Dr. Hunter knows what will look best. He's the professional."

"I don't think so, my dear misguided wife. My gut tells me he knows what's best for him. Not for you. Or for me."

"Dad's mad enough to hit Mom," Emilie said, "but he won't."

I walked to the edge of the patio and stared at the pool. "Don't you find it odd all of us but Alex want to hit Mom?"

"None of us will." Emilie stretched and headed for the door. "Dad's done yelling."

The front door banged when Whip left the house. Emilie and I went upstairs to unpack.

Hours later, Whip wandered into the kitchen where I washed the last of the pots and pans. I tossed him a towel and gestured at the stack in the dish drainer.

"Do you remember *Moonstruck*?" I put the last pan in the rack and turned on the dishwasher.

"That old Cher movie?" Whip wiped a skillet and handed it to me to put away.

"That's the one. Whenever Cher's family needed to talk, they went to the kitchen. Well, we're in the kitchen. We need to talk."

We sat at the table.

"I'm worried shitless about the power Hunter has over Merry." I'd been stewing over everything I heard Merry say about him since they met. "She said only he knows what's best for her. He'll make everything perfect."

"You heard the fight."

"Yes, but she's been unraveling for months. Wanting to be perfect is the last straw."

Whip frowned. "I gotta put a stop to this shit."

"High time. What are you going to do?"

"Confront Hunter. I'll make him listen to me."

"Think it'll work?"

"Has to. If not, my marriage is over."

CHAPTER TWENTY-SEVEN

Whip called Hunter and told him to stop operating on his wife. He was done. "I warned him that if he touched her again, I'd take legal action."

"What did he say?" I headed upstairs with an armload of clean clothes.

"He laughed."

With nothing more to be gained in the Hunter department and after many more late-night kitchen-table conversations, Whip went back to Peru. The kids and I returned to living with the ghost of Merry past. Over the next two months, Whip came home three times. On each visit, he found more and more of a stranger in his house. Hunter completely ignored the warning. Not only did Merry look different, she no longer acted like the woman he married.

During Whip's latest time in Peru, Merry left early one morning. She returned after I'd gone to bed. When I saw her the next morning, her profile was different. Not her face. Her chest. Merry had gone up three cup sizes. She wasn't wearing a padded bra.

She bleached her hair as part of change-Merry-into-a-stranger too. Something about the blond hair bothered me, but I couldn't figure out what it was. Besides, I had too much to worry about without adding Merry going blond and Emilie going purple to the mix.

I didn't tell Whip about the boob job. He'd see for himself soon enough.

I discovered more subtle changes in Merry's face. First it was the lack of lines in her forehead. Then no crow's-feet. Collagen and Botox treatments in addition to the surgical procedures? The smile commas around her mouth stayed, until they, too, disappeared when she came home with a new chin.

"Are you having this done in his office?" I confronted Merry after the chin entered the kitchen.

"It's outpatient."

When she tilted her face, half a dozen stitches showed underneath.

"You have an incision."

"Hey, don't make such a big deal out of it. Dr. Hunter shaved some bone to make my chin smaller."

I turned my back and walked out to the patio.

Hours later, I made a phone call.

"Eleanor? It's Maxine. I need a favor." I was back on the patio after dinner. It was dark, and the pool lighting cast its eerie blue glow across my legs.

"Anything."

"I need the name of your private investigator." I squeezed my eyes shut against the sudden burn of tears.

"You want Anthony Ferraiolli. He is the best. He always gets results." When Eleanor's youngest son got into trouble with drugs years earlier, she found Anthony through a mutual friend. He gave her the evidence she needed to confront her son. "It is never too late to call. The man does not sleep."

I wrote down the number and hung up. Then I breathed deeply and dialed.

When time for Whip's monthly return arrived, I drove Emilie and Alex to the airport to pick him up. He'd been able to catch an earlier connector from Dulles, so we had to scurry to be on time. I sent a text to Merry with the new information. No response.

"Shouldn't we have warned Dad about Mom?" Emilie asked while we waited for her father.

"He's not blind. He'll see soon enough."

We collected Whip and walked to the car, where Alex sat in front with me and dominated the conversation. Emilie snuggled close in the backseat and leaned her purple hair against her dad's shoulder. She spoke only when asked a direct question. I played Sphinx, my face neutral. Merry's car wasn't in the garage when we got home.

"It's Wednesday. She has appointments on Wednesdays," was all I said.

"She'll be home for dinner?" Whip sounded pissed.

"Maybe, maybe not. Most times she has dinner with 'friends' after her 'appointment.'" Only parents of a teenage girl could understand how much sarcasm one could put into a single sentence. Imaginary quotation marks hung in midair.

Alex ran out of news and was off IMing and texting his buddies. Emilie vanished. I raised an eyebrow and headed toward the kitchen.

Whip followed but not before sidetracking to the bar to pour four fingers of Scotch. He slumped into a kitchen chair. "What the hell's going on?"

Whip rubbed tired eyes. He'd dozed on the plane, but he didn't look ready to cope with the pile of shit I was about to lay on him.

I told him I'd hired Eleanor's private investigator, who had sent a guy out to follow Merry. He started from the house, tailed her to the Heritage Hotel in downtown Richmond, and took cell phone pictures of Merry with a man in the dining room. He followed them upstairs where they entered a hotel room. The desk clerk said they were Wednesday night regulars. You could plan your retirement on them.

"I had to be sure the report was true, but I couldn't go to the Heritage alone. I don't know many people here anymore. I called Johnny and asked him to go with me."

"Johnny? As in Johnny Medina?" Whip must have thought I'd segued into a different story.

"Focus, Whip. Johnny and I sat around a corner from Merry, ate dinner and watched."

"She's seeing Hunter." Whip guessed what was obvious to the kids and me.

"Who else?"

Hunter's name fit; he was a predator who exploited my daughter's fears to control her. I remembered Emilie's initial impression of the doctor's creepiness. I could add manipulative and unethical and lots of other adjectives if I thought about it hard enough.

"I'm not looking for approval or forgiveness." I pulled a large manila envelope from the desk drawer and set it on the table. "I have a written report and photos. The PI threw in a little something extra. Eleanor said it's the way they work. Get the goods and issue a gentle warning."

"He didn't rough the guy up, did he?" Whip rubbed his stubbly chin.

"No way. Two paragraphs in the paper reported a doctor came out of work one afternoon and found someone had shot up the engine of his BMW. The cops said it looked like a random crime. Probably kids out for a cheap thrill."

"Good one." Whip laughed. "Kill his car."

"I hoped I was imagining things, but I'm not." I wiped a tear away. "I'm sorry."

"It's not your fault. Merry's been weird since the accident." Whip clenched his fists; the muscles in his neck bulged. There it was again: "since the accident." "I'll handle it."

"I can help, Dad." Neither of us had heard Emilie come downstairs.

I poured iced tea and waved her to the table. Family council. Only Alex was missing.

"Mom and Mrs. Livingston had a big fight. Mom told her she was having an affair." Emilie stirred sugar into the tea. "Mrs. Livingston won't talk to Mom until she stops seeing Dracula."

"Dracula?" Whip frowned.

"Why Dracula?"

Emilie hadn't referred to the doctor as anything but creepy before. Now he had a nickname. Perfect, since Hunter's sucking the lifeblood out of our family.

"It's his teeth. He needs braces. The eyeteeth are crooked and snaggly. I have a bad feeling about him."

I leaned closer to Emilie.

"You can feel Mom when she's with Dracula?"

"Du-uh." Emilie sipped her tea. She got up and fetched an apple.

"Dracula totally scares me." Emilie polished the Gala on her T-shirt and bit into it. The apple responded with a satisfying crunch.

"Can you feel him too?"

"Of course."

"You think he's bad." Why I thought of Hunter like that, I didn't know, except he was responsible for what Merry had become.

"He's ice cold. All dark. Even when he and Mom are together, he's not warm or light. He makes her do things she doesn't want to. He, like, creeps me out."

Emilie knew a lot more about evil than she should.

Whip picked up the PI's report. "I'll take care of this, Em. You go back to being my daughter. Leave this mess to me."

After he left, Emilie turned to me. "Yeah, like I wish," and went upstairs.

I sat for a long time thinking about what to do next. I had no freaking clue.

CHAPTER TWENTY-EIGHT

Whip went to his den to read the report I'd already memorized. I hadn't wrapped my head around anything beyond the affair itself. The implications of Merry's actions were more than I could accept.

Pizza would have to do for dinner, because I didn't feel like cooking. Even if Emilie, Whip, and I weren't hungry, Alex, the human locust, would scarf down every last piece.

We chewed and swallowed in silence, while Merry's empty place screamed at us. Whip fled back to his den as soon as the pizza was gone. Alex volunteered to eat all of the pizza crusts, and Emilie volunteered to toss the box. I tapped on the den door. Whip had made a huge mess of his normally neat desk.

"She's totally fucked up my credit," Whip said even before I curled into a chair.

"Damn."

Whip waved at two stacks of envelopes. "Cleaned out two bank accounts. Checking account's all right, but my year-end bonus is missing. The kids' college funds are empty."

"How much?"

"Two hundred thousand, more or less."

"Shit."

"Maxed out three credit cards too."

"Double shit." I spoke more to myself than to Whip. "Will the bad news ever end?"

"Where the hell is she?"

"Probably out with Hunter."

Whip slammed his fist on the desk and shot out of his chair. He bounced from wall to wall, too upset to sit. Finally, he unlocked his gun safe and pulled out his cleaning supplies, along with a squeaky clean Sig Sauer pistol.

Shortly after ten, the garage door opened.

"She's home." I got ready to go up to my room.

"Stay."

"Need moral support?"

"More like someone to control me. Don't want to lose my temper. Might shoot her."

Merry rushed down the hall to the kitchen. I stayed in the den with Whip. Most of the time when Merry came in late, I didn't wait up to see what state she was in.

Whip didn't look up when his wife appeared in the doorway, a glass of wine held in front of her face. I kept my expression as bland as I could, but even I couldn't believe what she looked like. Her lips were bitten and swollen, and she had hickeys on her neck and partially exposed breast.

Who the hell does she think she's kidding?

Merry stared at the open gun safe. Then she spotted the gun in Whip's left hand, and the color left her face. The stink of gun oil permeated the small room. Whip picked up the Sig and popped the clip out. He looked down the barrel and pointed it at Merry. "So, you're home."

Merry slopped wine down her blouse, the red stain a stark contrast to her pale skin and purplish love bites. She fled up the stairs. The bedroom door clicked shut and locked.

"Has she no shame?" I was close to tears.

Whip pointed the unloaded gun at the empty doorway. "She looks like a burned-out crack whore."

The next morning, Whip wheedled and pestered me into agreeing to open joint accounts with him. We went to his bank and froze the current accounts.

"Want me introduce you to my management company?" I asked. "They handle all my checks and bill paying. I get a statement at the end of the month."

"After what I found rotting in my desk, gotta see everything. Won't feel safe if you and I don't control the checkbook. Don't want any possibility of her getting her hands on money without knowing about it."

"All right, but I have one provision. We use the Bank of America main branch downtown." I looked Whip in the eye.

"My Wells Fargo branch is closer."

"The president of my bank is a personal friend."

Whip shut up. We transferred everything that afternoon. Our actions, belated though they were, at least would prevent additional financial hemorrhaging.

CHAPTER TWENTY-NINE

The atmosphere in the house grew more toxic each day. Merry hid in her locked bedroom and refused to eat with the family or even speak to us. Most of the time she was passed out. We'd ceased to be part of her world.

Emilie moped around and looked physically sick, while Alex once again wandered around like a kicked puppy. Whip was a bundle of fury. All I wanted to do was get the heck out of Dodge, if only for a few days.

No matter how I tried to justify leaving for a week, I couldn't. Merry was volatile, and I didn't want the kids to be alone in the house with her while Whip worked. When Darla called, she proposed we take Emilie and Molly to the salon the next afternoon. Saved by the bell.

"Thank you, thank you, thank you, Darla." Relief overcame the desire to run away.

"I need to get my roots touched up, and Molly wants a manicure and a pedicure. She also needs a haircut before school starts."

The spa wasn't as good as going home, but at least we'd be out of the house for a few hours. "Em's going to be psyched. You're today's hero." I wanted to hug her.

"I'll take the girls overnight too. They can have a sleepover."

With one weight lifted from my shoulders, I told Emilie about the spa day.

"Terrific. Can I get pink highlights? How about a massage?"

We'd spend the entire afternoon away from the house. *Now what do I do with Alex?*

"Why don't you ask Mrs. Wheeler? Maybe she could take Alex and some of the boys to the paintball course."

This proves she read my mind. I looked into the most absurdly innocent brown eyes I'd ever seen. I tugged a lock of purple hair and went to call Mrs. Wheeler.

Only one thing marred a perfect girls' day at the spa. In the middle of her massage, Emilie had another of her feelings about her mother. All she'd say was I needed to talk to her father because the confrontation was ugly. I hugged her newly pink and purple head and sent her off with Darla and Molly.

I returned to an empty house. Even without Merry inside, the house stunk of anger. Whip's meeting with Merry in the family room had been confrontational. An upset glass was on the floor next to Merry's chair, liquid soaking into the Berber carpet. I wet a rag and sopped up the mess.

A brown stain on the white wall looked like Scotch. At the base of the stain was a shattered crystal highball glass.

We weren't going to get through this without someone getting hurt.

I found enough fresh veggies for a salad, so I didn't have to go to the grocery store. Whip wandered in just as I chased the last radish around my plate.

"Mind if I join you?"

"Sit. Get yourself a glass." Time for another Cher moment.

"Where's Em?"

"Darla took her home."

"Alex called. He kicked ass at the paintball range. He's over at Ben's tonight."

Whip took a large swallow of wine. I winced because this Zinfandel was too good to gulp. It deserved to be savored. Whip didn't look like he was in a savoring mood, though. "Reminded me you promised to take him to paintball. True?"

"Phooey. I forgot. I did earlier this summer. I'll do it soon."

"Doesn't know you can shoot, does he?"

"Not a clue. It'll be fun to beat the pants off him." Until that moment, I'd forgotten Whip knew I was a damned decent shot. "If I tell him I can shoot, he'll be all over me. He'll want to prove he's better."

"I talked to Merry."

"Kinda figured as much."

"She's impossible."

"Em warned me it didn't go well."

"Man, that girl knows how to understate something." Whip actually smiled. "Yelling and screaming was more like it."

"Who threw the glass? You?"

"You found it?"

"And cleaned it up. I figured the spilled drink was vodka and tonic. The lime slice kinda gave it away."

"She lied. She told me she was out with Darla Wednesday. She didn't like it when I laughed in her face." Whip's eyes narrowed and a muscle in his jaw tightened.

Merry told Whip what she did was none of his business. She'd do what she wanted. He could go to hell.

"Told her I knew she was fucking another guy. When she denied it, I picked her up by her blouse and ripped it halfway off. Neck and breasts were covered with dark-red hickeys and bite marks. Made me want to puke."

"I've never been through what you're going. I get your anger, though. Most of the time, I want to hit her. I haven't since she was thirteen and sassed me. Then I slapped her across the mouth."

"Tried to blame me for her affair. My fault because I was never home. All the usual guff about how wronged she was, how this other guy made her feel special." Whip searched for answers in his wineglass, but there weren't any. "When I asked where the money was, she told me it was none of my fucking business. I'd never find it."

"That's when you threw the Scotch glass?"

"Not quite. Called me pathetic. Said she never loved me. That's when I threw the glass." Whip hung his head, his shame at losing his temper overwhelming his normal stoic exterior.

"That's a lie." I wanted to put my arm around him, but Whip wasn't much of a hugger.

"Yeah. Hurt anyway. Took my truck and went down to the diner. Had to get away. Still can't figure out why she turned to Hunter."

"He's been playing her since the day they met. Feeding her shit with chocolate sauce and raspberries on it. She gobbles up everything he suggests."

Then it hit me. Merry's blond hair. Hunter's comment about thinking she'd be a blonde. He warned us he had his own agenda from the very first meeting. We didn't hear him.

Whip sat at the counter in the diner over a cup of coffee and a burger. He came up with a plan on how to move forward no matter where it led him. He pushed a stained napkin across the table with two fingers. He refilled our wineglasses and sipped the velvety red wine this time.

Whip wrote out a four-step plan. First, find the missing two hundred thousand dollars. I could help there. Maybe my friend at the bank could offer some advice.

Second, get copies of all medical bills. If Hunter submitted falsified records to the insurance company to get paid, they could sue him for fraud.

Number three, a family council.

"You come, too, Max. The kids gotta think we're united in trying to help their mother."

I tapped the stained napkin. "I love this last thing. Ruin Hunter. How are you going to do that?"

"Already sent letters to Chaminade and the state medical board. Violated his Hippocratic Oath when he had an affair with Merry while she was still his patient. Gonna do everything I can to make him lose his license."

"That's good. Make him lose his reputation and his livelihood."

"Coulda done something to prevent this mess from happening. Shoulda gone with her every time she went to see Hunter. Not that you didn't, but she saw him too many times alone. Woulda been able to stop his nonsense if I'd been home."

"Shoulda. Woulda. Coulda. Crappa."

What Whip said was true, but we couldn't turn back the clock and undo our actions.

"Too bad the PI only shot up his car." I put my plate in the dishwasher.

"Don't you start thinking that too."

Too?

CHAPTER THIRTY

I settled down in the family room to listen to a new CD and read. Whip continued with his forensic accounting in the den. He obsessed over the missing money. It never dawned on me Merry would actually come home. When I heard her at the door, I was surprised. I was shocked when she came into the family room, poured vodka and tonic, way more vodka than tonic, and sat in the chair where she'd spilled her drink earlier.

"I need to talk to you." Merry reeked of booze.

"I'm sure you do." I set my book upside down on the end table, folded my hands in my lap, and composed my face.

"Whip and I had a fight. He threatened me. He threw a glass at me. He tore my blouse." Merry whimpered.

"What did you expect?"

"He accused me of having an affair."

I almost doubled over with laughter. "I love it. Whip's been home what, barely two days? He sees what the kids and I've watched for weeks. You're running around all hot and horny after that sleazebag doctor. You're disgusting."

"How did you know?" Merry tossed back the last of her drink. She wanted more but for the moment was too disoriented to move.

"Dear God. You're out every Wednesday. You come home late and hide in your bedroom. You stink of sex and booze. Do you think I'm blind and stupid?" I walked over to my daughter and invaded her personal space when I stopped a foot away. "What the hell were you thinking?"

"Huh?"

"Don't play dumb with me." I refused to back down. "Are you out of your mind? Did you honestly think you'd get away with it? Did you think Whip would look the other way? Ignore what you were doing?"

Beads of sweat dribbled down Merry's forehead.

"You don't know what it's like."

"You're right. I don't."

"Whip called me a whore."

"Aren't you? You're cheating on him. I hope you're happy."

Merry gulped air. "I need to lie down."

"I'm not done. What're you going to do?"

"I have to talk to Andy. See what he wants me to do."

"Listen to yourself. 'I have to see what Andy wants me to do.'" I mimicked her like I did when she was a little girl. She hated it then; I hated it now.

"You're putting your future in Andy's hands? I don't get it." My voice rose and my face burned. "You've ruined a wonderful marriage. You had a good life, two great kids, and a mother who loved and respected you. I have no respect for you."

"How dare you!" Merry'd reached the end of what she was willing to hear.

"I dare because I'm your mother. I dare because you're wrong. You're going to be very, very sorry."

"You don't know shit about who I am or what I want."

Merry never saw my hand, but she felt its aftermath. For the first time since she was thirteen, I slapped her across the mouth hard enough to bring tears. I watched Merry gulp again and dodged. She ran to the sink and bent over. I left her to her misery.

CHAPTER THIRTY-ONE

Whip picked T.G.I. Friday's, one of the kids' favorite restaurants, for the family council. We arrived ahead of the crowd, so the usual din wasn't yet in full voice. Emilie and Alex were silent until we were seated at a table in back.

Alex started by saying he knew Merry was meeting Dracula in secret.

"It's yucky."

"How do you know?"

"I just do." Alex clammed up.

"Do you hate Mom?" Emilie asked.

The question seemed to catch Whip off guard. "No. Why?"

"I mean, look what she's doing to us. I hate her."

"Me too," Alex chimed in.

"I don't like the way she's acting." I didn't like where this was heading. "I don't think any of us really hates her."

"What do you feel, Dad?"

"Worried. I don't want Mom to hurt you two."

Whip leaned over to chuck Emilie under the chin but pulled back with less than an inch to spare. Just in time he remembered the unwritten ban about parent-originated public displays of affection.

"It's too late. She already has." Emilie wouldn't let the matter rest.

"Are you and Mom getting a divorce?" Alex finished off his last fry. "Can we share the brownie sundae, Dad?"

I smiled at the workings of an eleven-year-old boy's mind. From divorce to an ice cream sundae without a missed synapse.

"Sure." Whip waved for the waiter and ordered dessert.

"About a divorce. I don't know yet, Alex." Whip and I had avoided the word like the plague, and here it was, naked in public.

Emilie didn't say anything. I watched the kids dig into the largest hot fudge brownie sundae on earth.

"If you do," Alex had ice cream and fudge smeared on his mouth, "we're gonna live with you and Mad Max. We won't live with Mom and Dracula."

"You've decided?" I was amazed at Alex's flashes of maturity.

"Uh-huh." Alex shoved another bite of brownie in his mouth.

"Do I have anything to say about it?"

"Nope." Alex smiled a fudgy smile.

"So, what are you going to do, Dad?" Emilie broke her silence. "We don't want you to get divorced, but if you do ... Alex is right. We won't stay with Mom. It's not like she wants us anyway."

"I'll make sure you guys are safe."

"We're safe with you and Mad Max." Emilie. Wise beyond her years. "Make Mom understand what she's doing to us. Please."

CHAPTER THIRTY-TWO

Not long after Whip launched his four-step program, I was in yet another unending argument with Merry.

"I need help. I don't know what to do."

For a nanosecond, I thought she was being rational. "That's a crock! You know what to do."

"Huh?"

"Do you want to save your marriage?" I was getting dinner ready and turned from the cutting board. I had long since stopped worrying about poking Merry. No matter what I did or said, she went her own way.

"I don't know."

"Then tell Whip you want a divorce."

"I'm not sure I want one right now." Merry wailed and wrung her hands.

"Well, what do you want?" I took several deep-cleansing breaths.

"I don't know. I want a time-out."

"A time-out! Dear God, you want a time-out? To do what? Continue screwing Hunter?"

"Why can't I take a break? See if what Andy offers is better?" Merry became hysterical.

My uncontrolled laughter didn't help.

"Do you really think Whip will sit idly by while you pick and choose? Get real!" I pointed my cleaver at her. The pork ribs could wait.

"I thought you'd understand."

"Well, I don't. I think you want sympathy. Look it up in the dictionary. You'll find it between shit and syphilis."

"It's not like that."

The more Merry talked, the more she sounded like Emilie trying to convince me she'd study at a school-night sleepover. It didn't work for Emilie and wasn't working for Merry.

"Talk. To. Whip." I was a stuck record grinding on the same spot over and over.

"He won't stay in the same room with me."

"Do you blame him?" I put the cleaver on the counter. I was so angry I was afraid to be armed. "What do you expect?"

"I don't know."

"Whip's not going to sit around doing nothing. You're all but parading Hunter in front of him. You're lucky he hasn't locked you out." I regained some degree of calm. Years of practice took over. I was once again talking to a rebellious child. "Lord knows, I would have."

"But ..."

"Do you really think you can continue living here?"

"Why should I move? It's my house too."

"Do you think Whip will quietly go away? Leave the children with you? So you can move Hunter into his bed?" My voice rose on the last word.

"Andy's planning for us to go away."

"Has he asked you to leave your family?" I pinned Merry like a dead butterfly in a specimen case.

She walked around the kitchen, looking for an out. There was none.

"Has he?"

"Not in so many words."

"Has he asked you to marry him?"

"Not yet, but he will."

"Are you sure? How do you know he doesn't toy with women? Ruin their lives and move on to the next victim?"

"I just know. Andy's kind and caring and gentle. He'd never lie or hurt me. He loves me."

"What about Em and Alex? They know what you're doing. You're tearing them apart."

Merry didn't answer.

"You need to figure out what's important."

"I don't know what to do."

"There's no MapQuest for life, Merry. Look in your heart. Do what's right."

Dinner could wait. I shoved the ribs back into the refrigerator. I loved dramatic exits. I walked out of the room, back straight, head high.

I'd lied to Merry. Adults could have a time-out. I shut my bedroom door, threw myself on the bed, and ground my teeth. I wanted to be three again, to drum my heels and pound my bed with my fists. I wanted to wail in a full-throated temper tantrum.

For those few seconds, I wanted to go home and forget all about this godforsaken mess. I called Raney.

"A tantrum? You want to have a tantrum?" Raney laughed almost too hard to talk.

"Yes."

"Well, have one, damn it!"

CHAPTER THIRTY-THREE

Every time I stood in the doorway of Whip's office-den-bedroom, I started the conversation with "Whip, we need to talk." Confiding in my son-in-law had become a routine late night activity.

"Yeah." Whip shifted a pile of papers from my chair to the desk and waved me in. "Still a mess."

"Do you have ice in the bar?" I sat in my favorite and only chair and turned on the table lamp. The desk lamp threw too small a pool of light to chase the shadows from the corners of the room. Or from my mind.

"Sure do. What's your poison tonight?"

"Jack on the Rocks. Two fingers."

Whip poured Jack Daniel's for me and picked out a single malt for himself. We raised glasses across the room.

"Clink."

"Clink."

I gasped as the first sip of bourbon flowed down my throat. *God, it burns good.* "This whole mess sucks. I hate it."

"Yeah."

"Merry and I fight all the time. Gotten worse since I told her to dump Hunter." I was out of ideas about how to beat sense into my daughter.

"Yeah. Totally under his spell."

"You know Em's afraid of him, don't you?"

"Oh boy, that's an understatement." Whip sipped his Scotch.

I stared out the sliding glass door into an eerie blackness, my reflection glaring back at me. A frown deepened on my forehead. Whip must have forgotten to reset the timer on the garden lights because the pathway to the pool wasn't visible from where I sat.

"Gotta protect the kids."

"That's not why I came back, but it's why I stay."

"Can't thank you enough." Whip saluted me with a near-empty glass. Without asking, he set the Jack on the table next to my chair. We refilled as one.

"I'm contributing to the hostile home environment. I keep trying to reach Merry. Can't break through her walls."

"Well, you aren't creating the environment." Whip slid down on his spine and stared at the ceiling. "She is."

"Both kids spend too much time IMing or texting their friends rather than doing something active."

This hiding-behind-technology behavior bothered me, but there was only so much I could handle. I was pretty much full up, as my granddaddy used to say. I shivered. I turned and stared outside, half expecting to see Hunter staring in. The patio seemed empty, but I couldn't shake the feeling someone watched.

"Hired a lawyer today."

"Divorce attorney?"

"Yeah. Female, about four hundred pounds, been whupped with an ugly stick. The best damned divorce lawyer in town, according to Darla."

It made sense to call Darla. When her husband left with his secretary, Darla made out like a bandit.

"You work on the divorce. I'll follow the money. That's what they do in thrillers." I stood up.

"Are we in a thriller?" Whip's smile stopped at his lips.

"No, we're in a sordid family drama. I don't want it to turn into a tragedy." When I walked into the hall, the chill lingered.

Time to keep my promise to Alex. I invited him to the paintball range. I raided Merry's closet for a ratty pair of jeans, disgusting sneakers and one of Whip's T-shirts that should have been turned into a rag years earlier. Alex came downstairs in camo fatigues with his paintball gear in a matching backpack. I'd rent whatever I needed.

I slaughtered Alex. He learned two serious lessons about his dear old grandmother: I was a darned good shot, and I was ruthless in combat. I let him get in a couple of hits, but nothing like I did. Even after ice cream, he sulked all the way home. When I told Emilie and Whip what I'd done, they laughed until they cried.

"Where did you learn to shoot, Mad Max?"

I'd never told Emilie I knew my way around real guns. Same principles of taking aim and firing applied to paintball. "Africa."

"Alex will never live this down." Emilie mopped her face. "Tell me his friends weren't there."

"Can't. Ben Wheeler and three other boys. Got them too."

"So if one talks, they all have to confess they got beaten by an old lady."

"Who's an old lady?" I put my fists on my hips and glowered at Emilie. "Just for that, you get to fix dinner tonight."

I huffed upstairs for a hot shower.

CHAPTER THIRTY-FOUR

Another pattern emerged. I listened at night for Merry to come home, just like I did when she was a teen. I could relax only when I knew she was safe. One night I retired to my room after dinner to read and have a few moments of privacy when Emilie tapped at my door to tell me her mother was home at last. I glanced at the clock. Only nine-thirty.

"She's early. Guess Dr. Wonderful stood her up."

Much as I wanted to lapse into Mommy two dot oh, I didn't. Emilie was entitled to her opinion, even when it was disrespectful.

I went downstairs. "Em heard Merry come in." I walked into the den, sat in my chair, crossed trouser-clad legs, and leaned back.

"Saw her. Blind drunk." Whip knuckled bloodshot eyes. He looked so exhausted it about broke my heart.

"Remember how the Watergate co-conspirators got caught because the Democrats followed the money?"

Whip nodded. "I've been doing just that."

"Me too."

"Any luck?" I changed positions and tucked one leg under me. Men never understood how we women could sit on folded legs without losing circulation.

"Haven't found a damned cent." Whip reached into his desk and pulled out a stack of papers. "Here's where some of it went. She bought him a fucking car! Paid cash. A Hummer, no less."

"Jeez. Can she be that stupid? After Hunter's car was shot up, I never figured she'd buy him another." I rattled ice in my glass, my least favorite nervous habit. "She has more money than you know."

"Huh?" Whip asked.

"When my last husband, Reggie, died, I set up a trust fund for the kids and an emergency joint account for Merry. I should've told you."

For the life of me, I couldn't remember why I hadn't. Whip waved his hand as if my news was a gnat near his eyes.

I'd grown up in poverty on the family farm where money was so tight that every penny I spent squealed in pain. Years later, I heard Oprah Winfrey, then the richest woman in the world, tell of her terror of going broke and becoming a bag lady. She kept a large amount of cash on hand in case the worst happened and she lost everything. I tried to explain to Whip that most basic fear, the fear of having absolutely nothing.

"Anyway, Merry's bag lady account's empty."

"The damage?"

"Well over one hundred fifty thousand." I shrugged. "It kinda grew over the years."

"So, she's withdrawn between three hundred fifty and four hundred thousand. Where the hell is it?"

"I might have a clue, Dad."

Whip and I had been too engrossed to hear Emilie come downstairs until she spoke.

"You do?"

Emilie held a sandwich in one hand and a small black key in the palm of the other.

"A safe-deposit box?" I stared at the key, my mind slamming two and two together. "The money's in cash?"

"Where did you get that, Em?" Whip stared at the key.

"Mom's jewelry box. I wanted to borrow her gold bangle. I found this, but I'm not sure what it's for."

"You shouldn't be looking in Mom's things without her permission." A response so programmed I didn't think before I spoke.

"Yeah, well." Emilie rolled her eyes in a way guaranteed to annoy the crap out of her father and me.

"Em," Whip warned.

"May I see it?" I held out my hand. "Is there a name on it?"

Emilie shook her head. The key was blank except for a number stamped on the top.

"I wonder which bank it belongs to."

"One of those near the corner of Second and Broad, I think. Mom and I stopped one day weeks ago."

"Thanks. This helps a lot." I had to see what was inside the box.

"Me and Alex—"

"Alex and I." Again, an automatic response.

"So, Alex and I have been trying to figure out what she's doing."

"And?" I was curious.

"Got a good idea." Alex walked up behind Emilie. "Family council?"

"Is now," Whip said.

"Mom's going to leave us soon."

"How do you know?"

"Heck, I hacked into her cell phone. I've been reading her texts for weeks." Alex looked smug. If we didn't need every bit of information, I'm sure Whip would have exploded, especially over actions where he would have grounded Alex for life.

"Did you learn this at computer camp?"

"Well ..."

"What does she say?" Whip shocked me by dismissing the hacking infraction.

"All lovey-dovey stuff. Icky sexy stuff."

"Euw." Emilie wrinkled her nose.

"Stuff about the money being there. Being ready." Alex cracked his gum and blew a huge bubble. It burst on his nose.

"That reminds me. Don't go anywhere." Emilie dashed out of the den. In a couple of seconds, she returned with a handful of napkins.

"I found these in the kitchen desk." She handed them to me.

Girlish doodles intertwined with variations of Merry's name with Hunter's.

"Molly scribbles all over her notebooks just like this. But Mom? It's, like, so disgusting."

"'Andy and Kiki'? Who's Kiki?" Whip didn't touch the napkins.

I remembered the night in Merry's hospital room and shivered when a goose walked across my grave.

"It's who Hunter turned Merry into."

"But who is it?" Alex wouldn't let up.

"It's the answer to this whole mess," Emilie said.

"What do you suggest we do, guys?" I stared at the napkins. Emilie was right. I held the major clue in my hand.

"Break into the bank and steal the box."

I imagined Alex trying to pull off a bank heist with little more than his cell as a weapon. Had this not been so important, I would have laughed.

"Lock her in her room until she comes to her senses." Emilie offered a slightly less aggressive suggestion.

"Arrest Dracula." Alex overworked his gum. He really wanted to play detective. Maybe it'd be a good distraction.

"Figure out who Kiki is." Outwardly, Emilie appeared calm and analytical, but inwardly? How much of a toll was the family turmoil taking on her?

"Well, we can't rob the bank, but I think I can get into the box once we find it." I turned toward the window. Its black surface was impenetrable but reflected my pensive face.

"We can't lock her in her room. Even though she's not acting like a grown-up, she is one," Whip said.

"We can't arrest Dracula. He hasn't committed a crime," Emilie added.

"That we know of," Alex muttered. He went back upstairs.

CHAPTER THIRTY-FIVE

"Look, guys, don't want you involved. My problem, not yours." Whip shook his head and stared at Johnny and me in the IV Drip coffeehouse near the office. "I can do this myself."

"Sure you can. We're in this with you, like it or not." I stared him down.

Johnny spoke over the hissing of the milk steamer. "Hey, man, we're just here to help. We can arrange for Hunter to have a 'chat' with you."

"Talk to me."

"We want to mess with him, because he thinks he's gotten away with the affair."

"How are you going to do that?"

I told Whip he needed to go to Omaha for a meeting.

"Why Omaha?"

"Why not? You're not going anywhere. Merry will think you are. Leave the tickets on the kitchen counter. She'll see them."

"She'll run off to Hunter. We'll make dinner reservations at the Heritage Grille for the same night," Johnny said.

"How can you be sure they'll be there?"

"The PI says it's their only place. Besides, Alex reads her texts. It'll be too juicy an opportunity for her to pass up." I fluffed my new, shorter haircut.

"Once we're in place, I'll get him into the alley." Johnny grinned his lopsided grin. A scar from a boyhood knife fight slanted across his lower face and chin. It pulled the skin on one side of his mouth tighter than the other. "Then you can have your talk."

"Still don't like involving you."

"What are you going to do? Barge into the restaurant? Throw down a glove and call him out?" I thrust out my chin. No way would Johnny and I miss the big scene.

"Not in so many words. Planned to call his cell. Force him into meeting me."

"If that doesn't work?"

"Keep calling until the coward faces me." His plan leaked like a sieve.

"I don't think Hunter would meet you anywhere, but I can make him go with me," Johnny said.

"Our way's better," I said. "You're supposed to be away, so his guard'll be down. Time we wreck his plans, big time."

Johnny and I arrived at the Heritage Grille half an hour early and waited at the back edge of the parking lot. After Whip pulled up beside Johnny's truck, we stood in the lot for a final briefing. Johnny and I'd wait until Hunter went to the men's room. Johnny would follow and convince him to go with him. I'd call Whip to head for the alley behind the restaurant when everything was in place.

Whip was no longer fighting to get his wife back. He didn't want her, no matter what. He wanted revenge.

"Give me your cell." I stopped and turned back. "Take mine."

"Why?" Whip handed over his phone.

"Wait for my call."

With that, Johnny and I entered the restaurant. Whip stood next to Johnny's truck, a strange phone in one hand and nothing to do but wait. In less than an hour, I called.

"They're headed for the men's room," I whispered and thumbed the phone off.

I'd slipped out the front door right after Johnny went to the men's room. I rounded the corner just as Hunter staggered down the steps from the kitchen exit. Whip stepped out of the shadows. In the city glow reflecting off low-hanging clouds, Hunter clutched his stomach and gasped for breath. Johnny held him by the nape of his neck.

"What happened?"

"He was reluctant to come with me, but he changed his mind." Johnny released Hunter. The bastard swayed before regaining his balance.

"Son of a bitch hit me in the stomach," Hunter gasped. "What the fuck? You're supposed to be out of town."

"Life's a bitch when you can't trust the word of your married lover, isn't it?"

"She said—"

"What I wanted her to say." Whip took a step closer. "You prick. You preyed on my wife when she was most vulnerable. Told her you could make her perfect. Prescribed too many drugs. Suckered her into believing you were going to leave together."

"I never promised that." Hunter stood as upright as his bruised body allowed.

"Great. A prick and a liar." Whip inched closer and smiled as Hunter took a step back before bumping up against the solid wall of Johnny.

"You've been feeding her a crock of shit for months. Promising you'd bolt after she got her money."

"What the fuck are you talking about?" Hunter's eyes darted about.

"I never ..." Hunter edged sideways toward the light from the parking lot. Johnny blocked his way. The slug wasn't going anywhere until Whip was done.

"At least twenty messages about money. Is that it? Is this all about money? Are you planning to dump Merry once you have it?"

Distrust gave way to panic when Whip raised his hand to block the doctor's escape. Hunter made a terrible mistake. He swung wildly. Whip ducked but not fast enough to avoid Hunter's fist grazing his cheekbone. His signet ring cut an inch-long slice under Whip's eye. He stared at the weasel in front of him.

Whip hit Hunter a quick right and left in the face. The first landed on his cheekbone; the second broke his nose. Blood splattered over his white shirt. Whip hit Hunter at will, on the face, on his ribs, in his stomach. He struck him one last time in the gut before connecting with a hard uppercut. Hunter dropped to his knees, pitched forward, and threw up. Tears mixed with bloody snot and puke.

Whip stepped back until Hunter finished puking and rocked

back and forth whimpering. He leaned over and whispered in his ear. Whip planted one booted foot between Hunter's hands, lifted his foot, and stomped hard on the left hand. In a brief moment of total silence, I heard the metacarpals snap, followed by a shriek. Just at that moment, Merry ran around the corner of the restaurant. She tried to push her way into the alley, but Johnny grabbed her around the waist and lifted her off her feet.

"Let me go," Merry screamed. "He's killing Andy!"

"Not even close." Johnny tightened his grip when Merry kicked and flailed.

Whip walked over to Merry. "I warned you someone would get hurt. You didn't believe me. I'm through with you."

Johnny pushed Merry toward Hunter. We turned and walked out of the alley, Merry's screams followed us out to our trucks.

"Sounds like someone needs help." I linked my arm through Johnny's.

"Yeah. Someone should call nine-one-one, dontcha think?" Johnny said.

"Yeah, someone should." Whip wiped his hands on his puke-stained khakis.

If I was pumped on adrenaline, Whip was even higher. He shouldn't have driven home, but he insisted he was under control. He made it back and headed for the shower.

Half an hour later, Whip walked into the family room, clean but pale. Johnny and I had the bar open. Whip's hand shook so badly he could hardly hold the highball glass Johnny handed him. "Tell me what happened inside."

"We screwed with that asshole's head big time," Johnny said. "When we sent him text messages from your phone, he almost pissed his pants."

"Johnny told Hunter to 'leave my wife alone.' You should've seen his head on a swivel. He looked like Linda Blair in *The Exorcist*. He thought you were in the restaurant, but he couldn't find you." Now that I was calmer, I enjoyed telling Whip how clever we were.

"Hunter sent back a nasty-gram, warning he'd take legal action if you didn't stop stalking him."

"Stalking?" Whip chuckled. "I haven't begun to stalk him. Yet. His ass is mine."

"We waited until dessert and pinged him again. We told him to meet you outside. When Hunter went to the head, I followed. He was, shall we say, reluctant to take a walk, until his ribcage ran into my fist." Johnny picked up the decanter and poured himself three more fingers.

"Merry put on lipstick, oblivious to what was going on." I sipped my drink.

Johnny and Whip were intent on getting hammered. It must be a guy thing.

"So we messed with Hunter's head before you messed up his body." Johnny laughed at his joke.

"What did you say to him when he was on the ground?" I hadn't been close enough to hear.

"I wanted to hurt him, not cripple him. I asked him if he was right-handed. He is, so I broke the bones in his left hand. He'll be out of commission until it heals. He won't be a doctor much longer, either, if I have my way. At any rate, Merry no longer lives here. She's not to enter this house without my permission. Is that clear?"

"You should've thrown her out weeks ago."

"I'll be filing divorce papers tomorrow."

"Don't forget to change the locks."

Whip and Johnny raised their glasses in a mock toast. "Ding, dong, the bitch is gone."

I couldn't join in. No matter what, the bitch was still my daughter.

CHAPTER THIRTY-SIX

Whip filed for divorce. His attorney said it was lucky they lived in a state where he could charge Merry with adultery. It should be simple. Prove Merry was having an affair, identify the doctor, and it would be over.

Whip wanted custody. Merry and Hunter weren't going to raise his children, no matter what. Like all good attorneys, Mama Cass said it could be difficult because they had to prove Merry was an unfit or unwilling mother. Whip wouldn't have to pay alimony, though, if she lived with Hunter.

"Mom called," Emilie said at dinner. "She says you won't let her come home."

"She's right. Not after she chose Dracula over us."

"That's so wrong," Emilie said. "Dracula's evil. He'll hurt her. I just know he will. He's done bad things before, Dad."

"Do you have proof?" Whip wanted to believe Emilie but had told me he was uncomfortable with her premonitions.

"Not yet, but me and Alex, oops, Alex and I are working on it."

I wasn't sure they'd find anything useful, but I didn't discourage their efforts.

"She said she's getting her own apartment in the city." Emilie carried her dirty plate into the kitchen. "It's supposed to be very nice."

"I thought she was moving in with Dracula." Alex wiped his mouth on his napkin without any prompting from me.

"Guess not."

Emilie went into the family room to study, while Alex disappeared upstairs.

"That could really fuck up my divorce plans."

"How so?"

"If she moves in with Hunter, I won't have to pay alimony. I don't want to give her another dime."

I'd been scarce since Whip beat the snot out of Hunter. I kept busy, following up leads. Whip didn't know what I was doing. We'd laughed at the idea of me playing sleuth. He'd said at the beginning of the mess it was so out of character. Little did he know.

Johnny and I had just pulled up in front of the house when Merry swung the Infiniti into the drive and parked sideways across it.

"Not good."

"Yeah."

Merry tripped and nearly fell.

"She's drunk as usual."

Merry tried to unlock the door. When her key wouldn't work, she began pounding and shouting.

"She'll wake up the whole neighborhood if I don't stop her."

Before I could jump out of the truck, Whip opened the door and blocked Merry's way. She tried to push past him but was no match for his strength. Johnny's hand wrapped itself around my wrist.

"This is a guy thing, Max. Let them be."

"Let me in, you prick," Merry shouted.

"With that attitude, hell will freeze over before I let you in. I told you, you no longer live here." Whip stepped outside and shut the door behind him.

"It's my house, too, you asshole."

Front porch lights came on up and down the street. Whip grabbed her by the wrists and shook her until she stopped shrieking. I shrank down in the front seat, unwilling to watch my daughter's self-destruction.

"You made your choice when you chose Hunter over your family and me. Let me make this crystal clear. You. Do. Not. Live. Here."

"I need my clothes." Merry struggled, but Whip held her wrists in a bruising grip.

"Have your lawyer bring a list of what you want. Then and only then will I let you inside."

"I'll come anytime I damn well please, you bastard." Merry spit in his face.

"Wrong move." Johnny tensed, ready to help if Whip needed it.

Whip lost his temper and taunted Merry. "What's the matter? Has Dr. Wonderful thrown you out too? Well, my soon-to-be-ex-wife, you made your bed. Now go lie in it."

Whip released Merry's wrists and turned toward the door. Merry pulled a knife from her bag and slashed Whip across his back and arm. Blood dripped from his fingertips.

"*Jesus.*" Johnny was out of the truck and across the lawn before I could open my door.

When Merry raised the knife again, Whip shoved her backward and banged her arm against the porch railing until she dropped it into the flowerbed. Unarmed, she attacked him with her nails and raked his cheek where Hunter had cut him. Johnny grabbed her from behind and pinned her arms to her side.

Blue and red gumdrops reflected off Whip's face as two police cars rolled up. A patrolman shone his flashlight full in Whip's eyes to blind him and rested one hand on his holstered gun. He moved the beam to Johnny.

"What's going on here?"

The patrolman looked at the blood seeping through Whip's shirt. Merry's face was bloody as well.

Whip's shooting buddy Jerry walked up beside the patrolman. "I'll handle it, officer. I know this man."

"It looks like an assault to me. Better take him in for questioning."

"Me?" Whip burst out laughing. "She attacked me."

"Leave it, officer." Jerry stepped between the patrolman and Whip.

"But—"

"I'll deal with it. Go back to your route."

The patrolman walked back to his car.

"Okay, what's going on?"

Whip started to tell Jerry what happened when Merry burst out with, "He attacked me. He tried to kill me."

The accusation was so false Whip's mouth dropped open.

"Well, Whip here is bleeding like a stuck pig, and you have no marks on you, Mrs. Pugh. How do you figure he tried to kill you?" Jerry hooked his thumbs in his belt.

"He tried to stab me. I grabbed the knife to defend myself."

"Mrs. Davies, who's telling the truth?"

"Whip. Merry attacked him with a knife. She brought it with her. Johnny and I saw everything."

"Well, ma'am, I'm not one of them fancy CSI types, but even I can see someone who's been slashed across the back." Jerry faked a Southern redneck drawl. "You say you disarmed a man much heavier than you. Then he turned his back on a now-armed woman and gave you a perfect target for a cowardly attack. That how it happened?"

"Yes. No. I mean, he came at me with the knife. I took it away and slashed at him to protect myself."

"You're going to the station. You'll stay there until you've sobered up. Looks like you might have driven here under the influence. You can get into a lot of trouble with a DUI."

Johnny released Merry into Jerry's custody. The policeman spun Merry around and put plastic handcuffs on her. She yelled, kicked backward, and connected with Jerry's shin.

"Do you want to add assault on a police officer? Want to try for more charges?" Jerry lifted Merry, half-carried her to his car, and pushed her into the backseat. He returned to the bloody porch.

"Where's the knife?"

Whip reached over the porch railing to pick it up.

"Don't! Have you touched it?"

"No. Why?"

Without Whip's fingerprints on the weapon, Merry's assault accusation would collapse.

"I'll get a baggie," I said.

"She'll have plenty of time to sober up in the tank with the prostitutes and other drunks. If she's lucky, we'll have run in Looney Lucy too. She'll learn all about the end of the world."

I wasn't sorry to see my daughter arrested. It was past time for her to learn a major league lesson. A night in the drunk tank just might be what she needed. She was up a nasty creek, but only she could get herself out of this mess.

Jerry asked if he should call an ambulance. When Johnny said we'd take Whip to the hospital, Jerry took the knife and drove off with Merry in the patrol car. I was surprised later when we got home and found one of the neighbors had hosed down the porch. Funny, I didn't think once about fainting at the sight of Whip's blood.

CHAPTER THIRTY-SEVEN

"How are you feeling, Dad?" Emilie called from the doorway of the den.

"Wish I could say fine, but honestly, Em, not so hot."

"Do you need a pain pill or something?"

"Just took one, so I'll feel better soon." Whip turned in his chair and faced the door. "Come on in."

Emilie padded barefoot to the couch and curled up, both feet tucked under her. Whip shuffled papers around, and I sipped my drink until she began talking.

At first, she chatted about school and a big party coming up and how goofy Alex was acting over this girl texting him all the time. She didn't much like her dumb economics teacher; he had it in for her.

How refreshing it was to listen to the daily trivia of growing up. The feeling didn't last, but it was wonderful while it did.

"Dad, Mom called. She told me and Alex—sorry, Alex and me—she made a big mistake." Emilie chewed her lower lip.

"Which one?"

"Leaving for Dracula. He won't let her live with him."

I said nothing. One of my worst fears was coming true. Hunter had no intention of happily-ever-aftering with Merry.

"If Mom left Dracula, would you let her? Come home, I mean?" Emilie sat very, very still.

"No, Em. I can't trust her." Whip shifted in his chair.

"She tells so many lies. I never believe her, and Alex just laughs when she tries to tell him how wonderful her life will be soon."

"I've filed for divorce. I know you guys hoped we'd work it out and stay together, but it's impossible. I asked for custody. I went to court, too, and took out an order to keep her away from the house and you guys. She can only see you with Mad Max or me present."

"Oh, Daddy!" Emilie was twelve-going-on-thirteen again and flew across the room. She threw her arms around Whip. "I was afraid she'd take us away."

Whip's face went pale. Emilie's arms were across the deepest wound in his back, where he had more than forty stitches.

"We'll get through this. It'll be hard, but we'll make it."

"Pinky swear?"

They hooked little fingers.

"Pinky swear."

Emilie turned to me. I extended my little finger. "Pinky swear."

Whip worked late as usual. Alex was up in his room playing with his PlayStation. Emilie and I were alone in the family room. I took to locking the doors whenever Whip was out. I couldn't shake the premonition we were being watched. I didn't want to ask Emilie about it; if it were my long-standing case of the willies, I'd deal with it. She had enough to handle without me piling on more.

With nothing decent on television, we settled in for a long read. I made some chamomile tea, put some blues on the stereo, and curled up in my favorite chair, a grisly thriller propped on my lap. Emilie was stretched out on the couch reading a Judy Blume romance. We talked on and off, mostly off, grateful for a Simon and Garfunkel evening.

Just before ten, Emilie's book thumped to the floor. At first I thought she was asleep and the book had fallen from relaxed fingers. When I looked more closely, I saw she was wide awake, staring at the ceiling, trembling and unblinking. I rushed over and knelt on the floor beside her.

"What's the matter, dear child?" I'd never seen her so upset.

"I can't find Mom." Her whisper barely moved the air around her lips.

"You can't find Mom? Has something happened to her?" I leaned forward.

"She was happy. Then she was angry. Then she was afraid. Now she's gone."

"Gone like when she had her accident?" Something was desperately wrong.

"Not like when she was in her accident. Mom's totally not. Not here any longer." Tears flowed from the corners of her eyes, soaking her hairline.

"She's dead?" I hoped in my heart Merry was all right, but Emilie seemed to know differently.

"Yes."

CHAPTER THIRTY-EIGHT

Children who lose their parents have a name: orphan. Parents who lose a child have no name. They're just empty.

I'm empty.

Yesterday I buried my daughter. From the moment the police confirmed Merry's death until the last funeral guests departed, I had so much to do, so many lists to make, so many details to tie up, I couldn't think beyond the next step, the next meal or the next tear.

Between the time Emilie told me her mother was dead and the time Whip and I identified her body, Raney and Eleanor were on a flight to Richmond. I would have fallen apart if my two favorite Great Dames hadn't been standing beside me.

Whip's mother, Bette, watched the children and answered the never-silent phone. Everyone from friends to the curious to the press to the ghouls felt they had the right to invade our world of sorrow. Whip and I made the funeral arrangements while Bette and the Colonel organized the reception at the house after the funeral. Eleanor and Raney provided shoulders for me to cry on, a day trip to the mall with Alex to play video games, and different sounding boards for Emilie. Neither Merry nor Whip had prepaid burial plans like I had, so we winged it. Because the kids wanted to be a part of remembering their mother, I asked Emilie to choose some music and Alex to write the words he wanted to say.

I looked at Merry in her casket. Memories of happier pasts

flooded my brain, while tears poured down my cheeks. Raney held my right hand; Eleanor my left. Merry lay still, her spirit roaming far away from her body. She was a stranger, not the daughter I bore.

"There is no upside for this," Eleanor said.

"For what?" I mopped my face and snuffled into a handkerchief.

"For murder."

A pair of arms encircled my waist. Raney stepped aside and let Emilie wiggle in.

At last the funeral and burial were over. Raney and Eleanor packed up to return home to New York with my deepest thanks. Their presence let me lean on them rather than be the only rock.

"My heart is so numb, Eleanor," I said.

"I know, dear, but do not carry your troubles around like Linus with his blanket."

I tried to smile. That was just the way I felt—dragged down by life's sogginess.

"Let your emotions show, Maxine." Eleanor closed her overnight bag and turned to hug me. "It is important. It will help you heal. Emilie and Alex need to see what you are feeling too."

"You don't have to be strong every second of the day." Raney joined Eleanor in a group hug. "It's not the same as when Norm died. You have an extended family to help you."

Eleanor whispered in my ear. "Never mourn alone. Others must see your grief."

"Is this more of my doo-wop?"

"It is."

My dearest friends headed toward the door when the taxi's horn sounded.

Now, with Emilie, Alex, and me alone in the house, I couldn't move. I knew I should be doing something, but when I tried to get up, my face leaked. I retreated into my cocoon. The kids were as hollow as I was. I knew Alex was in his room texting his buddies, but I hadn't seen Emilie for hours. I thought she might be pruning in the tub.

Where was Whip? In the town jail. Accused of Merry's murder. Arrested immediately after the funeral. I thought of my beautiful daughter—the way she was before Hunter sank his teeth into her—

and of the wonderful man who married her and loved her right up to and beyond the arrival of evil. I was paralyzed. Yet I felt anger, rage, remorse, frustration, and disbelief.

Perhaps I wasn't as desensitized as I wished, but I viewed life filtered through burlap. I could see but not clearly, think but only linearly, put food on the table but had no idea what we ate. I couldn't do anything requiring "ahead"—thinking, planning, looking. I survived day by day, hour by hour. It wasn't healthy, not when I was the head of a fractured family. Murder had a way of grabbing your attention.

Children weren't supposed to be murdered in cold blood.

They weren't supposed to have a gun shoved against their head.

They weren't supposed to die.

They were supposed to mourn their parents when they passed at the end of a long and fruitful life.

Someone up there had a sick sense of right and wrong. I used to be a good Catholic but no longer. How can a compassionate Being expose an innocent person to such evil as Hunter represented and then do nothing to save her? Seeing Merry in her casket, I didn't know what I believed. If there was a God, She and I were going to have a long, serious talk about why She led Merry to her death. Yes, I blamed Her. I also blamed Merry, and I definitely blamed Hunter.

After the funeral, Whip's cop friend Jerry came to the house. They talked in the den for nearly two hours. I didn't know what was said, but when Whip emerged, he told me he was going down to the station to meet with the investigating officers. He said he'd be back by dinner. He wasn't.

Whip was in a cell. I couldn't believe it. The police took a DNA sample and searched the house and his office. They confiscated Whip's guns from the safe, clothes from the bedroom hamper, and other things I didn't see. The cops were so damned smug. As if they'd solved the crime of the century.

Fools! All they had to do was ask Whip. He'd tell them where he was and what he was doing the night Merry was killed. No, murdered. I have to get used to saying that.

My daughter was murdered.

CHAPTER THIRTY-NINE

When I thought about the last days of Merry's life, I wondered if I hadn't set a chain of events in motion that led to her murder. Did I somehow cause it? Was this an example of unintended consequences? I did what I thought best at the time to protect our family. Merry never mentioned the attack on Hunter's car, never suspected I was two degrees removed from it. I was pretty certain she didn't know I found out about the safe-deposit box or that it was empty.

I visited each of the three banks downtown near the corner Emilie remembered until I found the one where Merry rented the box. I was sure she hadn't emptied it yet because Hunter was still texting her about the money. I figured out how to talk my way into the vault to empty the contents of the box. Johnny and I discussed it over dinner, and he agreed with my scheme. We were the witch and the warlock, hovering over a bubbling cauldron, stirring and sniffing and muttering incantations.

I decided to use a little social engineering and all of my acting skills. I'd forged Merry's signature all year on school forms for Alex and Emilie, so I knew I could sign the card without hesitation. I was worried, though. What if I met a bank attendant who knew Merry? I sure didn't look like her any longer.

On the morning Merry was murdered, I wore a large floppy hat and huge sunglasses. Oh, and gloves. I made up a terrific story about a recent surgery, but the clerk didn't so much as look at me or say boo diddly. Had she looked closely, she would have been more than likely to remember the bold disguise rather than the face of the woman under the screaming pink polka dot hat.

The box was in both Merry's and Hunter's names. No surprise there. She was so obsessed with the bastard she couldn't see how she was being manipulated. Hunter opened the box three times, leading me to think he'd siphoned off some of the money. I signed the card and followed the clerk into the vault. We inserted our keys, and she left. When I lifted the box, I damned near dropped the thing on my foot. Heavy son of a gun. I opened it and found bricks of money. Lots of bricks. A pile of unwrapped money too. I emptied everything into my oversized bag, replaced the box, and shrugged the bag onto my shoulder, all but falling sideways under the unaccustomed weight.

When I returned home, I locked myself in my bedroom, dumped the contents of the bag on my bed and counted. And counted. Three hundred thousand. One hundred thousand plus short of the total I knew Merry took. A lot of the missing cash went into the new Hummer, but not all of it. I stuffed the money back into my tote and hid it in the back of my closet. Dumb maybe, but I couldn't think of a better place at the time. I would have to have it out with Merry when she discovered the empty box. We both ran out of time.

Lucky for me, when the police searched the house, they didn't go into my bedroom. Finding the money would have been awkward. They searched Merry and Whip's bedroom and Whip's office but left the rest of the house alone. If I'd have been a cop investigating a murder, I'd have turned the entire house inside out.

I couldn't help but wonder if Hunter had gone to the bank after I did. I imagined Hunter wild with rage if he looked at the signature card, which showed Merry visiting the box the day she died. Could finding the box empty have sent him over the edge?

At the time, I never thought taking the money would cause Merry harm. I thought I was being extremely clever. In the back of my mind, I half-hoped it would provoke a final argument between my daughter and Hunter. Maybe it'd lead to the creep walking out. Maybe it would jolt Merry back to her senses. I'd have given the entire wad of cash to charity to see their confrontation. I never thought he'd kill her.

I didn't have to think about who killed Merry and why she died. I knew it wasn't Whip. He'd have killed Hunter before Merry, yet he had already taken out his revenge on the bastard. Unless this was a random push-in robbery gone wrong, the killer had to be Hunter.

I needed to talk with Whip. He didn't know I had the money. After Merry was murdered, the police arrested him before I had time to tell him anything.

I woke up around four in the morning. I'd dreamed Whip was locked in a six-by-eight cage. It was no dream. I changed sopping wet pajamas and returned to bed, not to sleep but to plot.

At first, I wasn't allowed to visit Whip. The police told him he could see no one except his attorney, but they relented and let him see me at least once a day. Then they let me come in whenever I needed to. Wonder if my call to the chief of police had anything to do with relaxing the rules.

The police, all but his friend Jerry and maybe the chief, were certain he killed Merry. Case closed quickly and efficiently. Jerry knew he was innocent, but he was off the case because of a potential conflict of interest. They went to the target range together, and Jerry arrested Merry the night she stabbed Whip. Nothing, however, was going to get Whip out of jail.

Neither Whip nor I knew squat about what evidence the police thought they had. We needed a criminal lawyer. I wasn't about to let the court assign a public defender, so I did some asking around. I called Whip's divorce counsel the day he was arrested. Mama Cass didn't practice criminal law, but she gave me the name of the best criminal lawyer in Richmond. Next, I called an old friend, the president of my bank, for a recommendation. Both the banker and Mama Cass recommended Vincent Bodine.

"Don't let his mild looks fool you, Mrs. Davies," the bank president said. "Vince is a wizard in the courtroom. Give him the right circumstances, and he's a piranha."

"I found a good attorney. Vincent Bodine is supposed to be the best in the town." I blurted out the news as soon as Whip entered the interview room.

"Wish his name ended with a pronounced vowel. Wish they called him Vinnie."

"Do you think you need a 'connected' lawyer? Vincent Bodine isn't Italian."

"Nah. Feeble joke. No mob lawyer needed."

"He's coming in to meet you this afternoon. I'll be back, if you like."

"I like."

I ran my usual errands before presenting myself to the desk sergeant again. Vince was already in the interview room when Pete, Whip's jailer, opened the door to let me in. I'd talked with him by phone, so we shook hands.

I wasn't impressed with Vince's looks: middle height, mousy-brown, thinning hair, nondescript tan eyes, untanned skin. He was pale. No distinguishing features. Just pale.

Whip came in five minutes after I did.

"My sole responsibility is to prove the prosecution's case is wrong or expose enough holes in it to throw doubt on the jury." Vince laid some colored file folders on the table. Each had Whip's name on the left side of the tab.

"I didn't kill my wife," Whip said.

"Of course. I don't have to prove your innocence. I have to beat the DA."

"What about the possibility someone else killed Merry?" Whip's lowered brow warned me he didn't like what Vince said.

"Not my job, Mr. Pugh."

"Whip."

"Okay, Whip. I don't solve crimes. That's what the police do."

"How do we expose the real killer?" I, too, didn't like where this was going.

"You don't, Mrs. Davies. Leave Whip's representation to me. You could get hurt if you go chasing everyone you think may have killed your daughter."

Not everyone. Just Hunter.

"I don't want to sit in jail waiting for my trial. I want out now."

"Not much chance of that until I find out what you're charged with. No court will grant bail if the district attorney goes for murder or even manslaughter. I'll press for a date to hear the indictment within a few days. Afterward, the district attorney will have to turn over their evidence. Then we'll see what they have."

CHAPTER FORTY

Life didn't come with a user manual. When you faced something you'd never faced before, you made up the rules as you went along, but my family's future was too important to wing it.

From what Whip told me, the police weren't looking for anyone else for Merry's murder. Jailhouse scuttlebutt and local reporters said the police had the right guy. Maybe I could get Jerry to help. Off the record, of course.

I knew they were wrong. So did the kids. If the police thought they'd wrapped up the case with Whip's arrest, then we had to prove Hunter was guilty. We needed to find something incriminating in Hunter's background, but I had no idea what it would be, how to get it, or even where it might lead. Or what to do with it when, not if, we found the evidence we needed.

Darla called to offer support. She was torn up over Merry's murder, but I was clueless about how to use her. After Merry moved out, she called Darla several times, but caller ID helped Darla duck the calls. Listening to the voice messages she said was harder to avoid, though; the last one came in two days before Merry's murder.

"How could I turn my back on my chosen sister?" She sobbed.

I understood how she felt. "Who rejected whom? Merry dumped all of us after she fell under Dracula's spell."

"If only I'd talked to her. Maybe she was afraid. Maybe she was having second thoughts." Darla snuffled.

"Do you think she wanted to get away from Hunter?"

"I don't know," Darla wailed. "Likely not, but maybe I could have beaten some sense into her. It's probably wishful thinking. I always thought she'd realize what a mess she'd made leaving with that creep. What a horrible man."

Another stifled sob. Hunter killed my daughter, but outside of the immediate family, I thought I was a minority of one. I was relieved to find I had company.

"I saw them together in the hospital before one of her early surgeries," Darla explained, "when he put the move on her at her most vulnerable moment. I told Merry he was bad news, but she raged at me and told me I was jealous. She was going to be perfect, and I wasn't."

"I saw the same thing before the first surgery. She looked at him with big puppy eyes."

"Merry told me he kept correcting her manners, changing the way she dressed, telling her to go blond. He wanted her to change almost everything on the outside while he changed her face."

"He's a total control freak."

"It's more than that. He had an agenda and forced Merry to go along with it." Darla stopped snuffling. "Everything he told her to do, she did."

"I got that too. When I called her on it, she told me to get out of her fucking face. Her words, not mine."

Hunter's motives were his alone. Merry was nothing but a blank canvas on which to create his version of the ideal woman.

"Yes, she was totally under his spell."

"I've got to prove Hunter killed her." My hands were clenched. I wanted to put them around his neck and squeeze the life out of him.

"Whip had nothing to do with Merry's death."

"No, he didn't."

Whip took his revenge on Hunter, but I couldn't tell Darla about the fight in the alley.

"Thanks for saying it, though."

I promised to call her soon. For the moment, I wanted to put dinner on the table. I hung up and called the kids. As usual, it took several hollers up the stairs to pry Alex from his computer.

"We need to help get Dad out of jail." Emilie piled salad in her bowl and selected a small piece of roasted chicken.

Alex loaded chicken on his plate, along with a couple of pieces of lettuce. He started to say something when he caught my frown. He put some of the chicken back and added a scoop of salad. No matter how inadequate I felt as a detective, I wasn't inadequate in raising children. They needed consistency in my behavior, not a wishy-washy approach to house rules. I saved my uncertainty for the privacy of my bedroom. Echoes of Raney's earlier warning about not blowing this, my second chance at getting child rearing right, sounded in my head.

"Yeah. They've gotta arrest Dracula. He killed Mom." Alex's intense look scared me. I couldn't find the little boy in it. "Will Dad's new lawyer help?"

"No. His job is to defend Dad. We have to find the murderer."

"Wow! That's going to be, like, so cool."

"What can we do? We're just two kids and a grandmother." Emilie nibbled a piece of cucumber.

"I beg your pardon. Since when did I become just a grandmother?" I flopped back in my chair, placed my hand on my forehead, acting highly insulted. "You guys named me Mad Max. Well, I'm mad as hell. Your dad's not going to get railroaded."

"So, what're we gonna do?" Alex mumbled around a huge bite of chicken.

I wanted to remind him about not talking with his mouth full, but I decided to let it go. This time.

"Beats the heck out of me. We need a plan. I'm going to talk to Dad's cop friend. We have to start somewhere."

"We'll help."

"How?" I didn't want them involved any more than Whip wanted Johnny and me involved the night we set up Hunter.

"Well, we don't know much about Hunter. Alex, can you find out where he came from?" Emilie glanced at her brother, who smiled.

"I Googled him once but didn't find much. I'll ask Freddie how to find him."

"Freddie?" I cut a bite of chicken.

"He's my college mentor in my computer club. He was also at camp this summer."

"I see."

"We need to watch Dracula too. We don't want him to leave town or do anything stupid." Emilie picked up a cherry tomato between finger and thumb and popped it into her mouth. "We need to find out who Kiki is too. Remember the napkins?"

"I sure do."

"Let me work on that. It's important, but I'm not sure how." Emilie selected a piece of carrot and scrutinized it for imperfections.

I could do leg work; Alex could use his computer skills. Kids today were so much more resourceful than in my generation. They had to be, since they were bombarded with everything the electronic age could offer from the day they were born. Emilie could ... do what? I decided to let her figure it out for herself. She'd come up with something. Maybe she could watch Hunter by what she was feeling. I was curious to see where it would lead us.

We toasted with milk glasses. With my tiny army, I was more optimistic than I was a few days earlier.

CHAPTER FORTY-ONE

You'd think the police in this little upscale suburb in the middle of Virginia had a serial killer or a cold-blooded murderer in jail the way the media carried on.

"Wife Murdered!"

"Killed in Cold Blood!"

"Shot at Point Blank Range!"

I bounced between the jail and Whip and home and the kids. Emilie and Alex hid in their rooms, serious about their roles in our army, but they each spent way too much time on the computer. I listened when they wanted to talk, which turned out to be every night over dinner. On rare occasions, they actually found something to lead them in a new direction. I wished they'd spend more time with their friends outdoors, though. What an old fogey, thinking children play outside.

I was going nuts being trapped inside the house or car or interview room at the jail. One Saturday morning, I rousted the kids out of bed before ten, told them to put on shorts, packed up our three bikes, and drove to the public park. We rode miles on the bike path, swung on the swings, burned thighs on what might have been the last metal slide still in use, and tossed a Frisbee back and forth. I treated us to ice cream afterward. Later, Emilie confessed she felt loads better having spent half the day outdoors. This from the child who used to spend every summer day in or by the pool.

"We have to enjoy ourselves." I wiped my sticky fingers with a too-thin paper napkin.

"It's so hard," Emilie said. "I feel guilty having fun when Mom's dead."

"I know, but not having fun just because we've all suffered a huge loss isn't healthy. Besides, it won't bring Mom back."

"Hey, there's always room for ice cream." Alex polished off his double chocolate fudge cone.

Emilie and I laughed in agreement.

I had many loose ends to tie up, one of which was to clean out Merry's apartment. After Hunter told Merry she couldn't live with him, my daughter told the kids she had her own place. From the way she described it, it was a fabulous apartment. Emilie could visit "when it was convenient."

When the man from the rental office called, Emilie overheard the conversation and demanded she be allowed to go with me. I wanted to shelter her from the murder scene, but she gave me a look that was pure Merry and pure Emilie too. It was also pure me when she thrust her chin outward. I gave in. The force of her will made me welcome her company.

When I picked up the key, the agent told me to take Merry's junk away immediately, or he'd throw everything out. He had a crew coming in two days to scrub the place from top to bottom. He had a tenant ready to move in and every day was costing him money. Forget the fact Merry's rent was paid through the end of the month and it was only the twentieth. Forget the fact he had no right to tell me to clear the apartment out early. I'd be relieved to have this behind me, though, so I didn't argue.

"Oh, and don't expect to get the security deposit back either."

I didn't care.

We stood before the locked door, not knowing what to expect. The police seals were broken, so I didn't have to do that. I'd watched enough crime shows to expect blood stains, a room torn up, and fingerprint powder on every hard surface. I gritted my teeth and turned the key. The door stuck. I hugged Emilie for support before putting my shoulder against it. It swung open. Another deep breath, I clasped her hand, and we went inside.

The apartment, shabby in that rent-a-room-fully-furnished sort of way, was neat and clean. No blood splatter on the walls, thank God. No big blood patch on the floor.

"Not exactly the way your mom described it, is it?"

My granddaughter was pale and trembling, her eyes half-closed, a bead of sweat on her upper lip.

A chair rested on its side. Had it tipped over when Merry was murdered or when the police searched the room?

"At first, she was surprised and happy to see Dracula, because she didn't expect him. She'd just finished a bath. She didn't stay happy long, though. They argued," Emilie whispered. "Later they fought."

"What do you mean?"

A chill went through me. I shouldn't have brought her. If this haunted her, it'd be my fault.

"Dracula shoved her against the wall over there. He yelled at her."

"Do you know what he said?"

"He yelled about the money. I think he went to the bank and found the box empty. He said, 'Where's the fuckin' money?'"

I'd caused Merry's death.

"Mom tried to walk away, but he grabbed her from behind. He had something hard on his hand, the one he put under Mom's chin."

The cast. I was mesmerized by the faraway look on Emilie's face.

"Dracula demanded the money again. Then he put a gun behind her right ear and pulled the trigger." Emilie's chest heaved in a loud sob.

I pulled my granddaughter to me. She wept against my shoulder.

"That's when it all stopped. All my feelings. That's when Mom died."

No one had told the children any details of Merry's murder, other than she'd been shot. No one mentioned the shot behind one ear, so Emilie couldn't have learned it from overheard conversations. The papers hadn't reported that detail, either.

I held Emilie until she stepped back, wiped her eyes, and pointed to a spot on the rug.

"That's where the police found her. She wore that old pink bathrobe I gave her for Christmas years ago." Emilie's voice broke, but she steadied herself.

Another unreported fact. I freaked out. I suggested we look around, gather Merry's clothes, and leave this dreadful place. Something was wrong. If this was a crime scene, something was missing. At last, I got it: no trace of fingerprint powder.

I set the chair upright and stepped around a spot on the carpet. It wasn't blood, but spilled liquid dried near the sofa. I didn't want to think about what it was.

Emilie called back that the kitchen was early Goodwill, all mismatched dishes and cheap pots and pans. The fridge held some takeout containers, the food inside long taken over by gray-green fuzz. I tossed her a garbage bag. She emptied all of the food out of the fridge and cupboards and marched the trash out to the dumpster.

I took the bedroom and bath. I didn't expect any surprises. Someone had pulled out every drawer in the chest and thrown the contents across the floor. The police hadn't reported finding the place torn apart. Instinct took over, and I reached down to fold the clothes before Emilie stopped me.

"Wait a minute. The police didn't do this. Dracula did."

"Are you sure?"

"I feel him searching this room. He didn't find what he wanted. It was later, though. Not the night he killed her. He came back for the money. Why's the money so important?"

I reminded her about Merry putting money in the safe-deposit box. After all, she found the key. I also told her Dracula couldn't get his hands on it, because I had it.

"He was after it all along."

Emilie took several pictures of the ransacked bedroom with her cell phone. She returned to the living room and took a picture of the end table before sending the photos to Alex.

I looked at the blouse clutched in my hand and at the rest of the clothes scattered about. Most were new and too young looking for Merry's age. They were hers, though, and I didn't want to leave them to be thrown away by uncaring strangers. I folded underclothes, blouses, dresses, skirts, and pants. Some of the blouses were soiled. I rooted around in the closet until I found Merry's suitcases stacked in the rear behind a pile of dirty laundry.

I looked for her jewelry box, the one I delivered to her lawyer so many weeks ago, but it wasn't there. What happened to the four-carat diamond ring Whip gave Merry for their tenth anniversary?

Where were the diamond heart-shaped earrings? What about my mother's gold watch?

"Do you see her jewelry case?"

Emilie shook her head.

I started a list of questions for Vince. The first was why the police hadn't dusted the living room for fingerprints. They said the crime scene didn't look like a robbery, yet the bedroom was a shambles. If they'd let me in at the time, I'd have missed the ivory-inlaid ebony jewelry box Whip brought back from Africa.

Emilie walked over to the bathroom door and looked inside. I followed. The bath was shabby, and at the same time it was quintessential Merry—full of potions and salts, lotions, and cleansers. Even before Hunter, she was manic about the latest skin products, wrinkle-prevention creams, exfoliants—whatever was new and expensive. Merry single-handedly helped beauty products become a multibillion-dollar-a-year industry. In that way, she was just like her mother.

Something was wrong, but for the life of me I couldn't see it. Emilie stared too. I packed cosmetics in the suitcases with the clothes and took one last look. Then it hit me. "If she'd just emerged from the bath, as the police think, where's the bath sheet?"

"Maybe Dracula wrapped what he took in it."

Another question for Vince.

I sat on the couch for a moment and waited for Emilie to rejoin me. I thought about other things that should have been there. Her cell. Where the heck was it? Her handbag. Did the police take it as evidence? Or for safeguarding? More questions.

I could get nothing more from the room that had never seen a professional cleaning crew, no matter what the rental agent said. There was nothing of the fabulous apartment Merry told Emilie she'd rented. I put my hand down to brush some crumbs from the brown-striped couch. Merry loved to snack in front of the TV. My face grew tight and my eyes leaked in sorrow, anger, and frustration. Emilie held me this time as we cried for a life cut short. We'd never stop missing a daughter and a mother. Sometime later, I wiped my eyes and opened the door.

An elderly white-haired woman waited in the hallway. She about spooked me.

"Are you related to the poor woman who was killed?"

"My daughter."

"My mother."

"I live next door."

Just what we need—a snoopy neighbor.

"These walls are so thin. I've been waiting since I heard you come in. Would you like a cup of tea?" She smiled at Emilie, who nodded. We introduced ourselves. I pulled the door closed behind me and followed the woman into an overly furnished apartment. A sunnier mirror image of Merry's, it was stuffed with early-American maple, chintz, and ruffles. She poured from a kettle already boiling. She carried a tray with cups, a teapot, and a plate of cookies into the living room.

"I'm Mrs. Curry. I've lived here for thirty years. I've seen residents come and go, but I've never had a murder happen next door."

Emilie gave the woman her full attention.

Mrs. Curry might be a lonely shut-in excited by the murder, but a cup of tea would soothe our tired souls.

"You don't look like your mother."

"I used to."

I noted the bitterness and felt sorrow for my grandchild. My mind drifted while our hostess nattered on, until she said something that swept the cobwebs away.

"Mrs. Curry, you just said you were home the night Merry was shot."

"Of course. I never go out after dark alone. It's not safe, and I don't drive at night."

My friend Eleanor was the same. Closing in on seventy-five, she went out after dark if she took a taxi or one of us drove.

"As I said, these walls are so thin. I tried not to listen, but his voice was so loud. Your daughter sounded like she knew him, but she sounded scared. At first I couldn't hear most of what they said, but I heard the anger. Later, I heard more of the conversation, such as it was."

I had a brief image of Mrs. Curry holding a water glass against the drywall to listen more clearly. I stifled a smile. "Why do you say she was scared?"

"Because she kept begging him to calm down and not hurt her."

"Did you hear anything else?" With a trembling hand, I put the delicate porcelain cup back on its saucer. I was afraid I'd snap the handle.

"He cursed a lot, like so many of the young do today."

"He was young?"

"After you reach eighty, almost everyone's young. I could tell from his voice he wasn't my age, so by the process of elimination, he had to be young." Mrs. Curry patted her white hair. For a second, I saw Julia McKenzie as Miss Marple of PBS's *Masterpiece Theater*. I smiled.

"As I was saying, he cursed. He kept asking where the money was."

I jumped. *Is this the proof we need that Hunter killed Merry?* I knew where the money was. Whip didn't, not until after Merry's murder. Emilie froze.

"You know what that means?" Mrs. Curry refilled our cups.

"I do. Can you remember his exact words?"

Mrs. Curry closed her eyes for a moment and then leaned forward. "He said, 'where's the fuckin' money?' Then I heard a noise. I thought he slammed a door, but I now think it might have been a gunshot."

"Do you remember what time it was?"

"Oh, yes. It was a little after nine. Maybe nine-fifteen. A repeat episode of *CSI* had just started."

"Mrs. Curry, have the police talked to you?" Emilie asked.

"The police? Why, no, they haven't. I assumed they arrested the killer. The papers said he's in jail." She shook her head. "Such a tragedy."

"Mrs. Curry, you've been so kind to offer us tea and tell us what you heard. Would you be willing to talk to my son-in-law's lawyer?"

"Of course."

I took one of her hands in both of mine and stroked the tissue-thin skin of advanced age. "You've given us hope. Please don't believe everything you read. The man in jail, Merry's husband, Emilie's father, my son-in-law, did not kill my daughter."

I carried the tea tray into the tidy kitchen and rinsed the pot. I set the cups on an embroidered tea towel, and we took our leave.

When we stopped at Merry's apartment to pick up the suitcases and a couple of bags of clothing, a small, darkish object at the edge of the couch glinted in the harsh overhead light. A key. I wrapped it in a tissue and tucked it into my handbag. I knew where its brother was.

CHAPTER FORTY-TWO

After coming off the emotional rollercoaster of cleaning out Merry's apartment, I wanted to tell Whip about Mrs. Curry right away. I'd been going to the jail every other day or so, but I didn't want to wait until my next scheduled visit. We were lucky because the police relaxed their restrictions and allowed me nearly unrestricted access. Could Whip's friend, the police chief, have stepped in? I hoped so. We might need that connection again later.

The booking area roiled with a dozen people under arrest and their handlers and lawyers who shouted to get the attention from the desk sergeant. Ten minutes after I arrived, Pete unlocked the door from the cells. Once again, I looked around the interview room. It would look less like the room of no hope from a bad film noir with a fresh coat of paint to hide stains, streaks, and years of handprints. I was so wound up I blurted out everything we learned almost before Whip took his usual seat.

"Odd. If your Miss Marple overheard Hunter demand the money, doesn't it prove he killed Merry?"

"Not really. Remember, you didn't know I'd cleaned out the safe-deposit box until after you were arrested."

"Yes, but we didn't tell anyone. Hunter had access."

"Hunter made a mistake." I reached into my handbag, pulled out a tissue, unwrapped the key, and showed it to Whip. "Merry's key is in my bureau. This was on the floor in her apartment."

"This should prove I didn't do it." Whip's eyes flickered. "Why didn't the cops find it? I thought they searched her apartment."

"I don't think it was there when Merry died. There's more." I told him about the missing jewelry, cell phone, and handbag. "Her bedroom was trashed. The police didn't mention that. Most important, I found no trace in the apartment."

"What do you mean, 'trace'?"

"We always see fingerprint powder used at a crime scene on television, don't we? The CSI people grab jars of powder and brushes when they test solid surfaces. They don't clean up afterward, do they?"

"I don't think so. Ask Jerry. He'd know."

"We found the normal accumulation of dust on the hard surfaces but no fingerprint powder. If they'd conducted a thorough search, wouldn't you think the police would have found this little key? After all, I found it, and I'm no professional." I returned it to an inside pocket in my handbag. "I asked Vince for the police report. I want to see if they mention the state of the bedroom."

"Why?"

"Em says Hunter came back. She thinks he went to the bank and found the box empty. He got so angry he confronted Merry and killed her. The police tape was ripped. Em knows he did it. He ripped the bedroom apart. When he didn't find the money, he threw the key on the floor and left."

"You may be right. How can we use this?"

"I'm not sure. That's Vince's problem. Em took pictures and sent them to Alex. See, the bedroom's ruined. The living room's normal." I laid a stack of photos in front of Whip.

"Here's where I found the key." I pointed to the edge of the couch.

"Give these to Vince."

"Of course. You can't imagine how weird it was standing where Merry died. I hoped for some kind of sign, a ripple in the Force, anything, to let me connect with her. Some people believe the spirit of a murdered person remains near the place of death. I couldn't feel her presence."

I bet Whip wanted to laugh because I'd hoped for a sign to help me with my grief. Maybe the key was it, and I was too earthbound to see it.

Vince arrived with news just as I was getting ready to leave. Whip would be arraigned in two days at which time he'd enter his plea. Afterward, they'd see the prosecutor's case.

Things weren't moving as fast as Vince originally predicted. Whip had sat around far longer than was usual. The idea of a rapid trial didn't carry as much weight when a murder was involved. The police could delay as long as they continued to build a case against him.

"They'll probably go for manslaughter, although the district attorney might try to make this a signature case to support his bid for re-election."

"Why?"

"He hasn't won a murder trial in four years. He could go for murder two, but I don't think that's likely. He needs a conviction on which to hang his campaign."

"I don't see how they can charge Whip with murder," I said.

"The district attorney will try for as high a profile case as possible."

"Any chance they'll let me go?" Even to me, Whip didn't sound hopeful.

"Snowballs in Hell, Whip."

"Terrific. A political volleyball to satisfy some prick's ambition. Where's the justice in that?"

"Cut the crap. Justice and politics repel each other. We'll ask for dismissal on lack of physical evidence."

I told Vince about my visit to Merry's apartment. He made little of the fingerprint powder, but he jotted a note to look into it further. Maybe we could get this thrown out on sloppy police work. "Here are the photos Em took at the apartment yesterday. Will you compare them with the official police file?"

Vince put them in a new folder he labeled "Apartment."

"Now, do you want the charges dismissed? Or do you want to be found not guilty?"

Good question. No one was found innocent, just not guilty. I could split that hair seven ways from Tuesday. I already knew what Whip's answer would be.

"Dismissed."

"I agree. We want the charges dismissed with prejudice."

"With prejudice?" I'd never heard that term before. It didn't sound good to my non-attorney ear, though.

"If the charges are dismissed with prejudice, you can never be charged for the same crime again. If charges are dismissed because of lack of evidence, the police can and probably will keep the case open. If they ever find anything, they can come after you again. There's no statute of limitations on murder."

We spent another hour going over what to expect and made a list of the clothes Whip wanted me to bring. At least he wouldn't be led into the courtroom in chains and an orange jumpsuit. Much as I hated to have Emilie and Alex hear their father charged with killing their mother, I wanted him to see the kids, talk to them, and hug and kiss them. I hoped he'd get the chance.

CHAPTER FORTY-THREE

I putzed around making dinner and trying to figure out what to do next. Alex was upstairs, and I hadn't seen Emilie since I got back from the jail. She might be taking a nap. God knows, she must be emotionally drained from going to her mother's apartment. I needed a nap, too, but early to bed would suffice.

Dinner wasn't quite ready when Emilie and Alex came downstairs together. Odd. Standard practice was to call them several times, particularly Alex. When he was online, the world could end and he'd only become aware of it when the power went off.

The kids were deep in conversation. Emilie put a pad of paper upside down beside her place at the table. Without being asked, they got out four settings.

"Four? We're having company?" I'd made enough pasta and sausage to feed a small army. Alex was going through another of his growth spurts and inhaled everything biodegradable.

The doorbell rang, and Emilie went to answer it. I was pleased when Johnny entered with a bottle of Tuscany Rustico cradled in one arm. He kissed me on the cheek, ruffled Alex's hair, and leaned against the counter.

"Rumor has it you're making spaghetti." Johnny winked.

"I called Uncle Johnny, Mad Max," Emilie said. "We need a family conference, and Dad's not here."

Hmm, a conspiracy. One I hadn't concocted. I put salad on the table, filled bowls with pasta, meatballs, and sausage, and ladled my homemade sauce over it all.

We ate and chatted about junk and nonsense. Whenever I looked at Johnny, he just shrugged and glanced at Emilie and Alex. I knew who was in charge of this scenario.

Emilie and Alex cleared the table without prompting.

A first.

That left me alone with Johnny and half a bottle of wine. I refilled our glasses and smiled over the rim. Johnny's eyes twinkled. The dishwasher started. We waited for the kids to return.

"I called Uncle Johnny because we need his help." Emilie plopped back into her chair. "He always helped Mom when Dad was out of town."

I was glad Emilie found Johnny's presence as comforting as I did.

"I talked with Mr. Zimmerman, too, because we'll need Uncle Johnny during the day sometimes."

"You called Tops?" Johnny raised his left eyebrow. "He's okay with this?"

"Why wouldn't he be? He said we can borrow you whenever we need. He promised to do anything he can to bring Dad home."

"Great!"

Johnny told me just after Whip was arrested he was worried about getting away from the office without being AWOL.

"Remember, Mad Max, you said we need a plan. Anyway, me and Alex ... jeez, I mean, Alex and I started a list of stuff we know and stuff we don't know." Emilie put the pad in the center of the table.

Johnny and I poured over the list.

"Great start, guys," I said, "but not everything's accurate."

"Like what?" At eleven, Alex hated to be told he was wrong. About anything.

"Like we don't know Dracula took Mom's jewelry. We think he did."

"Well, we know he killed Mom. Mrs. Curry heard it." Emilie stared at her list.

"Mrs. Curry heard someone shoot Mom. She didn't see anyone."

"He had to have done it." Alex's voice rose in frustration.

"I agree."

"What Mad Max's saying, Alex, is we don't know these things.

We think they're true, but we have to prove them."

"All we really know is Dad didn't kill Mom." Emilie looked crestfallen.

"Your father would never have killed your mother. If he wanted to kill anybody, it would have been Dracula."

"The police think Dad did it, though." Emilie sighed.

"They're idiots," Alex said.

The police were fools if they thought Whip capable of murder. *No, wait.* We were all capable of murder, given the right circumstances, but Whip wasn't capable of cold-blooded murder. Not the cold-blooded murder of the mother of his children, no matter how angry and hurt he was by Merry's betrayal. I'd never believe he could have done it.

"We've got a lot of work to do before Dad can come home." A pattern emerged in what we were missing. The task was daunting, but we should be able to do it if we made baby steps and worked together.

"May I see the list?" Johnny reached out his hand. "Let's see if I can make it more accurate. Then we can decide how to get the answers to the unknowns."

Johnny drew three columns on a clean piece of paper and moved things around.

"Jeez, we don't know much, do we?" Emilie looked discouraged.

"It's not all that bad. We know your dad didn't kill your mom," Johnny said. "He worked late that night."

"Were you there all the time?"

"No. Tops and I left around eight-thirty, after scarfing down some pizza."

"Dad doesn't have an alibi for the time Mom was murdered, does he?"

None of us wanted to admit the lack of a verifiable alibi. There it was, front and center and unavoidable, the pink elephant in the kitchen.

"Not really. Let's say you left just after eight-thirty. Let's agree Mrs. Curry is right about the time *CSI* started. It'd be a real stretch to get from the office to Merry's apartment on the far side of Richmond near Chaminade." I steepled my fingers under my chin.

"He could do it, but he'd have to have been flying," Johnny agreed.

"Wonder if there were any construction delays on I-95 that night."

"I can find out." Alex had something else to pursue.

Emilie told Johnny about our visit to the apartment and Mrs. Curry's remark about the money. We left that as a known, because we had an earwitness. Plus we had pictures from Emilie's cell.

"The police have pictures too. They'll be presented at trial. Vince'll see them after Dad's arraigned."

"When's that?" Emilie had a small catch in her throat.

"Day after tomorrow. I assume you want to go."

Three heads nodded.

"So, what else do we know? Do we know what kind of gun killed Mom?" Alex, Mr. Serious, asked. "I mean, Dad has lots in the safe. Was one missing?"

"It was a twenty-two. Dad's guns are all nine-millimeters. We know where they all are."

"Whew!"

I was surprised by Alex's reaction. Did he harbor a tiny doubt his father wasn't innocent? I stared at him. No, he was just relieved his father's guns were a different caliber. Simple as that.

Emilie stared at the list. "Has anyone sold Mom's jewelry? If it turns up in a pawn shop, we should be able to find it."

"Could be on eBay. I'll check." Alex seized on another way to use his computer skills.

"Good idea. I'll hit the pawn shops." Johnny echoed Alex's enthusiasm.

"We had insurance riders and pictures, so when we find it, we can prove the jewelry was Merry's."

"If the police didn't see the messed up bedroom, doesn't that prove Dracula came back?" Emilie dwelled on that point. "After all, we didn't break the police tape."

"It just proves someone came back, not necessarily Dracula."

"There are two more questions," Emilie said. "Why was Dracula turning Mom into Kiki?"

"Kiki?" Johnny's pen was poised to add to the list.

"We don't know who she is," I answered.

"Kiki's a person?"

"We think so." Emilie told Johnny about finding napkins of doodles with "Kiki and Andy" along with other variations of her name with Hunter's. She rolled her eyes. I let her get away with it this time, because I agreed with her assessment of her mother's silliness.

"It's also Dracula's password."

"His password? On what, his computer?"

Alex blushed bright red and picked at a crumb on the table. "Um. Yeah."

"Alex Pugh, you are not to do anything illegal. Do you hear me?" I was furious. "My grandson is not going to end up in jail next to his father. Do you understand?"

"Yes, ma'am," Alex mumbled.

"I'll work on Kiki." Emilie saved Alex from more of a tongue lashing.

"There must be a thousand more things, but I can't think straight."

The effects of the wine and the stress of the day were hitting me. Funny, I didn't mind saying I couldn't think straight. Like Eleanor said, I didn't have to be the only strong one all the time. Johnny was here. I could lean on him.

"Good time to stop. Do you want to give each of us our 'to-do's'?" Here was strong, tough Johnny asking for his "honey-do" list. I burst out laughing.

"Let's divvy this up and see where it gets us. I'll ask the police about the stuff that's missing—Merry's purse, cell phone, and jewelry box."

"I'll help Alex with the jewelry." Johnny wrote their names next to each task.

"Alex can find out where Dracula came from and who he is," Emilie volunteered.

"Yeah," Alex nodded.

"You guys can help, but you have to make me a promise." I put on my sternest, most grandmotherly voice.

"Promise what?" Emilie and Alex shared a wary glance.

"If I feel there is so much as a nano-inch of danger to any of this, you'll stop playing detective at once. Pinky swear?"

"Pinky swear." Emilie clearly didn't like it.

"There's no such thing as a nano-inch," Alex sassed.

"Whatev-ah." I rolled my eyes in perfect mimicry of Emilie. "Pinky swear?"

I had to drag it out of Alex. "Pinky swear."

We reached across the table and hooked little fingers. We were a team with two priorities: proving Whip innocent and Dracula guilty.

"Let's go get Whip out of jail," Johnny said.

"I'll type this up and put it on the fridge, so we can track our progress,"

Alex grabbed the paper and ran upstairs. "'Night."

Emilie kissed and hugged me. "Thank you. For everything. I love you."

"I love you, too, dear child."

She kissed Johnny on the cheek, surprising the heck out of him.

"Well, we have some place to start, don't we, pretty lady?" Johnny took my hand and held it. "You look about done in."

"I am, but I'm not too tired for a nightcap and a hug."

CHAPTER FORTY-FOUR

Whip looked good in his own clothes instead of jailhouse orange. Even for a day. I took his suit, shirt, tie, and underwear early the day of his court appearance. Alex wanted his father to know he polished his loafers for him. Add a jail haircut and shave and Whip looked almost normal. That was, until I remembered why the changes: his court appearance to plead not guilty.

An hour before the hearing, the police led Whip through an underground corridor into the adjacent two-century old courthouse where Vince and I waited in a conference room. The transport cop removed the plastic handcuffs and locked us in. Vince said Whip would make a good impression. "We've been fortunate to draw one of the more centrist judges on the bench, Mary Rhonda Garrison."

Vince went over the protocol of what to expect once again.

"You'll come in through a side door. You won't be able to speak to your children, friends, or other family."

"Why not?"

"Think of this as prosecutorial posturing. The district attorney can and will do everything in his power to diminish your position." Vince shut his briefcase. "Just be glad you aren't in a jail jumpsuit."

Not much more would happen at the initial hearing. The prosecution would present the charge, which Vince believed would be manslaughter.

Whip would say, "Not guilty."

Vince would ask for bail or release on Whip's own recognizance. They'd post bond and surrender his passport, because he was neither a threat to the community nor a flight risk. And Whip would be out.

Nothing went according to plan. The prosecution asked for murder two and remand. No matter what Vince said, he couldn't convince the judge to grant bail.

"Not on a murder charge, Mr. Bodine," the Honorable Mary Rhonda Garrison said for the second time.

"But, Your Honor ..." Vince got no further. He fell silent when the judge pointed her finger at him.

The judge sided with the prosecution. So much for being a centrist.

Whip returned to his home away from home—the jail cell. Vince said he'd be over after he petitioned for an immediate release of the evidence. I followed Whip to the jail to wait for Vince; Johnny took the kids back home.

I was with Whip when Vince arrived, his face red with fury.

"The district attorney plans to try the case himself. George Weed never prosecutes murder two. It has to be his re-election campaign. He lost his last high-profile murder case."

"What happened?" Whip ping-ponged around the room, too hyperactive to sit.

"He tried a guy who killed his parents and boss in front of a dozen witnesses. Sad but true, most of the physical evidence was compromised by sloppy police work and thrown out."

"What happened to the guy?"

"He was released, left town, and murdered his in-laws out in West Virginia. He killed a cop in a shootout before the police nailed the son of a bitch with a couple of dozen well-placed bullets."

"So, reading the tea leaves, Weed's going to eviscerate Whip to prove he killed Merry. In cold blood? Or premeditation? A crime of passion?" I squirmed on the hard wooden chair.

"Premeditation. He doesn't think it's a crime of passion."

"Bullshit!"

"Calm down." Vince laid several new colored file folders on the table.

"How could it be premeditation? What about the evidence?"

"I have a partial list and asked for the police photos. I should get the rest of the evidence next week." Vince handed over a single sheet of paper. "I don't see how they can build a case out of this."

Whip scanned the list and handed it to me.

Nothing unexpected. Whip's fingerprints were found in Merry's car—naturally, since he bought it for her and maintained it. None in her apartment—he'd never been there. A blue shirt with gunshot residue the police took from the dirty clothes hamper. An old New York state registration for a twenty-two caliber handgun. An inventory of the nine-millimeter guns from the safe.

"Here's the first thing wrong, Vince." Whip pointed to the twenty-two. "That gun was stolen from a locked case in the trunk of my car more than four years ago. I filed a police report. I bought it for Merry, but she never liked it. Funny, isn't it? She was killed with a gun similar to the one I got her for her own protection."

"I'll pull the police report." Vince made a cryptic mark on his legal pad.

"I have one with the insurance claim in my filing cabinet."

"I'll bring it, Vince." I'd do whatever I could.

"That'll help, but it's not evidence the gun was stolen. It's evidence you reported it stolen."

"So I was planning to kill Merry for more than four years? Bullshit!"

"The other guns were all registered?" Vince didn't miss a beat. He ran a manicured finger down the list.

"Absolutely. Even before the Brady Bill, I registered every one of them. I haven't owned an unregistered gun since I was a kid. My dad had an old thirty-eight we used for target practice. I have no idea what happened to it. Hell, he may still have it."

"Don't mention any unregistered guns. Even as a kid. Even if you owned one before guns had to be registered. It's no use planting any seeds of doubt in a juror's head. Look over the list of guns the police impounded. The police compared them with your known permits. One's missing."

"It's not missing. I shipped the Glock to the worksite in Peru. Steve can fax the Peruvian permit. It's still there."

"Can you prove it?"

"Sure, why?"

"It sounds like Weed intends to make a federal case out of that gun. Just like the twenty-two. He wants to show a pattern." Vince made a note in his neat handwriting. His ever-present legal pad filled up with single words and short cryptic phrases. "Maybe you were planning to get rid of your wife for a long time."

"I repeat, the Glock's not missing. It's all legal and locked in my safe in Peru. I couldn't have sneaked it back into the country, because I came home with a small carry-on. American Airlines can pull my records, if necessary. Since September Eleventh, no one's been allowed to board a plane with a weapon. Besides, the Glock's a nine-millimeter, not a twenty-two."

Vince ignored Whip's outburst. "What about the shirt the cops found in the clothes basket? Any idea how the GSR got on it?"

"Easy. Two days before Merry's murder, I competed in a tournament at Saunder's firing range. Beat the police chief and the head of the detective squad. Everyone knows me. Shoot there as often as I can."

Whip always wore the same shirt, his lucky shirt, in competition. "Why?"

"I like to keep my skills sharp."

"Have you ever fired your gun at a person?" Vince made another mysterious entry on the pad.

"Twice. Once to scare a robber off down in South America. Once in Africa."

"And in Africa?"

"This militia guy chased two of my native crew with a machete and an AK forty-seven. Him or my crew. I chose him."

"He died?"

"Direct shot in the heart."

I'd never heard this before. *Boy, I don't know as much about my son-in-law as I thought.*

"That doesn't have any bearing on Merry's murder."

"It would, if Weed tries to prove you're violent."

"Does he have evidence of Whip's violent nature?" I picked at a loose thread on my sleeve.

If the district attorney got wind of Whip's fight with Hunter, it might support his theory. I wanted to make sure he never did. Johnny, Whip, Hunter, and I were the only living witnesses to the beating, and Johnny and I weren't about to volunteer any information. From the lack of charges against Whip for assault, I doubted Hunter wanted to admit his married lover's husband beat the snot out of him.

"Not that I know of."

"What about a statement from the guys at the range?"

"It doesn't hurt to have the chief of police vouch for you." Vince smiled the tiniest of smiles. Whip didn't.

"Before we move on, what do you know about GSR, Vince?" Whip asked.

"Not much. Why?"

"My shirt should be covered with microscopic trace particles of lead, barium, and antimony. Fired between six- and eight-hundred shells that day. Both in practice before the competition and during it."

"Okay." Vince made a note but didn't appear to see a pattern. I did.

"Should have trace all over the front and both sleeves. Merry was killed by a single shot fired from someone standing beside or behind her. Trace would be on the right sleeve, with a little on the front maybe, if the murderer touched the shirt. There would be very little."

"You could have worn a dirty shirt, just to throw the police off."

"Jesus! What about my alibi?"

"Full of holes, Whip. Mr. Medina left right after eating the pizza, right?"

"Yeah."

"That was around eight-thirty?"

"Eight-thirty. Maybe eight forty-five."

"Mr. Zimmerman left about the same time?"

"Yeah. Maybe a couple of minutes before Johnny."

I didn't like where this was headed. I could see Whip didn't either.

"The coroner set your wife's time of death between nine-thirty and ten-thirty. That gives you enough time to get up to her apartment and shoot her."

"But Mrs. Curry heard the gunshot about nine-fifteen. She said a rerun of *CSI* had just started. The coroner must be wrong."

"Shit on a shingle!" Whip exploded over my comment.

"What are you doing, Vince?" I wasn't pleased with Whip's attorney playing good cop-bad cop.

"Just asking the kind of questions the district attorney will ask at trial. If I anticipate his line of attack, I can prepare Whip and other witnesses. We want to get our story out our way and not have to rebut the prosecutor's spin."

"Makes sense." I didn't have to like the tactic. Still, it was effective and made us think through what we said about each piece of evidence.

"So far, the case is all circumstantial, but juries have convicted on less. We'll get through this. In my career, I haven't let an innocent man be convicted. You aren't going to be my first."

"While you're getting the statement from the guys at the range, talk to Mrs. Curry." I reinforced my request to have her deposed.

"I will, but she didn't see anything."

"She heard the killer's voice. Might be able to tell you it wasn't Whip if she hears his."

"Anyone else?"

"Not that I can think of."

"One more thing. Whip couldn't get to Merry's apartment from his office on I-95 if he killed her at nine-fifteen."

"Huh?"

"Alex checked the Department of Transportation Web site for that night. Only one lane westbound was open. Tie-ups were over an hour."

"That's good. Now, think of what else we're missing. You've got a lot of time on your hands, Whip, so get busy." Vince packed his legal pad and folders, shook our hands, and knocked at the door.

"Yeah, like I'm going anywhere soon." Whip's being the target of a power-hungry district attorney didn't go down well.

"We need your help, too, Whip." I told him about our small army of four.

"Four? Who's the fourth?"

"Johnny."

"Don't tell me you're dating my best friend." Whip tried and failed to look scandalized.

"Okay, I won't. Back to business. If we want to prove Hunter killed Merry, we can't do it alone. Think about what we should look for."

"What's Hunter doing now? Is he still around? Is anyone watching him?"

"I'll find out." I made a note in the small notebook I kept with me at all times. I wasn't about to tell Whip Alex was still monitoring his cell and Emilie was "feeling" what Hunter was doing.

"You guys gotta get me outta here."

"We're trying everything we can think of. Help us. Tell us what we're missing."

"Don't want to go through life with everyone looking at me like I'm a killer."

"That's part of the problem. If we don't pin this on Hunter, it could be your reality."

"I know. I'm scared shitless, Max." Whip walked to the grubby window and stared through countless fingerprints. "People have been convicted on less."

"Not if I have anything to say about it."

"Just don't bring your private detective back. Wouldn't do me much good if he got caught tailing Hunter."

"Tony Ferraiolli's boys don't get caught. Still, I see what you're saying. We'll do a lot of sleuthing ourselves. If I think we need him, I'll get him back. You won't have a say in it."

"Just be safe. Hunter's a loose cannon. I don't want him to kill any witnesses."

I kissed Whip on the cheek. I hated the forlorn look on his face. He could be in jail for months.

CHAPTER FORTY-FIVE

I stared at Alex's questions stuck on the refrigerator. So many unknowns.

The police remained uncooperative. When Vince asked about the missing items, he got stonewalled. The party line was, "Pugh's guilty. Your questions are noise in the system, so forget about it."

I blew on my coffee. The surface rippled. I took a sip and still burned the tip of my tongue. Shoot, that'd blister. I stared again at the list.

"MM? MM? Where are you?" Alex shouted.

"MM?"

Alex thundered down the stairs, his oversized sneakers not sneaky.

I looked up. "Who's MM?"

"You. Oh, sorry. When Em and I text each other, we call you MM."

"Why?"

"Shorter than Mad Max."

"Gotcha."

"And it's better than Grandma," Alex sassed.

"You got that right." Then what Alex said hit home. "Hey, wait a minute. Do you and Em text each other when you're both in the house?"

"Sure."

"Your bedrooms are on the same hall, separated by your bathroom." I set my cup on the kitchen table.

"So?"

"So, no more. Get up and walk over. No texting within the house."

"Ah, come on, Mad Max."

"No. Your butts are glued to your chairs too damned much as it is."

"Okay."

"Now, what's up?"

Alex held a fistful of crumpled papers. He threw himself into a kitchen chair. Emilie strolled in a few seconds later and went to the fridge for sodas. After they opened Diet Cokes, Alex spread out his smooshed papers.

Could he have found something?

"This is, like, totally surreal," Alex started.

"Alex's been looking for Dracula." Emilie watched her brother stare at the printouts.

"Have you found him?"

I was determined to play the game. Humor him. Keep him focused. Deep inside, though, I doubted he'd come up with anything substantial.

"That's the problem. I found a bunch of Draculas. I don't know which one's him."

"What do you mean, a bunch?" I wanted to snatch the printouts, but I held back. "Alex Time" was slower than mine.

"I Googled him, but Andrew Hunter's too common. I got tons of junk. I found several Andrew Hunters who are doctors."

"How many are plastic surgeons?"

"At least five."

"Five?"

No wonder Alex was confused.

"Well, five with a name that's a variation of Dracula's. See."

My grandson pushed the papers across the breakfast table. I saw his problem: Dr. Andrew R. Hunter. Dr. R. Andrew Hunter. Dr. A. Randall Hunter. Dr. Randall A. Hunter. Dr. Randall Andrew Hunter.

"I see. How do you suggest we narrow it down?"

Emilie stared at the table, her eyes unfocused. She sat motionless for several long seconds. "We don't."

"We don't?" Now I was confused. I reached for my coffee cup.

"We don't narrow it at all. They're all him."

"That doesn't make sense. Look." I pointed to one of the printouts. "Here's a news story about a Randall A. Hunter who graduated from UVA Medical School. Another about an A. Randall Hunter who graduated from USC Medical School. A third about an Andrew R. Hunter who graduated from St. George's University Medical School in Grenada."

"Where's Grenada?" Alex belched and earned a frown for his exuberant efforts.

"It's a small island in the Caribbean with a medical school. Americans go there when they can't get into a school in the States."

"Is that legal?" Emilie whispered a small burp.

"Sure. To practice medicine, you have to pass state medical board exams. Dracula must have passed at least one." I picked up two of the printouts and laid them side by side.

"These dates are off." I pointed at the stories. "Dracula couldn't have graduated from UVA and USC two years apart."

"Then he's lying."

Alex got up and returned with the cookie jar.

"Yes, but where? And why?"

"Or how many times? About what? I bet we find out he's a serial liar." Emilie helped herself to a peanut butter cookie.

"Or a serial killer." Finding and stopping a serial killer would be right up Alex's fantasy-sleuth alley.

"So, this guy has several aliases. What does that tell us?" Emilie sipped more cola.

"He's got something to hide," Alex suggested. "I'll Google him again. Oh, guys, I found a way cool site called 'rottendoctor.' It lists doctors who've lost their licenses or who are under investigation for all sorts of stuff. You can also post stuff."

"Your dad sent letters to the state medical board and the hospital several weeks ago. He told them one of their doctors was having an affair with a patient. That's so against the rules." Why I hadn't thought to tell the kids earlier, I didn't know. Now they deserved to know everything I did.

"I'll post a question. Maybe there's other stuff about Dracula." Alex grabbed his papers and thundered back up the stairs. "Could be he's been sued for malpractice."

"I wonder if there are other sites like that. I'll look." Emilie took her soda and another cookie and walked out of the room. She threw a question over her shoulder. "Have you found Mom's cell phone yet?"

"No," I called toward the retreating back.

"Did you call the number?" Emilie's voice drifted from midway up the stairs.

I picked up my phone and speed dialed Merry's number. It rang half a dozen times before it was answered. I steeled myself to listen to her recorded voice. What I heard was someone's raspy breathing. I hung up and stared out into the backyard. I called back and it went right to voicemail. The someone who answered had turned the cell off.

CHAPTER FORTY-SIX

Time for my daily report to Whip. Once the police let him read the newspapers, he suffered mixed emotions when Merry's murder returned to the front page following his arraignment. The media continued to brand him a cold-blooded wife killer, guilty as charged. One opinion columnist for the *Richmond Times-Dispatch* wrote he should plead out, save the county the cost of a useless trial, and take his punishment like a man. The columnist had spoken to a cop but wouldn't identify his source. He hadn't questioned Vince. He hadn't tried to interview Whip, and he sure as heck hadn't reached out to me. I was pissed off about Whip being tried and convicted *in absentia* by some newspaper hack doing a shoddy job.

Whip was in one of his nastiest moods when I showed up with the news about Hunter's multiple personae.

"So, he uses aliases. Big fuckin' deal. Does the medical board know?"

"I have a call in to them."

"Wonder what else he's hiding."

"No idea, but there's more. I think he has Merry's cell. When I called, I could hear raspy breathing."

"Sure it was Hunter? Not someone who may have found the phone?"

"My gut says he kept it. When I called right back, I got voicemail. It was creepy."

Did Hunter keep trophies of all of his victims? Sick, but so was creating his brand of perfection only to destroy it.

"Get a printout of her last calls. You'll know if someone's been using it. Don't forget her text messages."

"Already done." Or I could just ask Alex.

"Wonder where Hunter was before Chaminade. Told me when we met he was here on a one-year teaching fellowship. Probably why Merry thought they'd move."

"Alex's working on Hunter's history. He's found contradictory stories about where he went to medical school. He found where Hunter worked, though. He's tracking leads in three states."

Even though I knew Alex was hacking into Hunter's accounts, I couldn't encourage my grandson to break the law. We had a long talk when I let him know in no uncertain terms we were living in extraordinary times. I'd only tolerate him hacking into Hunter's cell or computer to help his father. Alex promised, but he might have had his fingers crossed behind his back.

Whip was in enough trouble for all of us. I didn't want Alex or Emilie, or for that matter, Johnny, doing anything illegal, but I'd overlook a little social engineering. If it helped the cause. After all, I'd pulled off a bank heist. Sort of. Right now, I could rationalize anything short of murder. Maybe even that if it got Whip out of jail.

"Em hasn't said much, but she took Merry's PC from the kitchen desk to her room. I'm sure she's reading every e-mail."

"Has she found anything?"

"Other than lots of proof Merry was having an affair with Hunter, no. They sent lots of raunchy e-mails and text messages back and forth. We already knew about the text messages. Now, we know what they said in e-mail too."

"Hunter texting anyone else?"

"Not that we know of. Alex figured out his computer password, so we can read his e-mails too."

My turn to cross my fingers behind my back.

I didn't want Whip asking too many questions, so I plunged ahead. "At any rate, we're trying to get answers to our 'fridge list.'"

"'Fridge list'?"

I handed Whip the list of questions. He laughed at our level of organization and the assignments.

"Johnny's helping? Tops okay with this?"

"He sure is. We can have Johnny any time we need him."

"Have you found Merry's purse?"

"No. The police don't have it."

"Wonder if Hunter took it with the cell."

"I'm betting on it. The purse is most likely long gone in a dumpster somewhere. The police said it wasn't in her apartment."

"Merry kept all her passwords written on a card in a side pocket. Never could remember the alarm settings for the house."

"Phooey. The security system. Hunter could get in. I'll call as soon as I get home. Have the company reset the codes."

"Good idea."

"Why won't the police give us more information? They're no help at all."

"They don't have to help. They have their killer behind bars."

More bitterness. I hated the police department's myopia and narrow-mindedness as much as Whip hated putting his family through this mess.

"Johnny's checking on her jewelry?"

"He's looking at pawn shops in a twenty-mile radius around Richmond." I winked. "He didn't want me going into such notorious establishments."

"Hell, like you're afraid of anything. You little witch. Let him feel big and brave and strong, didja? He-man protecting the shrinking violet from seedy places?"

Whip laughed for the first time in days. A belly laugh that brought tears to his eyes. He couldn't stop, especially when I did my best Scarlett O'Hara-eyelashes bat.

"Why, Rhett, how can you even think such a thing about little ol' me?" I waved an imaginary fan to cool my flushed face.

When Whip had caught his breath, he told me he just realized the importance of two truisms: The truth will set you free, and laughter really is the best medicine.

"Corny and unoriginal, but I don't give a damn. Feel more like myself for the first time since Merry's murder."

"Murder sure has a way of sapping energy." I turned serious again. "Put those gray cells to work. I can't do this alone."

"You guys are doing fine."

Rare praise, huh? Time for a come-to-Jesus moment.

"I'm making this up as I go along."

"No guidebooks on how to solve a murder, huh?"

"None that work. I've never felt so helpless, so out of control."

"Know what you mean."

"Not only don't I have all the answers. I don't have all the questions. I don't know what I don't know. I need you to add to the list, give us suggestions. Help in any way you can. It's your freedom."

I left a copy of the list with Whip. My time was up, and Pete would soon shut us down.

"I have to run. I'm meeting Johnny for lunch. He has a lead on my mother's watch, the one I gave Merry. I may get to visit a pawn shop this afternoon."

I winked as Pete opened the door and blew Whip a kiss as I left.

CHAPTER FORTY-SEVEN

"Hello, pretty lady," Johnny rose and kissed me on the cheek. I was late getting to Applebee's.

"Sorry, traffic was wicked. I forgot they're setting up the Celtic Festival at the high school."

"No problem. I just got here too. What have you been up to?"

I told Johnny I'd just come from the jail.

"How's Whip holding up?"

"He's okay, but I told him he had to help. He can't sit around on his butt all day getting fat on all that gourmet jailhouse food."

Johnny laughed. We ordered and sipped iced tea while we waited for our salad and burger. Me, the spinach salad, of course; Johnny, the burger. That man could eat more food than even Alex. He never gained an ounce. His doctor was satisfied with his overall health. I waited for him to tell me what he'd found. It took no more than two bites of burger and a few fries.

"I'm pretty sure I found your watch. I must've walked into every pawn shop in Richmond. It was closer to Chaminade than I thought it'd be."

"I brought a picture of Hunter."

"How'd you get that?"

"Alex found a news clip. It's grainy, but he's recognizable."

"Terrific."

"Let's see what the owner says when we tell him the watch was stolen."

"It doesn't matter. If it's yours, we call the police. Let the insurance company settle it."

"Right."

We drove through Richmond as quickly as traffic allowed after lunch. I was impatient and nervous. What if it wasn't Merry's watch? What if it was? Either way, I'd learn something; I just didn't know what.

"I was here two days ago about a watch. I don't see it." Johnny frowned.

"I put it in the safe. The guy who pawned it said he'd be back. I ain't seen him."

I breathed as silent a sigh of relief as was humanly possible. I was keyed up to the point where I'd burst if I didn't see the watch right this second.

The pawnbroker returned from the back room, my grandmother's watch draped over his left fingers. Before I took it, I wanted the shop owner to look at the back.

"Do you have a jeweler's loop?"

"'Course." He opened a drawer and pulled out a small loop and clipped it over the right lens of his small gold-rimmed glasses. "What am I looking for?"

"On the back should be an inscription: 'For Josie at sixteen.' There was a date, but it's almost worn off."

"Got it."

"Josie was my grandmother."

"So this is yours?" The pawnbroker dangled the watch over three long fingers.

"I gave it to my daughter on her sixteenth birthday, as my mother had to me. She had it with her when she was murdered."

"Oh my God. Not the woman who got shot? I didn't have nothin' to do with that."

"We know you didn't. We just want to find the son of a bitch who killed her daughter." Johnny's face showed less expression than a Mayan sculpture. "We'll need you to talk to the police. Okay if I give 'em a call?"

The pawnbroker handed over his cordless phone. "Number five on speed dial."

"Thanks."

I wandered around the pawn shop. I'd never been in one before and wasn't sure what to expect—probably something dark, slightly dank, and seedy. I didn't expect something crowded with goods but bright, sunny, and scrubbed clean. Every countertop was polished.

"Easier to isolate fingerprints if I get robbed." The owner tracked my every movement. I looked over my shoulder at the owner. I couldn't imagine anyone messing with anyone who looked like a weightlifter. Would have to be a nut case.

I thought about the watch's recent history. Next in line was Emilie, but her mother wouldn't be the one to give it to her. I'd have to. That wasn't supposed to be my job. Damn Hunter! He took so much from my family.

"Real sorry about your daughter, ma'am. Don't deal in stolen goods. If I'd known this was hot, I'd have kicked the guy's ass—sorry, butt—out the door."

I believed him. I reached into my bag and pulled out Hunter's picture.

"Is this the man who pawned it?"

The pawnbroker ran his hand across his shaved scalp and barely glanced at the print. "Nah."

"Will you take another look?" Johnny asked.

"Don't have to. Guy was black. Darker than me."

"Crap." Johnny swore as he hung up the phone.

"Yeah, didn't fit my normal clientele. Why I remembered him. Stood out, know what I mean?"

"No, I don't." Johnny picked up Hunter's photo.

"Well dressed. Slacks, polished shoes, dress shirt. Most of my guys wear oversized jeans, sneakers, and stadium coats. Guy didn't fit. Coulda been one of the doctors at Chaminade. Get 'em in here all the time. 'Specially just before payday."

This well-dressed black man's identity was another question for the fridge list.

"Seen this guy, though." The pawnbroker tapped his finger on the print. "Came in a few weeks back looking for a gun."

"A gun?" Johnny stopped lounging against the counter, ears pricked up, every sense on red alert.

"Yeah. Filled out the paperwork but never came back after the waiting period. Musta got someone else to sell him a piece."

"Was it a twenty-two?"

"Nah. Wanted a Walther. Wondered if he had some kind of James Bond fantasy going." He nodded at the locked gun safe. "Didn't have one, so he filled out paperwork for that Glock."

"You still have the application?" Johnny asked.

"Sure. Seemed strange, though. Wasn't a Glock kinda guy."

"There's a Glock type?" Could the pawnbroker take a look at someone and tell what kind of gun he or she was likely to own?

"Sure. Target shooters mostly. Gang members, but they don't buy. They steal."

"Uh-huh."

"Cops too. Fairly standard piece, only cops don't buy from a pawn shop. Get 'em issued."

While the pawnbroker shuffled through his file, I asked, "What kind of gun would I want?"

He didn't raise his head. "A twenty-two or thirty-eight."

"Why?"

"Hand's too small for most three-fifty-sevens or nine-millimeters. You'd use either a twenty-two or a thirty-eight. Maybe a thirty-two. Probably a revolver. Nothing big or heavy. Here it is."

My hand shook as I took the crumpled form. I looked first at the name to see if Hunter had used his own name or an alias. Randall A. Hunter. Yes, a known alter ego.

I was surprised he used his "real" name, until I saw the driver's license information. Of course, he'd have to produce identification. No occupation was given. We already knew his home address and now we added a date of birth and Social Security number. I wrote the new information in my notebook.

Wonder if either's real. Alex'll find out.

"Was this approved?" Johnny peered over my shoulder.

"Sure. No problem. Just the guy never came back."

Guess the date of birth and Social Security number are real.

"Look at the date." I pointed to it and showed Johnny.

"Three weeks before Merry's murder," Johnny said. "Looks like he was getting ready."

"Looks like he was getting ready for something." I was troubled about Hunter wanting another gun.

"Yes, but why use a twenty-two then?"

"If you ask me, a twenty-two'd make more sense. Like I said, not a Glock guy. Hands are too delicate. If he don't know how to use the thing, he'd shoot out the damned ceiling."

Johnny and I had learned all we could from the pawnbroker when I thought of two more questions.

"The guy who brought in the watch. Other than being black and well dressed, do you remember anything else about him?"

"Six feet, skinny, short hair slicked back, glasses, foreign accent. Didn't recognize it. Oh yeah, he had a triangular scar on his left cheek. That help?"

"It does. Any chance you still have the tapes from the two visits?" Johnny nodded up at the security camera.

"Nah. System wipes the disk at the end of the week."

"One more question, if you don't mind. Mr. ..."

"Smith. John Smith." The pawnbroker pointed to his business permit. "Mother didn't have much imagination."

The police arrived. I filed a report and watched them seal the watch in an envelope. The senior officer gave me instructions on how to reclaim my property.

"Mr. Smith, if I wanted to sell a large diamond ring and some diamond earrings, where would I go?"

"Broad Street or West Cary. Lots of jewelry and antique shops over there buy estate jewelry."

"Mr. Smith, I can't tell you how helpful you've been. Thank you." I reached out the hand too small for a three-fifty-seven.

"Hope you find the guy who killed your daughter, ma'am. No one should have to go through that." The pawnbroker gripped my hand.

I left the shop with Johnny, gratified by kindness from a stranger. Mr. Smith didn't have to help or offer me sympathy. I swallowed a lump in my throat.

"Pretty lady, I gotta get back to work. Drop you at your car?"

"Fine. I want to change and do some shopping."

"You look great to me." Johnny draped his arm across my shoulders.

"Yes, but I'm shopping for some expensive jewelry. I want to look the part."

"You always look like a million bucks."

I couldn't believe Johnny said that. I glanced over to see if he was joking. He never looked more serious. "You're too sweet. At least we have one answer for the fridge list."

"Plus several more questions. Would you like to go to dinner and catch a movie Saturday?"

"I'd love it. I'll need a break from playing sleuth by then." If the circumstances had been different, I could get used to being an amateur detective. I was almost having fun.

"Just what kind of sleuthing do you have in mind?"

"First, see if Hunter sold the rest of the jewelry. Then figure out how to find the black doctor. I bet he works at the hospital."

"I don't like this. He could be Hunter's partner." Johnny paused to look at me.

I shook my head. "Hunter's a loner."

"And if you find this doctor?"

"I'll try and get the hours he works. Then you can talk to him."

"Oh, I get it. You do the easy work. Then, send in the muscle to rough him up." Johnny grinned and flexed his free bicep.

"Not at all. He might be more willing to talk to you than me. You can be most persuasive." That earned a squeeze of my shoulder.

"Find him first, and we'll flip to see who interrogates him. How're you going to get the hospital to give out personal information?"

"I can't decide between ditzy blonde or dotty old lady. Depends on my mood when I call."

Johnny's laugh boomed across the busy intersection. It startled a family in front of us. A little girl glanced over her shoulder. I smiled, waggled my fingers, and watched her duck behind her daddy's leg.

CHAPTER FORTY-EIGHT

My feet hurt all the way to my butt!

I'd hiked up and down Broad Street, in and out of antique and jewelry shops all afternoon. In high heels, no less. Of all the stupid pet tricks.

I was in my best Lauren Bacall form. She was my image of what a lady of means should look like—tall, slender, elegantly dressed. I couldn't do tall at just under five foot four, but nothing else was wrong with my Bacall impersonation. Hiding behind her was a harmless enough affectation. Besides, I loved her style. I just couldn't complete the image. I was allergic to cigarette smoke.

Since I was asking about multi-carat diamond rings and earrings, I wanted to look like I could write a check for thirty thousand dollars without blinking. In reality, I was a woman of means in any attire. I could write a check for more than thirty thousand any day of the week.

I didn't look like anyone else in the upscale shops, however. None "looked the part," yet many tried on rings and necklaces pricey enough to keep a junkie in crack for a year.

In Barney's, a permanent fixture on Cary Street for over a century and the finest jeweler in the city, I waited for the senior clerk. I looked around the shop at the lighted counters glittering with precious stones, gold, and silver. The rosewood and glass displays were far removed from John Smith's pawn shop but were every bit as polished.

I was perturbed when the clerk I wanted to speak with pulled necklace after necklace out of a case for a jeans-wearing, booted and belted urban cowboy leaning on the glass counter. I struggled to keep a straight face when he decided on a two thousand dollar diamond and pearl drop and pulled out a wad of cash. He took his gift away in a pretty brown box tied with a yellow ribbon, as much of a local trademark as Tiffany's pale blue box and white ribbon were in New York.

So much for "looking the part." I could have dispensed with my men's cut silk trousers, my fedora, my cashmere sweater, and my three-inch pumps and not had sore feet, but I wouldn't have felt right. Lesson learned.

The senior clerk smiled her welcome and moved to the counter where I stood.

"I understand you've been waiting for me. How may I help you?"

"Well, you can start by reminding me not to judge people by looks alone."

The clerk chuckled. "We get all kinds. Until Tex pulled out his money, I had no idea he could afford anything. He fooled me too."

"At least it wasn't a waste of your time."

"Now, let's not waste any more of yours. You're looking for something special?"

"I'm Mrs. Davies." I held out my hand.

"I'm Mrs. Evans."

For some reason, I felt it proper to introduce myself, even though I held no fantasy anyone would connect me with my departed husband. Mrs. Evans shook my hand. Without further preamble, I pulled a glossy color photo from my tote and laid it on the counter. "I'm looking for this ring."

"Yes, Mrs. Davies, it's one of ours."

"One of yours? You mean you have it here?" I felt my heart give a little hip hop. Would I soon hold the ring Whip gave Merry for their tenth anniversary?

"I mean, it's our design. We made six before we retired it." Mrs. Evans waved her hand toward a display of rings. "We sell only our own designs in this case. The other cases hold commercially manufactured, albeit high-end, pieces."

"Why would you stop making such a stunning ring?"

"At the time, we were in a dreadful recession and the demand for stones as large and perfect as this was not high on most people's priority lists."

"I see."

"Our master designer wouldn't modify the setting for a smaller stone, so we retired it."

"Have you seen one like this recently?"

"It's funny you should ask. Mr. Barney said a gentleman tried to sell one to us a few weeks ago."

My heart was on a racetrack. My pulse pounded in my throat.

"But Mr. Barney didn't buy the ring?"

"No. He keeps records of who buys the originals. The man presenting it for sale wasn't one of them."

"Do you know if he called the police?"

"You'd have to ask him. Generally, he reports such incidents."

"If you wouldn't buy the ring, where might the man go?"

"I'd try Heirlooms over on Broad. George buys jewelry and doesn't ask as many questions as we do."

I nodded and put the photo back in my purse.

"One more question. Were you here when the gentleman came in with the ring?"

"No. I'd just returned from lunch and wasn't behind the counter."

My face registered my disappointment. *Crap!*

"I did get a good look at him, though. Will that help?"

I held up the grainy photo of Hunter.

"No, the gentleman was black."

"Thank you. Thank you very much." I took Mrs. Evans's hand in both of mine.

I left and walked four blocks to Heirlooms. The shop wasn't as upscale as Barney's, but its display cabinets contained many expensive pieces. I went to the back of the empty shop where a white-haired jeweler kept watch from a high stool. It didn't take long to spot the ring and earrings, since both were in a locked wall case behind the counter. I could see them from where I stood.

Being tired, footsore, and cranky, I dispensed with all but the basic formalities. I laid my photos on the counter and told the jeweler I reported the items stolen to both the police and my insurance company. I implied with no guilty conscience they were stolen as part of a brutal crime.

The last point got the jeweler's attention. He stammered and bumbled and dithered, before admitting he didn't ask for proof of ownership. He bought them for thirty-five percent of their value.

"Let me guess. The seller was a well-dressed black man with excellent manners and a triangular scar on his cheek." I was confident, if not cocky.

"No. He was white."

"Is this him?" I held up the same photo I'd shown at every other shop.

Squinting at the grainy photo, the jeweler turned it toward the sunlight streaming through the front window. "Could be. He spun a tale about his wife having cancer and needing the money for her treatment. I didn't believe it for a second."

"Why?"

"Ma'am, I've heard every tale of woe in my forty years in business. I don't care why someone wants to sell jewelry, but I've developed strong radar for lies. Like Pinocchio, he could have grown a very long nose."

This fit what we were putting together about Hunter's lying psychopathy. I wanted to kill him, but that would lower me to his level. I'd be happy to trap him and let justice prevail.

I lay in my chaise. Fading daylight danced across the pool. A light breeze rippled the surface and lifted the barest hint of chlorine into the air. I reached for my glass of Pinot Grigio.

I was alone. Alex was at a pizza and computer game party at a neighbor's house with five other boys. He wouldn't be back until ten-ish. Emilie went to a movie with friends; she, too, was due back around ten. Curfew time. Whip was still in jail. Merry was still dead.

I was too tired to think about the black doctor. I needed to find him, but he could wait. My brain was as dull as the pain in my feet was sharp. We'd made significant progress, though. I wanted to write up my notes and give them to Vince for his records. I didn't care if the attorney pooh-poohed our amateur efforts; he was going to get everything we learned as fast as we learned it.

I stared at the pool as it darkened with evening. What was I doing back in Riverbend? I left the South two husbands ago for a life of glamour and excitement. When Merry was hurt, I came back to take care of her until she was on her feet. Months later I was still here, raising two children and trying to get my son-in-law out of jail.

I'd practically lived in Europe with my second husband, Frank, in and out of museums, historical sites, and antique shops. Reggie, my last husband, was unconventional. We went on safari in Tanzania, watched sunsets over Cape Elizabeth, relaxed on our sailboat off Key West, snorkeled on the Great Barrier Reef, and sipped Singapore Slings on the veranda of the Raffles Hotel. We indulged in global adventures all the time.

Now I was once more in the South, too far from an ocean or a mountain or a savannah for comfort. A soccer mom. Or, rather, soccer grandmom. Too far in spirit from adventure.

If the district attorney convicted Whip, I'd be raising kids for another decade alone. Even when we got Whip out of jail, free of all charges, I'd more than likely still be raising kids. I could no more abandon them than I could fly. Nope, I was in for the count.

CHAPTER FORTY-NINE

"Can't tell you how fuckin' bored I am. Every day's the same—dull, mind-numbing, no stimulation. Feeling more and more helpless. More and more like a caged animal. Less and less hopeful. Plus I'm pissed. So little I can do to help myself."

This was the longest speech Whip had made in weeks, a sure sign of his state of mind. He rattled on about the dirty walls, the tasteless food, and the lack of good conversation. Except for what he had with Vince and me, he had no one else to talk to. On the positive side, his body was rock hard. He couldn't do much in a standard-sized cell, but hundreds of push-ups, crunches, and other exercises kept him toned.

"I'd give my left nut to get out of here. Back out in the open."

I couldn't imagine what it was like for a man who came alive in the dust from a construction site, who hoisted heavy rolls of cables onto trucks and slept in a trailer or tent on a job site, to be locked in a claustrophobic cell.

"I'm so homesick to get outside. Get some fresh air. I can almost smell the dust and hot diesel fumes of earthmoving equipment."

"Are you as homesick to get home? To be with your children?"

"What do you think?"

"I don't know."

The job came first; the family second. Months ago, I accepted Whip's priorities. It was a mountain I wasn't willing to die on, as the Marines said. Whip was what he was. Only he could change himself.

I couldn't.

As had become a habit, I waited in the interview room with Whip for Vince who was two hours overdue. Whip had run out of things to complain about and lapsed into despair-tinged silence. When the door opened, I thought we'd both pounce on Vince. Or rip into him for causing even more anxiety.

"Sorry. I got tied up in court. The judge read us the riot act. He loves to hear himself talk and talk and talk. I felt sorry for the court clerk. Her fingers were down to bare bone after the tirade."

"Glad he's not my judge. If he doesn't like you, the mud might splatter on me."

"He's fine." Vince waved aside Whip's concern. "He doesn't carry a grudge from case to case. He takes each on its merits and is fair. We'd do well to draw him."

"You mean I won't have the same judge as before?"

"Maybe. Maybe not. It depends on docket congestion and who's next when we get a trial date. We may have an evidentiary hearing with the first judge, but she may not be the trial judge."

"I didn't like her. She thinks I'm guilty as sin."

"That's not true. She heard the district attorney say he had enough evidence to bind you over for trial. That's all she needed."

"Did you file another bond petition?" Whip would lose his mind if he didn't feel sunshine on his face soon.

"Yes, but don't get your hopes up. With nothing new, no judge will grant bail."

"Christ!" Whip sighed. "So, what's up today?"

"A shred more evidence from the district attorney. They're very slow to show their hand. Eventually, we'll get everything."

"How long is 'eventually'?" I, too, was angst-filled because of the endless stalling by the district attorney.

"Very soon."

"Is that why you want to push for the, um, evidentiary hearing?" This bad case of political gamesmanship took away Whip's freedom. "I wouldn't need a hearing if you could prove Hunter killed Merry."

Vince frowned and reached into his briefcase for his stack of colored folders. *Gun Permits, Autopsy Report, Restraining Orders*, and *Glove* were written on various tabs.

Vince opened the autopsy report folder first. "Did you know your wife drank heavily? She had a high level of alcohol in her system, well above the legal limit."

"Doesn't surprise me. Hit the bottle hard before she left. Drunk most of the time until she met Hunter."

"What about drug use?"

"Lots of painkillers and antidepressants after the accident. Why?"

"She tested positive for cocaine and other opiates. Heroin too."

"Opiates I can understand. Took Oxycontin for months after the accident. But cocaine or heroin? Must have been recreational."

"She had four times the normal Oxycontin dosage in her system."

"Cumulative?"

"I don't think so. It could be she took too much or someone gave her too much either the night she died or over a longer period of time." Vince glanced at the autopsy report again.

That shook me. Was Hunter drugging Merry without her knowledge? I had one more reason to get even. Whip already wanted Hunter's reputation; I wanted his soul. I was glad Whip kept silent. Making a threat probably wasn't a good idea when he was sitting in jail. I didn't think prim-and-proper Vince would approve.

"There was a fresh bruise on the left side of her neck just under the chin, but no defensive wounds on her hands. She could have been partly or mostly incapacitated when she was shot."

"If she knew her killer, why would you expect defensive wounds?" I had difficulty following Vince's line of thinking.

"Knowing your killer doesn't prevent you from defending yourself. Merry should have had some marks, at least a broken fingernail or skin under her nails. There's nothing else in the autopsy and toxicology report."

"Except Hunter shot her behind her right ear."

"We don't know that, Whip." Vince seemed weary of this discussion.

"You said there was a bruise on the left side of Merry's neck."

I had been thinking about the autopsy while Whip and Vince argued. Emilie, too, felt something hard under her mother's chin.

Vince flipped to the second page of the autopsy report. "Yes. A fairly large one."

"Not post mortem?"

"No. Is this important?"

"Hunter had a cast on his left wrist the last time I saw him." I was relieved Vince stared at the report when he made a note on his legal pad. I physically crossed my fingers in my lap.

"That's interesting. I'll check it out." Vince folded his hands on the table. "Now, what can you tell me about the threats against your wife?"

"What threats?" Although Whip promised Hunter he'd be on his ass every step of the way if he got anywhere near his family, he'd never threatened Merry.

"According to this deposition, Darlene Livingston told the district attorney Merry said you threatened to hurt her because of her affair."

"That's crap! I was furious with Merry's actions, but I just wanted her to get the hell out of my life."

"We'll have the deposition thrown out, of course. It's hearsay and can't be corroborated."

"Why would Darla testify against Whip? She and Merry had a major league fight over Merry's affair. As far as I know, they never spoke again." Darla became a crusader for marital rights after her husband's infidelity. She wouldn't tolerate any of her friends screwing around on a spouse.

With nothing else new, Vince straightened his files and put them back in his briefcase.

"Hold it, Vince." Whip grabbed the folder marked "restraining order" and flipped it open. It was empty. "Why's the TRO still here?"

"The assistant district attorney said it has bearing on your trial."

"I don't get it. Were there two restraining orders? One I don't know about. How would the one I took out help their case?"

"Restraining orders carry a lot of weight with most judges."

How does Whip's taking out a restraining order on Merry help the prosecution? She attacked him. He has the scars to prove it. I was getting dull-witted with all the time I spent in this place of last resort. Someone was confused. It wasn't me.

"Yes, but the only TRO I know about is one I took out on Merry to keep her away from me and the kids. I told you about it earlier."

"Don't you have a copy?"

"No. I was waiting to get it from the district attorney."

"I'll bring it tomorrow," I said.

"It's beginning to look like Mr. District Attorney Weed is putting together another sloppy case."

Vince stood and signaled the guard. Pete escorted Whip back to his cell.

CHAPTER FIFTY

Every time I met with Vince or Whip, I left more despondent. Evidence trickled in from the district attorney's office in dribs and drabs, but nothing pointed to having enough grounds to petition for a dismissal. We finally got one pressing question answered: The cops didn't dust Merry's apartment for prints because the killer dropped a glove with a little GSR on it. With no DNA and no fingerprints on it, the police couldn't connect it to Whip through physical evidence. The assistant district attorney seemed convinced he wore two pairs, one inside the other. The only prints on the right glove belonged to Merry.

The police figured Whip used his left hand to hold her and his right hand to shoot her. Easy figure, even for Riverbend's crack police force. Like the vast majority of people in the world, Whip was right-handed. It was a safe guess. Since he was right-handed, the GSR would be on a right-handed glove.

The gun was a problem, though. The district attorney was obsessed with the "missing" Glock. Forget the fact it was legally in Peru. Forget the fact Merry was killed with a twenty-two. They harped on the fact Whip once owned a twenty-two. The Glock remained "missing," regardless of the fact a faxed affidavit from Charlie proved the Glock was legally in Peru. I didn't get it. Neither did Whip.

"Remember, Whip," Vince said for the millionth time, "the

district attorney will blow a lot of smoke to keep the jury wondering if you could have murdered Merry, especially when the evidence is entirely circumstantial."

We already knew the district attorney planned to enter Whip's original divorce filing as well as the one counter-filed by Merry. "With Merry asking for ten thousand dollars a month in alimony, you'd have grounds to get rid of her."

Whip rubbed tired eyes. We'd been over this before. Way too many times.

"I told you Merry said she was leaving with Hunter. My divorce attorney said I wouldn't have to pay alimony, no matter what she originally asked for. I just wanted custody of the kids."

I couldn't for the life of me figure out why the divorce papers had any bearing on Merry's murder.

"Don't be naïve."

"I'm not being naïve. Mom and Pop raised me to tell the truth, no matter what. That's what I'm doing." Whip pounded his fist on the table and took his frustration out on Vince. "What happened to reasonable doubt? What happened to 'If it doesn't fit, you must acquit?' What happened to innocent until proven guilty?"

"The district attorney will use innuendo and insinuation to plant half-baked ideas in the minds of the jurors. I have to refute them. My job is to provide the best defense possible and represent you fairly and justly."

"It's just not fair."

"The law isn't fair, just impartial."

"What about the jewelry?"

"What about it?"

"Johnny and I found it. Hunter sold the ring and earrings a couple of days after the murder."

"So? It doesn't prove anything. He could always say she gave him the jewelry because she needed money. You cut her off, remember. He'd probably claim he hadn't seen her for over a week before her death. He worked long hours at the hospital, no time off. I can't take the risk, remember?"

No matter what we said, Vince wouldn't depose Hunter, because it could become the smoking gun to convict Whip.

"Do you really want to risk his testimony? Especially if he's the serial liar you claim him to be."

While I wanted Hunter on the stand with Vince grilling him, I couldn't take the risk. "No."

"No," Whip said.

Whip was in another piss-poor mood when I dropped by a day later with an updated fridge list tracking our progress. Whip's enthusiasm was so obviously faked I called him on it.

"You're a dreadful liar, Whip Pugh."

"You guys have done a lot. Sorry. In a shit-eating mood. Can't fully appreciate it today."

I left minutes after I arrived, hurt and frustrated. Whip needed to snap out of his funk. I didn't need him dumping his freedom on me the same way he dumped Merry and the kids shortly after Merry's accident. He needed to get in the game. Now. Maybe he needed a pity party. It should bore the crap out of him and put him in a better mood.

What if we lose? Whip could go to jail for a very long time. Who would raise Emilie and Alex? Not Bette and the Colonel. They'd raised their own family, as had I, but the Colonel's health still wasn't good in spite of his triple bypass. I'd have to continue to step up. Months ago, I accepted the fact my role was permanent—at least as far as I could see into the future, no matter what happened to Whip at trial.

The likely next step for us was a short but intense trial. "Don't expect court high jinks like at O.J.'s trial, on *Law and Order* or on *Perry Mason*," Vince warned at an early meeting. "Most murder trials are dull and mundane, full of sordid details. DAs provide just enough evidence for the jury to come to a decision."

Until we went to trial, Emilie, Alex, and I continued working on the fridge list, regardless of whether Whip thought we were doing anything to help or not. We were; he was just too discouraged to see it.

CHAPTER FIFTY-ONE

"How's Dad?" Emilie popped into the kitchen where I was marinating a London broil.

"He's been better." I turned the steak, recovered the bowl, and put it back in the refrigerator. I stared at the list. "He was pretty depressed today. He tried to hide it but couldn't."

"Wouldn't you be depressed if all you could do was sit and worry?"

"You're right. I would." I stretched my shoulders to relax the tension. "We're both pretty down."

"Dad hasn't asked all the questions, has he?" Emilie twisted a lock of pink and orange hair.

I blinked. Emilie was right. Parents and grandparents don't know everything. Shoot. I wasn't sure I didn't know what I didn't know.

"Did you tell him how much we've done?"

"I did. He's so proud of you. He'd rather you guys just be kids." Time to lighten the mood. "How long's it been since you took a swim?"

"It's getting too cold to swim."

"Not true. The pool's heated. It's really warm today. So, again, how long since you were in the pool?"

"I don't know. Not this week."

"Okay, last one in does the dishes for a whole week."

I tossed the kitchen towel on the counter and sprinted for the stairs. Emilie shrieked for Alex to get his suit on and get into the pool. I heard Alex's shouted reply, as I shut my door.

I'd never changed so fast in my entire life. I raced down the stairs, took an extra second to kick off my flip-flops and dove into the water just as Emilie barreled through the family room door. Alex followed on her heels and gave his famous Tarzan yell before cannonballing into the cool water.

"No fair, you had a head start." My granddaughter came to a dead stop at the edge of the pool.

"Today's lesson one more time: Life's not fair. You're younger than I am. You should have beaten me." I knifed my hand against the surface and sent a plume of water outward to soak her from the waist down.

"Water fight!" Alex whooped and splashed his sister as she dove into the deep end. When she surfaced, both Alex and I pounced on her. I tickled her while Alex pushed her under.

We laughed and splashed and shouted. I let Alex and Emilie win the water fight. After all, I won the dishes challenge fair and square. When we all clung to the side of the pool, weak with laughter, Emilie admitted choosing a suit slowed her down. I didn't have that problem. One suit here. One choice.

"Hey, is this a private party?" Darla and her daughter, Molly, stood at the side gate. I waved them in. Emilie sloshed over to her best friend and gave her a sopping hug. The girls ran inside to find a suit for Molly. I toweled off, pulled a wrap around my shoulders, and dropped into a chaise, Darla next to me.

"I wanted to stop by. Molly insisted she had to see Em. I should have called."

"Since when have you had to call first?" She was uncomfortable. I knew why.

"You know the assistant district attorney deposed me?"

"Yes. We both know Merry lied about threats from Whip."

"That's what I told her, but the little witch was so nasty. I can't imagine what she has in mind, but she hates Whip."

"Vince says she has all the charm of a rattlesnake that needs a root canal."

Darla laughed the rollicking laugh I missed. She'd been one of Merry's best friends once. She was still one of mine.

"You did the right thing. When they ask, you have to answer the questions truthfully. We all do."

"I knew you'd understand. How's Whip doing?"

"Some days are better than others. Today was an 'other.' Tomorrow will be a 'better.'"

Darla lay back, her face turned toward the autumn sun. She closed her eyes, relief relaxing the strain lines. "In spite of the fact I disapproved of Merry and Hunter, I miss her like hell."

"So do I. Every day." We reached out and held each other's hands.

Molly and Emilie chattered their way into the water and began swimming laps. Both girls displayed the wonderful firm tone of youth. My granddaughter swam back and forth without effort. She made flip turns at each end of the pool.

Emilie and Alex were fish who grew up in pools and began swimming as babies. Not as fluid, Molly soon tired and climbed onto a float. Alex would dump her in the water before long.

I invited Molly and Darla for dinner. Johnny was coming over too. It was time to expand the get-Whip-out-of-jail army. Over lemonade, vodka tonics, and lots of food, Johnny and I brought Darla and Molly up to speed. I had some news: I'd discovered the identity of the black doctor.

"Which role worked?" Johnny cut into his steak. Alex matched him bite for bite. My two men certainly could pack away the food.

"Dotty old lady."

"You, a dotty old lady?" Emilie and Molly burst into giggles.

"Well, I played the role perfectly." I huffed. "'This nice young doctor took such good care of me, but I can't remember his name. He was young and had this most wonderful accent. He wasn't on duty when I was released. Can you help me find him? I want to thank him personally.'"

I raised the tenor of my voice, quavered a bit to make it sound old, stumbled over my words, and sent everyone at the table into hysterics.

"His name's Francis Patterson, a resident in internal medicine."

"Going to send in the muscle?" Johnny wiped his fingers on a napkin and flexed his biceps against his black T-shirt.

"I'm rethinking 'muscle.' I want Dr. Patterson to know what a snake he helped. I want him to know he hocked stolen property for a murderer."

"Do we know Hunter stole the watch?" Johnny mopped the last of his marinade with a roll and popped it into his mouth.

"No, but Patterson doesn't know we don't. If he thinks he's in trouble, he might talk. He could be a dead end, but at least we'll put the fear of God into him."

"Let me talk to him." Darla cut in. "I need to help."

"Good idea."

I didn't want to go to the hospital. If I ran into Hunter, I'd rip him apart.

"Our turn. Let us tell you what we've learned," Emilie started.

Alex talked around a mouthful of baked potato. "Hey, some of what we know I found out."

"Alex, don't talk with your mouth full."

My reaction was so programmed I was unaware I'd spoken until he mumbled, "Yes, Mad Max."

"Me first." Alex wiped his mouth on his napkin.

There was hope.

"Dracula's résumé claims he graduated from at least three different med schools. I e-mailed them to see if he's telling the truth. I haven't heard back yet, but it's only been a week."

"Good job." I was impressed with his ingenuity.

"While Alex searched for Dracula, I found several Web sites devoted to missing people. There are lots of group sites to help families of murder victims. I think it's a way to find Kiki." Emilie looked proud of herself—rightfully.

"Who's Kiki?" Darla asked.

"We don't know, but I asked anyone who knew someone named Kiki to contact me," Emilie continued.

"Any luck?" Molly joined in.

"Well, it's been a few days since I posted my question, but so far I've had a couple of dozen e-mails. One man knew a Kiki, but he had nothing to do with Dracula."

"He?"

"Yes. A guy from college trying to find a friend he's lost touch with. We're sure Kiki's a she. Several people lost dogs named Kiki and hoped I'd found them. Then I got an e-mail today with some promise. At least, it's from a city near where Dracula practiced medicine."

"How do you know?" Johnny asked.

"The writer said she lives in New York."

"And his résumé," Alex spoke up, "says he worked at Mount Sinai in New York, at New Jewish in Pittsburgh, and the Cleveland Clinic before Chaminade. I sent e-mails to confirm this too."

"Do I want to know how you got his résumé?" I asked.

"Um, probably not." Alex grinned.

I dropped the subject.

Johnny stared out the window into the darkening night.

The hairs on the back of my neck rose.

Alex went on. "Anyway, I started snooping around in police records, 'cause so much stuff's online today. I looked for any missing person named Kiki." He made a face. "I struck out. Nothing."

"Was Dracula married? Before he came here?" Molly asked.

"I dunno." Alex looked chagrined he'd missed an angle. "I'll check."

"What about your e-mail lead, Em?" I hoped Emilie wasn't trying to catch fog in a butterfly net.

"I just got it. I sent a note back immediately and asked if she had a photo. Maybe she could e-mail it."

"You're sure it's a woman? I read so much about predators on the Web." Darla sounded doubtful.

"Don't worry, Mrs. Livingston. I'm not using my own YouTube or MySpace accounts. I set up a new e-mail address. I also found this site for mothers who've lost children through tragedy and asked about Kiki, even though I'm not a mother. I lost my mother, so I figure it's all right."

"It is," Darla said.

"It's so sad reading about their losses," Emilie said, "but Kiki's the key to this whole mess, so I have to try everything."

"I agree." Johnny looked serious and intense.

"It's like she's going to help. I totally feel it." Emilie believed this message was different.

"Let me know what else we can do." Darla rose from the table and carried dishes into the kitchen. Molly followed.

"Don't bother. Em has graciously volunteered to do the dishes for a week." I winked.

"I didn't exactly 'volunteer.' I lost a race." Emilie stuck out her tongue but got up to clear the table.

"We'll help." Darla and Molly carried the remaining bowls and plates into the kitchen, where Emilie rinsed and stacked them in the dishwasher.

After Darla and Molly left, and the kids retreated to their rooms to check e-mail, Johnny stared through me with the strangest expression on his face.

"She's close." Johnny paused. "I've been thinking about this a lot. I have a gut feeling there's more than one Kiki."

"You too, huh."

"Yes. You called Hunter a predator." Johnny spaced his words. "I think he seeks vulnerable women and remakes them into Kiki. Then he gets rid of them when he realizes they aren't the original."

"How'd you come to this conclusion?"

"After Alex found Hunter's multiple aliases, I started searching. Now we know where he worked, it's worth seeing if there were murders of young women near those hospitals."

That would mean Hunter killed before. That thought was chilling but couldn't be willed away.

"We need to cast a wider net. Look at cities between here and New York. You and Alex need to find other unsolved disappearances along the route to Riverbend." I rattled ice cubes in my empty glass.

"Getting the goods on Hunter is like nailing Jell-O to a tree. He's so damned slippery."

"All the more reason to stop him before he leaves town. Or picks his next target."

"He may already have selected his next target. We have to stop him before he can act."

Fear made the hair on the back of my neck stand up and dance the cha-cha. I wasn't as sensitive as Emilie, but Johnny was right. Hunter had killed before and would again if we didn't stop him.

CHAPTER FIFTY-TWO

I woke up full of piss and vinegar, ready to get back to the fight. Darla was going to Chaminade to talk with the black doctor that afternoon. I had a list of loose ends to run down. Before I got started, though, I got a call from the jail. Whip wanted to see me as soon as possible.

As soon as I walked into the conference room, it was evident this was a better day. Whip skipped the hello part of our meeting before plunging into a profuse apology for his behavior the previous afternoon. He'd bottomed out. Overnight he shook off the blues and was once again thinking straight. He started firing off questions for Johnny, determined to help nail Hunter.

"We might lose track of Hunter." Even with Emilie feeling what Hunter was doing, I worried he'd leave town.

"You mean, he could disappear?"

"Yes. Alex monitors his cell and e-mail. Hunter doesn't seem to be doing anything interesting." I leaned against the table.

"I asked Jerry early on if the police ever looked at him. Talked with the cops from my case. They're off working on new stuff. No interest in Hunter." Whip rubbed his chin. "If he moves on, we might never catch him. We can't let that happen."

"I called Tony Ferraiolli. His guy's coming back to keep Hunter under surveillance."

Whip agreed. Not that it mattered what he thought.

I needed someone on surveillance.

"Can Johnny find out where Hunter worked before?"

"Already have that. Alex traced him to Mount Sinai, New Jewish, and the Cleveland Clinic."

"Terrific."

"Yes, we're checking references."

"How'd you get Hunter's résumé?"

"Alex hacked into his computer." Under normal circumstances, I would have locked the kid in his room until he turned eighteen, but these were far from normal circumstances.

"Wanna bet Alex has everything we need on Hunter? We just don't know what's important yet."

"Probably. He turns up more nuggets every day."

"Can you contact the state medical boards where he worked? See if there're any complaints filed against him? Has he been sued for malpractice? Has anyone complained about unethical behavior? Like affairs with patients?" Whip's questions ricocheted all over the place.

"Malpractice, huh? Good idea. Alex's monitoring a Web site called 'rottendoctor.' He found several complaints about Hunter. We know Hunter killed Merry. Let's say Kiki's a person. He tried to remake Merry into her. He'd soon have realized she wasn't anyone but Merry."

"Merry was a mistake that had to be destroyed." Whip looked so sad my heart almost broke.

"Something like that. Johnny and I think he's killed before. We're looking for unsolved murders."

"If there are similar crimes, think we can link 'em?"

"If he used the same gun. If we can find it. Em's focused on Kiki. She's been working overtime. Posting questions on dozens of different sites. Getting lots of responses."

"Good. Anything on Hunter's financial status? Where's his checking account? What's in his savings account? Maybe get a copy of his credit report."

I didn't answer, but my mental hamster was running at full tilt. I knew what to do. If Alex didn't already have Hunter's financial records, he would soon. He loved real-life mysteries as much as he loved the Internet.

Whip looked alive. He'd beaten the bogeyman. He and I were

once again a team functioning with a shared urgency. I wished I could get a computer into the jail so Whip could help more.

"Mad Max! MM! MM! Come here!"

I was meditating after a hard Pilates workout when Alex's cry shattered my quiet. I scrambled to my feet, called "coming," and went down the hall to his room. It was its usual mess with the added attraction of piles of crumpled, discarded printouts. This attested to how involved my grandson was with his find-the-bastard-and-stop-him role.

"Look, MM. Look what I got!" Alex jabbed at the screen. "Look!"

An e-mail from NYU, Hunter's first medical school. The dean wrote that Randolph Andrew Hunter had been a student but left in his third year.

Randolph?

"I got one from Dracula's second med school too. He graduated but left and finished his internship and residency in Grenada."

I was puzzled. Chaminade bragged Hunter was a graduate of these schools, so it seemed they hadn't verified his résumé. Shame on them.

"He lied on his résumé." Alex was fixated on Dracula being a serial liar, maybe even a pathological one.

"Wonder why he left NYU early." I wanted to know everything Hunter had done. Were we getting closer to an epiphany? My gut said "yes."

"Some police departments have their blotters online, but this goes back too far."

"Did you notice what name he used? Randolph? We had Randall."

"Uh-huh." Alex clicked through several screens and found letters from the second medical school: Andrew Hunter, no other name or initial.

I patted Alex's shoulder and withdrew to my room, proud he was plowing ahead in unraveling the persona of Randall-Randolph Andrew Hunter. I settled into an easy chair and picked up a book but didn't open it. I leaned my head back, closed my eyes, put my mind into neutral, and let my thoughts go quiet.

I might have dozed. As you get older, mini-naps are refreshing. I awoke more hopeful because we had a better understanding of

Hunter's past, which held the keys to his current and future actions. Had he been thrown out of medical school? Had he been charged with ethical violations? Just as I had a hunch we'd find missing persons in his past, I had an even stronger hunch we were closing in on the end of this nightmare.

Three days after Alex received the e-mails from the two medical schools, Emilie wandered out onto the patio where I wrote letters. I still wrote letters. Putting fountain pen to beautiful stationery and shaping my thoughts was one of my favorite pastimes. I liked writing in my journal too. I wasn't about to be a blog person. I capped the pen and set my portable desk aside.

Emilie stared at a printout. Then she handed it to me and wandered over to the patio railing. She spoke not a word.

I was alone with a piece of paper. I steadied myself and read:

Dear Emilie,

I don't know why I am writing, but I might have some information to help with your search. I want you to know how difficult this is for me.

My dear friend Brenda came across your search for someone named Kiki.

I knew a Kiki almost two decades ago, Kiki Gustafson, a freshman at Columbia. She dated my son Randolph when he was a third-year med student at NYU. Kiki was a lovely young woman with a winning smile, a gentle personality and a quiet manner.

She was Randolph's opposite—he was outgoing, athletic and talkative. They dated for about a year, fell in love and got engaged. They were on the way to my apartment one evening to celebrate when a car ran a red light and hit their cab broadside. Kiki took the brunt of the blow, smashing her face into the back of the front seat.

Even though he was still a student, Randolph assisted with the emergency surgery. No one asked if he was a doctor. Kiki was dreadfully injured, and it was a busy night, so they welcomed an extra pair of hands. From what he told me, the surgery started normally. Kiki had broken so many bones in her face, but they were repairable. Unfortunately, she also had a bruised heart no one detected. She went into cardiac arrest and died on the operating table.

Afterward, Randolph withdrew from NYU, convinced he killed her. I lost him to depression for several years. I didn't know where he was until he sent me a letter from Grenada where he finished his residency. He was a plastic surgeon.

Eventually, Randolph moved to Pittsburgh and married. I went to the wedding, but we had a huge fight, and I haven't spoken to him in nearly a decade. Until Brenda found your post, I am ashamed to say I hadn't thought much about my son in years. I tried on and off to reach him in the beginning, but he didn't return my calls. When he got a new cell number, he refused to give it to me.

I don't know if our Kiki is the one you are looking for. I hope I've helped. Good luck, my dear. Please let me know how things turn out.

Sincerely,
Paula Hunter Goodman

My hands shook when I finished Mrs. Goodman's letter. Emilie found Kiki, who died under the hands of her fiancé. Hunter lied by omission in not telling the attending surgeon he was a medical student. That violated medical ethics.

My guess? He was kicked out of NYU, but the dean of students couldn't say so. Our litigious society too often buried the truth under politically correct language.

Emilie turned, tears in her eyes. "He killed her," she whispered.

"That's not what Mrs. Goodman says."

"He killed her. He didn't murder her, but he killed her as sure as he murdered Mom." Tears poured down Emilie's tanned cheeks. She came over and threw herself into my arms. "Oh, Grams, he's so awful."

Grams? I held her, rubbed her back and let her cry herself out.

CHAPTER FIFTY-THREE

Even though we were on a roll, finding Kiki upset me more than I expected. My first inclination was to tell Whip, but I sat on the news for two days. I was as shaken as Emilie and needed space to cope with my emotions. I did the logical thing—I asked Mrs. Goodman if I could meet her in New York.

When I got to the jail three days after Emilie received the original note, Whip entered the conference room and stopped dead still. Unlike my usual practice, I wasn't sitting at the scarred oak table, the fridge list in front of me. Instead, I leaned my forehead against the smudgy window that faced the back alley and didn't turn around. I knew he wondered what the hell happened, why I was missing in action for two days.

I whispered, "We found Kiki."

"Say again."

I turned and looked Whip in the eye. "We found Kiki. Or rather, Em found Kiki."

Whip fell into the straight-backed wooden chair, his face full of hope. "Have you talked with her?"

"No, but I've talked with Hunter's mother."

The tiniest breeze would have knocked Whip off his chair. His face showed he couldn't believe what I'd said.

"His mother? How ...?"

I took a couple of steps to the table and sat on its edge. "You know Em posted questions on several Web sites about Kiki."

"Yeah."

I handed him the message.

"That's incredible! We have the whole story now."

"There's more." I pointed to the bottom of a second message. "She sent her phone number. I've met her." I moved to a chair.

"You met her? She lives nearby?"

"She lives way out at the end of Long Island, retired and spending her time gardening. I flew out and talked with her yesterday. She told me the entire story about the original Kiki and her son's resultant depression."

"You told her about Merry?"

"Of course. Both what we know and what we suspect." I rubbed at the stiffness in the back of my neck. Mrs. Gordon and I lost our children too early. We had much in common—pain, loss, anguish, and a survival spirit.

"Many years after Kiki's death, Hunter married a lovely young woman with dark auburn hair and green eyes named Lydia-Marie Mendoza in Pittsburgh. Mrs. Goodman met her once early in their relationship. Didn't see her again until the wedding a year later. By then, Lydia-Marie had new eyes, cheeks, and chin. In fact, she looked almost exactly like Kiki."

"Dear God, you were right. Hunter's resurrecting a ghost. Merry was just the latest. Where's Lydia-Marie?"

"No one knows. Mrs. Goodman told me her son called Lydia-Marie 'Kiki.' Lydia-Marie thought it was cute. She didn't know she was the second Kiki."

I remembered the napkins in Merry's desk with Meredith "Kiki" Hunter doodled on them. At the time, I thought she was making up a new persona to go with her new face. Had I known Hunter controlled her every move, I would have tied her to a tree in the backyard or had her committed to a mental hospital until she was cured of any infatuation with this cretin. Or until he moved on to his next victim.

I reached into my tote and pulled out an envelope, yellowed and tattered from much handling. I handed it to Whip. In it were a series of pictures: Hunter as a child, Hunter in a Little League uniform, Hunter at a piano recital, Hunter in a cap and gown. The hairs on Whip's arm stood up.

Looking at the original Kiki and Lydia-Marie was like looking through a distorted mirror at Merry. Each had similar eyes and cheeks. Both were blonde. Lydia-Marie's unaltered lips were fuller than Kiki's. Because I studied the photos on the plane home, I was no longer vulnerable to their impact. Whip wasn't.

Whip dropped the photos on the table as if his hands had been splashed with acid.

"Mrs. Goodman knows we think her son's a cold-blooded killer. She promised to do whatever she could. She told me how worried she was when Lydia-Marie disappeared. Hunter said she went to visit her family in Mexico. Decided to stay."

"Could it be true?"

"Highly unlikely. Lydia-Marie, her parents, and her siblings were all born in the US. Her grandparents are dead. No family in Mexico."

"So, what do you think happened to her?"

"Mrs. Goodman stayed in touch with her after the wedding, even though Hunter forbade it. Lydia-Marie was strong-willed. She wasn't about to be bullied. Mrs. Goodman kept her letters. She'll send them if we need them." I couldn't sit any longer. I walked back to the window and watched police cars enter and leave the parking lot as the morning shift ended and the afternoon shift began.

"Wonder if we can find Lydia-Marie's body." Whip mumbled. "If Hunter gets rid of his mistakes—and Merry was a mistake—he must have gotten rid of Lydia-Marie too."

"Alex is searching for unsolved crimes between here and New York. Do you have any idea how many police and sheriff jurisdictions there are?"

"Too many to count."

"You've got that right. Alex is focused on unsolved murders of young women in or near the hospitals where we know he worked." I rubbed tired eyes. I was almost as drained as I was the week of Merry's funeral.

"Hunter shot Merry behind the ear with a twenty-two. Have him look for similar crimes. For missing women too." Whip joined me at the window.

"Will do."

"Try smaller jurisdictions."

I was too exhausted to ask why.

"How are you holding up? You look beat."

"I am. Once Mrs. Goodman contacted Em, she was up several nights puking. It's nerves. She feels Mrs. Goodman's pain. She's overwhelmed."

I stared through the mesh sandwiched between two panes of glass. I wanted to hide how worried I was about Emilie's health. Whip had enough on his mind without fretting over something he couldn't change.

"Used to think her feelings were fantasy. They're real, aren't they?"

"They're very real. Do not underestimate that child."

"Does she know how to control them, the feelings?"

"No. I'm looking for a New Age, hippy-dippy shrink. Maybe from California. Doubt there's anyone local. I might have to call every shrink in the phonebook. Ask what their sign is. Or if they've read Carlos Castaneda. Do they believe he turned into a crow? Come to think about it, that might not be a bad idea."

Whip laughed.

"Seriously, I've been reading about some of the newer trends in psychotherapy. We need someone experienced in dealing with a sensitive. Not a sensitive teenager, but a true sensitive. Em's gift has to be trained, or it could destroy her."

I stowed the photographs in my tote. Pete opened the door to the interview room.

"Time's up."

CHAPTER FIFTY-FOUR

I was more worried about Emilie than I let on. I told Whip the truth about looking for a psychiatrist, but I didn't tell him I'd called experts all over the country. Dr. Silberman was helping the kids develop the day-to-day coping skills they needed to get over their mother's murder, but he'd already told me he had no experience with sensitives. He, too, was making calls.

Finding a New Age shrink was on my list as far back as when we began going to Dr. Silberman. I was about ready to tackle the search when Hunter murdered Merry. No way could I put this off any longer. If there was a rock I could turn over, I would.

I regretted ignoring Emilie's initial response to Hunter when she said he was evil. Perfect twenty-twenty hindsight. I shouldn't have.

I pulled into the drive and went upstairs to look for the kids. The house felt too silent for my peace of mind. Alex's room. Empty. Emilie's. Empty. I trotted downstairs to the kitchen table where we always left notes. Empty. No text messages on my phone. I called each kid's cell. No answer. My vivid imagination ran wild with thoughts of bloody bodies and car wrecks and perverts kidnapping children. I jumped half out of my skin when my cell rang.

"Mad Max?"

Alex. My knees felt weak as I struggled to control my voice.

"I just got home. Where are you?" I sounded cross because I was scared.

"At Danny's. We're playing video games. I forgot to leave a note. I left my cell on my desk. Stupid me." The beeps and tire squeals of *Grand Theft Auto* sounded in the background.

"Don't do it again."

"Okay."

"Where's Em?"

"I dunno. She was on her computer when I left. Maybe she went to the library."

The library? The bookstore, maybe, but the library? I didn't remember the child going to the library once this summer. I wished she'd spent her summer rereading the *Harry Potter* series like her friends rather than playing sleuth.

"Be home in time for dinner. We're having hot dogs and beans."

"Yippee. I'll be home by five-thirty."

"Dinner will be at six-thirty. Have fun."

Much as I disliked Alex playing video games in a darkened room on a day when the sun was shining and the air was Indian-summer warm, at least he was safe. I'd worry about long-term damage to his psyche from *Grand Theft Auto* later.

So where's Emilie? She didn't answer her phone. Unheard of.

She wasn't at Molly's. I called her other friends but came up empty. I paced the family room, more worried about her than Alex. I was haunted by an early memory of Emilie meeting Hunter. I remembered how he said he could work miracles with her because she was so young. Had Hunter snatched her? Dear God, I couldn't cope with that.

Emilie returned just before five with a laden backpack, her face flushed and sweaty. Torn between anger and weak-kneed relief, I crushed her before I sat her down with lemonade. We had a heart-to-heart talk about taking her phone, leaving notes, and getting permission to visit friends beforehand.

"You had me worried. I wondered if Hunter—"

"Don't worry. I pretty much know where he is all the time. He's nowhere near me today."

"Don't let him get too close. I don't want him living rent free in your head." I couldn't shake my fear, even if Emilie knew where Hunter was all the time.

"Neither do I, but I can keep track of him better than anyone else."

For now. When Tony's man was on the job, I'd rest easier.

"I blew out of here so fast I never even thought about a note." Emilie looked stricken and excited at the same time.

"Where's your phone?"

"Oh, shoot." Emilie dug into her backpack. "I turned it off. Sorry."

"Where have you been?" I stared at the bulging backpack.

"I went over to the university."

"Virginia Commonwealth?"

"No. University of Richmond."

"You rode your bike all the way over there?"

"Uh-huh. I've been e-mailing a teacher through a paranormal Web site for weeks. I learned about her at camp this summer. I just found out she teaches at U of Richmond, so I asked to meet her."

"Okay. That's why you forgot a note. Does she know Dracula?"

"She never met him, but after she answered me, she did a reading on him and saw five dead bodies."

"Is she a psychic?" Hope rose for the first time since I'd entered the empty house.

"I'm not sure. Maybe. At any rate, she knew things I didn't, so I went to meet her. She's like me, but she 'sees.' I 'feel.'"

"Can she help?" Mental fingers crossed.

"Well, she had some ideas for Alex's research. She saw at least five bodies. The first is Kiki. One is Mom. She saw all but Kiki shot in the same way. Oh, we should look for Jane Does."

"Dad and I came to the same conclusion this morning. Tell me more."

Emilie described her search for a psychic. She heard from dozens of kooks, many interested in doing a reading, "for a fee, of course."

"Don't worry. I didn't use my real e-mail. I set up a special account through MySpace."

That relieved my worry a little. "This teacher communicated with you through MySpace?"

"At first. She responded to the e-mail address I used to find Mrs. Goodman. At any rate, she said she might be able to help, but she wants to meet you before we go any further."

Emilie handed me a card: "Dr. Angela Schwartz, Professor of Philosophy."

She could still be a crank emerging from the woodwork to prey on hapless victims of crime. Or she could be real. Or somewhere in between. Emilie sensed she was real, which was almost, but not quite, good enough for me. I needed to vet her before I'd let my vulnerable granddaughter get more involved.

"Thanks. I'll call her. What's in your backpack?"

"Books Dr. Schwartz loaned me." Emilie opened her pack and dumped several books about psychics onto the table. I recognized two but not the rest. One on how mediums helped police departments looked academic.

"Pretty heavy stuff, huh?"

"No worse than the books you've been studying." Emilie grinned. "Busted!"

Over our supper of hot dogs and beans, Emilie told Alex about Dr. Schwartz and her suggestion he widen his hunt to include Jane Does. He'd been concentrating on people whose names we knew; Jane Does might offer another avenue. We had to try everything.

We knew what happened to Kiki, and we knew Lydia-Marie's maiden and married names. Alex searched for mention of her everywhere. So far, all he'd found were engagement and wedding announcements and a few photos in the *Post-Gazette* of the happy couple at charity events. Otherwise, Lydia-Marie Mendoza Hunter didn't exist.

"She's dead. You know that, don't you, Mad Max?" Emilie said.

"I'm afraid so, but Alex'll find out. At the very least, we might be able to help her family."

The more we peeled away the layers of the Dracula onion, the more complex he became. The more evil he became. He was a broken soul, who turned to the dark side after his initial loss.

"Don't tell me it'll bring closure. I hate that word."

"So do I, Em. There's no such thing. We can end the uncertainty. If you go through life wondering what happened to a loved one, it has to be worse than accepting the finality of death. At least then you can bury the body, mourn, and move on."

"That's what Dr. Schwartz said. Lydia-Marie's dead. Her family doesn't know it. That's one way I can use my gift. To help other families through the pain of loss."

I was beginning to like this Dr. Schwartz, unmet and sight

unseen. "Did she say you could use your gift for people who are alive?"

I didn't want Emilie facing a life of darkness, of "I see dead people" like in *The Sixth Sense,* the old Bruce Willis movie. I didn't want my family living through that plot.

"Yes. I don't know if I want to learn how to use it. It's more a curse than a gift."

I put my arm around my granddaughter's shoulders. "Can you ignore it?"

"No more than you can ignore breathing." Emilie's smile was quavery. I gave her a squeeze and sent her upstairs while I called Dr. Schwartz.

CHAPTER FIFTY-FIVE

Whip asked for a speedy trial when he entered his not guilty plea, so we expected courtroom antics to begin within three months. Now, at the two-month-and-three-week mark and closing in on November, we still hadn't seen all the evidence. I was growing more and more agitated with the criminal justice system when every day passed with nothing new.

Whip whirled on Vince the moment he entered the interview room. "I want my fucking life back."

I remained seated but shared Whip's urgency. My son-in-law stood with his back to the grubby window, his arms crossed over his chest.

Vince went through his standard routine; he pulled file after color-coded file out of his briefcase while Whip ranted. He opened his yellow notepad, uncapped his fountain pen, and folded his hands at the edge of the table. And waited.

"Are you done now?"

"I should say I'm sorry, but I'm not. Are we getting stonewalled?"

"Yes."

"All we have is an evidence list. Is that normal?"

"No."

"Then what the fuck's going on?" Whip threw himself away from the wall and paced, mimicking the frustration of countless criminals and innocent men who sat in this room before him. "I want outta here."

"Max and your family are doing more than I am? Is that it?"

The fury went out of Whip with the explosive blast of a punctured balloon. He collapsed into a chair. I remained planted in mine. I opened my mouth then closed it. This was between Whip and his attorney. They had to settle their differences in a guy way.

"No, that's not it. Well, yes, that's part of it. At least they're trying to prove Hunter killed Merry."

Vince looked at me. "We've been over this before. If and when you bring me something that will stand up in court, I'll add Hunter to the witness list. Without proof, Whip could be sued for making false accusations."

I was defeated by Vince's logic.

"Why don't I have a trial date?"

"Because the district attorney is stalling. He might ask for a contingency, but the election season is looming. He's running way behind his opponent."

"Does he try and stall until after the election?"

"He could, but that would be a bad political maneuver. If there's one thing you can count on, it's that District Attorney Weed is a political animal."

"The election's not for seven more months," I said.

"Since we haven't seen the evidence, my guess is he's delaying because he's got real problems proving the case."

"Well, no shit. Like having the wrong man sitting on his ass in jail." Whip waved his hand at the thin pile of folders. "Anything new here?"

"Not really."

Whip flipped open the top folder. I could see the contents from where I sat. "Glove." There was a single piece of paper inside written in Vince's crabbed hand. It documented a conversation with an assistant district attorney who said they found a glove on the floor of Merry's apartment.

"Do we know any more than they found a plastic glove?"

I had this bizarre image of a yellow Playtex kitchen glove.

"No. Just that the district attorney says the killer wore two pairs of gloves," Vince said.

Whip set the nearly empty folder aside. Next in the stack was titled "Divorce Papers." "We've been over both of these already."

"Stop sounding so angry, Whip. It could work against you in court."

"Well, I'm pissed."

"Vince, are there more than one set of divorce papers? I mean, we gave you what Whip and Merry filed." I stared at the folders, wondering if we'd ever get to a consistent set. Did the district attorney have a different set than we did? Or were they reading them completely differently?

Whip flipped through more folders. He stopped at the last one. "Temporary Restraining Order."

"Why's the district attorney still holding onto this? Didn't you tell him he had it ass-backward?"

"Weed's been ducking me. He's turned all the prep over to his hotshot assistant district attorney, Julie Hamada. She won't meet with me or return my calls, either."

"I took out the TRO on Merry, not the other way around. Max brought you a copy. I can prove she was a threat to me. She attacked me with a knife on our front porch after I locked her out."

"There's a police report?"

"Sure. Ask Jerry Skelton, the officer who responded to a call from my neighbors."

Whip repeated the messy story of the attack. Then he shrugged out of his orange jumpsuit, pulled up his T-shirt, and turned around to reveal the ugly scar left by Merry's knife. "I'll sign a release for the emergency room. They have photos."

It was puckery, and the scars from the stitches required to close the wound were still visible.

Vince stared at the curved scar. "Your wife did that?"

I stared too. I hadn't seen it since Whip's back was covered in blood on the front porch of his house.

"She came by the house, drunk and stoned. Got violent when she found I'd changed the locks. Got arrested for assault. Spent the night in the drunk tank. It's all well documented. The next day I took out the TRO to keep her away from me. Protect the kids. I didn't know what else to do."

"Mr. Medina and I were eyewitnesses," I said.

Vince gathered the scattered folders, straightened them, and replaced them in his briefcase. He made one last note on the pad. Whip busied himself pulling the jumpsuit back into position.

"Time to ask the judge for an evidentiary hearing."

"It's way past time." Whip's anger had lessened, but it hadn't dissipated. "The district attorney's case is a house of cards, isn't it?"

"It sure looks like it. I think we can get a judge to agree. No weapon, no DNA, no fingerprints, no paper trail of threats. The divorce papers, the TRO, the police report for the call at your house—as you say, all ass-backward."

"What are our chances?"

I stood to walk out with Vince.

"Looking a helluva lot better than they were two hours ago. I'll charge stonewalling by the district attorney. The documents they built their case on tell a very different story from the one they've been leaking to the press. Without a murder weapon, this should collapse. Wish me luck."

"Get me the hell out of here."

"We will," Vince and I said in unison.

In the corridor, I handed Vince another small packet of information we'd gathered on Hunter. "For future use" was all I said.

CHAPTER FIFTY-SIX

"I found at least five Kikis." Alex plopped on the end of my bed, another fistful of printouts crumpled in his left hand. I was folding and putting away clean laundry. I pushed the pile aside and sat on the bed too.

"*Five?*"

"I found three more. There may be others."

"May I see?" I pointed to the papers, my heart pounding. Maybe Hunter as a serial killer wasn't such a far-fetched idea after all.

"Whatcha got, Alex?" Emilie followed her brother into my room.

"What do you have, Alex?"

"You sound just like Mom."

"Well, who do you think taught her? Me. So?"

"What do you have, Alex?" Emilie sighed and repeated the question using correct grammar this time. She sat cross-legged on the bed beside me.

Alex spread the pages on the coverlet. The pictures weren't clear.

"Here's Dracula with a young woman at a party in New York. It's dated about a year after the original Kiki died."

Emilie and I stared at the grainy photo. My granddaughter shivered. Hunter with a pretty little blonde by his side. The caption identified him as "Dr." Randall Hunter, but he had yet to finish medical school. The girl wasn't identified, but she wasn't Lydia-Marie, either.

"We need to find her."

"Good luck," Emilie said.

I raised an eyebrow, but she concentrated on the papers and didn't look up.

"Hey, I got this far, didn't I?" Alex sulked.

"You did, indeed." Without Alex's digging, we wouldn't have so much on Hunter's background. "Go on."

The next was a news article with a lovely studio portrait announcing the engagement of one "Randall Andrew Hunter, M.D. to Lydia-Marie Mendoza of Vera Cruz."

Vera Cruz? According to Mrs. Goodman, Lydia-Marie was from Pittsburgh.

What was amazing was how little Lydia-Marie looked like Kiki—darker hair, rounder eyes, and a very different mouth. Why would she undergo plastic surgery when she was a natural beauty?

"Okay. Here's the wedding picture. Lydia-Marie is Kiki, complete with blond hair. Just like Mrs. Goodman said." Emilie and I already knew about the transformation, but seeing it made Hunter's obsession impossible to ignore.

"Just like Mom. Even to the blond hair." Emilie and I shivered. Geese walked across my grave.

Alex next handed over a printout from a small-town police station in central Pennsylvania with the barest of details about the death of a young woman, a twenty-two caliber bullet wound behind the right ear. A hiker discovered Jane Doe's skeleton buried in the woods in a shallow grave. The only distinguishing characteristic was evidence of possible plastic surgery on her cheekbones. Or, it could have been marks from an animal.

"That Jane Doe stuff worked." Alex puffed himself up.

"Lydia-Marie," Emilie paled but was determined to see the rest. "We've gotta contact those cops and let them know what we suspect."

"I already did." Alex was smug. "I haven't heard back yet. It's been a week."

"If we don't hear by Tuesday, we'll give the police a call, okay?"

"This one's different. Here, Dracula's standing next to a Penn State student at a local hospital charity event. In the caption she's identified as a youth organizer, no name. Could be she's in the picture by accident, though."

"Why?"

"This girl's black. She'd look dumb as a blonde if she was Dracula's next target."

"Where is she?" Emilie couldn't wait for Alex Time.

"Disappeared from school. Her parents listed her as missing. After a couple of stories in a local paper, nothing. Guess the papers don't follow stories about missing black women as much as they do for missing white women."

"Whatever gave you that idea?"

How had my grandson become so cynical at the ripe young age of eleven? Kids grew up faster in this media-enriched culture than I had.

Alex shrugged. For him, it was probably a truism.

"I found over a dozen stories about Lydia-Marie, the wife of a doctor, and two on the missing black student. It might be accidental, but if she's missing, we should ask. Dontcha think?"

"I think."

"That's all."

"That's a lot. You've done a lot."

Alex's Internet mining continued paying off.

"I found two more police reports of Jane Does killed with a twenty-two and dumped in the woods. One was shot in the head, but the other was shot in the back of the neck. See?"

The woman shot in the head was white, about twenty-four years old, and had been dead for several weeks before a mountain biker found her body. Animals had been at the corpse. What was left were parts of the torso and the head. Possible surgical scars on the face, but again the marks were inconclusive. This time, I shivered. It wasn't Lydia-Marie. It might be the unnamed white girl.

The woman shot in the back of the neck was found in the woods in a shallow grave. This time, though, there were scraps of clothing and a glove nearby. No report of plastic surgery. The woman was either black or Latina. The Penn State student. I just knew it.

"Do they put autopsy reports online?" Emilie asked.

"I haven't found them. I'd have to hack into their systems to get that stuff."

"No hacking into police records." Could I make my point any clearer? I could overlook Alex hacking into Hunter's computer but nothing else.

"'K," Alex mumbled.

I raised an eyebrow and glared at him.

"How do we get these police departments to pay attention?" Alex asked. "I called one, but they knew I was a kid and blew me off."

"Figures," Emilie retorted. "What do we know?"

"Now, now. Just because you're kids doesn't mean you aren't seeing what the professionals missed. After all, they're small-town departments with limited resources."

"Isn't that the point, Mad Max?" Emilie asked. "All the bodies of the women Alex found, these Jane Does, were hidden in woods where local cops would be handling the investigations."

"That's true."

"Then why kill Mom in the city?" Alex asked.

"Because he made a mistake," Emilie said. "Maybe he's gotten away with so many murders, he got cocky."

"That could be." I looked at the timeline. "Let's assume Hunter killed Lydia-Marie, the white girl and the black student. Between Kiki and Lydia-Marie there's almost five years. The white girl came between them. Before Lydia-Marie died, Dracula was with her for two years. The black girl went missing a couple of months after Lydia-Marie. Then there was Mom less than a year later. He's speeding up."

"How do we know he isn't looking for another Kiki now?" Alex asked.

"He is."

I didn't like the expression on Emilie's face nor the matter-of-factness of her statement. I told Alex what Hunter said when they first met, about starting plastic surgery on her right away so she'd be perfect by the time she was grown.

Alex fidgeted with the printouts. Something was bothering him, but he didn't seem anxious to talk about it.

"Was he setting Em up if he failed with Mom?"

"No, but he's always on the lookout for the perfect Kiki. He saw something in Em's face he liked."

I didn't want Alex or Emilie living in fear of Hunter stalking them. I knew something neither of them did. My helpful PI was keeping tabs on Emilie to be sure Hunter didn't come close. I couldn't tell Alex about Tony Ferraiolli's man, because it would have been too juicy a secret to keep. He'd have to blab to his friends.

"Can Johnny help with the cops?"

"Let me try first. Maybe they'll listen to a grandmother."

"You sure don't act like a grandmother," Alex said, "most of the time, that is."

"If I ever start to, you let me know."

"You bet!" Emilie and Alex chorused in unison.

"Well, would it be too grandmotherly to suggest ice cream sundaes to celebrate Alex's hard work?"

"No!" With a whoop, Alex was off the bed and thundering down the stairs before Emilie and I could move. We followed more quietly.

CHAPTER FIFTY-SEVEN

I spent another sleepless night thinking about Hunter's victims. We wouldn't get any attention from the rural police without having the gun. What if we gave them the ballistics report on the bullet that killed Merry? If it matched, maybe we could generate enough enthusiasm to get them to look into the cold cases more carefully. We needed the gun to clear them. Most important, we needed it to get Whip off.

First thing in the morning, I called my faceless PI and told him what we suspected. He asked me to leave copies at the front desk of the Comfort Inn out on I-95. I could pick up a copy of Hunter's latest movements at the same time.

I made two sets of copies at our local library. I didn't know why, but I didn't want Alex to do it even though his printer made copies. I added more information to one set, sealed the envelope, and asked Johnny to meet me for lunch.

Over burgers I told Johnny about Alex's suspicions. I told him about leaving copies for "Joe the PI." I put the second envelope on the table beside my coffee cup.

"This one's for me, isn't it, pretty lady?" Johnny could make me feel better even after a sleepless night that left unpacked luggage under my eyes.

"Can you follow up for us? I called two police departments but didn't get much further than Alex did. Each listed a dead Jane Doe 'killed by person or persons unknown.' End of story without physical evidence."

I must have looked discouraged, because Johnny reached across the table and took my hand.

"Which we don't have. Yet." Johnny patted the back of my hand with his own work-hardened paw.

"Vince gave me the ballistics report." I left my hand where it was.

"I have a copy?"

"It's in the envelope."

"What about the report from 'Joe the PI'?"

I removed my hand, opened Joe's sealed envelope, read the written report, and looked at the stack of photos. I wanted to faint or vomit or both. I handed them to Johnny.

It took a full day to recover from the PI's report. I didn't want Whip to worry more than he already did, so I didn't give him a copy. All he could do was worry—and worry wouldn't help us a whit. I set a copy aside for Vince. When I got to the jail, Whip was once again wrapped in his own cloak of despair and missed my distraction.

More bags under my eyes than at an airport claim area. Even my tried and true remedy—hemorrhoid cream—didn't work.

We were still waiting for a court date. The district attorney tried to block the evidentiary hearing, but the judge who reviewed the filing gave him two days to comply. No more stonewalling or he would have to answer to her. The hearing should unlock the cell door.

I updated Whip about the case we were building against Hunter. Johnny disappeared after our lunch to visit rural police jurisdictions in the Northeast. I finished my report just as Vince walked in and set his briefcase on the table. From his barely controlled excitement, I knew we had the date.

"The district attorney missed the deadline yesterday. I saw the judge an hour ago. We're on the docket for Tuesday."

I wanted to hug him, but Vince Bodine was the least huggable man I'd ever met. I settled for a huge grin and Whip for a handshake. Vince gave us the schedule of events, the time Whip was to be ready, etc. Maybe it'd all work out. I still harbored doubts about Vincent Bodine being a piranha in court, as my friend the bank president called him. To date, he'd seemed too passive. Now I wondered if a slow and steady tortoise wasn't the right way. Please, just a hint of the piranha, a bit of sharpened teeth, to make me feel better.

"I hope this works," I said.

"It will. By this time next week, Whip will be a free man." Vince turned at the door. "Feeling better?"

"Yes. I'll feel great when two things happen."

"Two things?"

"Yes." Whip nodded. "When the judge dismisses the case and when the other half of my team proves Hunter killed Merry."

Whip smiled at me. Vince did, too, because he'd come around on the unlikely possibility we just might find proof of Hunter's guilt. Like a cat finishing a bowl of cream, I grinned back. After all, I knew more than either Whip or Vince about Hunter's activities. I had "Joe the PI's" report.

CHAPTER FIFTY-EIGHT

Late the night before the evidentiary hearing, there was a tiny tap on my closed bedroom door. I was thinking about the New Age book I was reading and somewhat annoyed at the interruption. Given the unnatural state of affairs in which we found ourselves, I had made concessions to my privacy. For one, I no longer slept in the nude but had returned to wearing silk pajamas. For another, I answered every late night tap at the door.

"Yes?" I laid my book on the nightstand.

"Mad Max, it's me, Em," came a soft whisper.

"Come in." I was Mad Max again, not Grams. This might be important, but it wasn't a crisis.

"I wouldn't have knocked, but I saw your light on."

"Dear child, climb under the covers and talk to me."

Emilie crossed the room after shutting the door. She crawled into my bed and shoved pillows around until she was propped next to me. She laid her head on my shoulder like her mother used to when she was little and I read her to sleep. I kissed her freshly shampooed hair and searched for the baby-clean smell of infancy. It wasn't there.

"Are you happy here, Mad Max?"

"I'm not sure what you mean." I wanted to know what was bothering her before I tried to answer. No use guessing and being wrong.

"When Auntie Raney was here, I overheard her talking with Auntie Eleanor about your mantra."

"You mean, 'I'm not living in the South again and I'm through raising kids.'"

"There's another?" Emilie tickled my side.

"No, only one." I tickled her back.

"Are you going to leave us? I mean, you're back raising kids again."

"Not until you don't need me anymore."

"That could be a long time." She fell silent for a moment. "I mean, like, even when Dad's out of jail, he travels all the time. He can't stay here and raise us."

"I've talked with your dad. He's concerned too. Let's get him out of jail first. Then we can have a family conference. Sound okay?"

Emilie nodded against my shoulder. She wasn't very relaxed, though; something else was bothering her.

"Why don't you like living in the South? I mean, you were born near Richmond and grew up here. Didn't you have a happy childhood?"

"My childhood was schizophrenic. Kind of like yours. We were happy until my daddy got hurt. He was never the same after his accident. Kinda like your mom's accident and death changed everything. Life was very difficult."

"You stayed for a long time after." Emilie seemed to be struggling to fit together pieces of an incomplete puzzle.

"I did indeed. I married your grandfather Norm and raised your mother and Uncle Jack on the other side of Richmond. Even after your grandfather died, I stayed until your mother and Uncle Jack were grown. I met and married Grandpa Frank a few years after Grandpa Norm died. Grandpa Frank was a Richmond native. He loved to travel and infected me with a critical case of itchy feet."

"Bet it wasn't athlete's foot, was it?"

My turn to tickle Emilie again. "After Grandpa Frank and I moved to New York, I realized I loved living with the rhythms of the city than in the slower life of Richmond."

"So, do you still hate the South?"

"I don't hate it. You and Alex are here. Where else would I be?"

Emilie was quiet for so long I thought she was sleeping. She wasn't. "It's not over, is it, Mad Max?"

"If you mean your dad's trial? No, it's not, but it should be tomorrow."

"That's not what I mean. I mean it's not over with Dracula."

"No. It won't be over until we stop him." Wanted dead or alive. Long ago I passed beyond wanting anything less than him dead or locked away forever. I couldn't live with myself if he harmed another woman.

"He's looking for the next one."

"Yes."

"Why does he try to remake Kiki? Doesn't he know changing our looks will never be enough? Inside, we'll never be Kiki. We're Lydia-Maria and Merry and Em."

Hmm, Emilie included herself in the list of "Kikis."

"Because he's mentally ill, dear child. He's broken in spirit. He's obsessed with his memory of Kiki's physical perfection. He gets as close as he can only to realize his new creation is flawed. Like a mad artist, he destroys his masterpiece. If he didn't, he'd have to accept she's gone. He can't do that."

Emilie didn't say anything. Again I thought she'd dozed off, but apparently she was thinking. "Do you remember when we talked about closure?"

"Uh-huh."

"Dracula will never get closure. Kinda like Mom and Dr. Silberman. She wouldn't admit she needed help, so Dr. Silberman couldn't help her heal. Dracula won't admit it, either."

I agreed.

"Dracula hasn't accepted responsibility for what he did in the operating room. He's like a ghost trapped on this side."

"Except he's alive." I peeked around the bedroom, looking for Casper or some other kind of ectoplasm. Nothing.

"Physically, maybe. His spirit's dead."

Hunter wasn't a whole person; he lacked an essential aspect of humanity. "How did you get so world-wise?"

"By watching you and Mom."

I could add nothing.

"He's not done with me, either," Emilie whispered. "He wants me next."

We trembled until the bed shook.

"I won't let him get to you. Do you want to go stay with Grampop and Gramma? Or I can take you and Alex to New York where he'll never find us."

"If I run away, he'll escape and find someone else to transform into an imperfect Kiki. I can't let that happen." Emilie's teeth chattered. "I just want him to leave me alone. I feel his presence. It's ice cold. He's like a mad thing in my head."

This was way too damned creepy. I needed our hippy-dippy medium, but two in the morning wasn't a good time to call.

"Have you seen him?"

"No, but he's seen me. I feel him. Sometimes he's close. Sometimes he's far away."

"Have you talked to Dr. Schwartz about this?"

"Sure. She's helping me keep him away, but it's not always easy. He won't give up."

I told her about "Joe the PI." "I'll have him keep closer tabs on Hunter. He'll protect you too." I hoped I sounded reassuring, but I sure as hell didn't feel reassured.

Emilie was right. Hunter wouldn't quit. If Whip wasn't released after the hearing, Emilie, Alex, and I were going to New York. My Upper East Side apartment would be safer than Riverbend until this all blew over—or until we had enough proof to put Dracula in jail.

"Let's not think about it tonight. Remember what Scarlett O'Hara said? 'I'll think about it tomorrow. Tomorrow is another day.'" We chanted in unison.

At six the next morning, the phone startled me out of a lack of sleep-daze and caffeine-induced trance.

"You should have called me," Dr. Schwartz said.

CHAPTER FIFTY-NINE

I nearly laughed when I saw Whip appeared decked out in his Tuesday-go-to-court clothes. It was déjà vu all over again, except his suit no longer fit. The pants were too tight across his thighs, the waist was too large, and the suit jacket strained across his shoulders. Working out like a fiend had paid off. With a shave and a haircut, Whip looked transformed. Underneath his clothing, though, I was pretty sure he sweated like a pig.

I couldn't wait for the hearing to be behind us. I ran a million scenarios through my head: The judge would be prejudiced and keep Whip in jail; the judge would be enlightened and read the district attorney the riot act; the judge would be fair and let Whip go. If I flipped a coin, it would have landed on its edge. I twisted in my chair in the holding room and jumped at the slightest sound.

After what seemed like a hundred years, Vince entered the room with the biggest smile I'd ever seen on his face. A huge smile for Vince was a minor-league curl of the outer corners of his mouth. Today's corners pointed skyward. Piranha teeth glinted.

"What?"

"Time for an old-fashioned district attorney ass-whipping."

"We've got 'em?"

"And how. This is going to be fun."

A trial attorney's idea of fun was entering a courtroom with a portfolio of district attorney bait. My idea was driving Whip to a restaurant, going out for dinner with the kids and letting him sleep in his own bed.

"Two minutes." A court official knocked on the door.

"Showtime," Vince said.

"See you inside." I hurried to the seat Emilie held for me. The courtroom was packed with the ghoulish and just plain curious.

A policeman led Whip in. Alex, Emilie, and I were in the front row behind the defendant's table. I felt more confident than I had in months. Alex squirmed and waved; Emilie looked very serious, hopeful and fearful, all at once. The Pughs were in the second row. The Colonel gave a thumbs-up, Bette a tight smile. We chatted with Whip and waited.

The prosecution trickled in and settled down. This time George Weed glad-handed his way down the center aisle. Ever the politician, the district attorney exuded Old Spice-scented confidence. Julie Hamada, who led the arraignment, was bumped to second chair, with a black attorney I didn't recognize in third.

The district attorney and two assistant district attorneys for an evidentiary hearing? Outrageous waste of time and expense.

Miss Hamada arranged and rearranged her files and looked smug. The third assistant district attorney was expressionless. Whip glanced at Vince. *Hmm.* A district attorney butt-kicking in front of two of his staff was going to be fun after all.

Fifteen minutes later, the bailiff called the court to order. "All rise."

Everyone stood, and the judge entered. Vince had told us we'd drawn Judge Hamilton, but he failed to mention this judge was a woman too. I stared at her as thoroughly as I did a piece of art I wanted to add to my collection.

Gray-white hair curled at earlobe level. Black robe, of course, collar of a white blouse, a broad gold band on her left hand, a diamond ring of no small size on her right. Watch and gold studs. Very little makeup. I couldn't decide if she'd be a ball-buster or fair. God, I hoped fair.

We were so wound up we all jumped at the sound of the gavel, all but Emilie, who looked calm and serene.

"The court will come to order. This is case number zero-three-five-four-nine-eight, People versus Winston I. Pugh. This is an evidentiary hearing requested by Mr. Vincent Bodine, counsel for the defendant. Are we ready to proceed?"

"We are ready, Your Honor, although we'd like it entered into the record this is a waste of the court's precious time and wholly unwarranted." George Weed stood and smiled at the judge.

"So recorded. The court appreciates your interest in our precious time, Mr. Weed. Let it be recorded my precious time is being wasted because the district attorney's office hasn't released the evidence as ordered. Let me further remind the district attorney the law will be followed in my court. Do you have further comments?"

Round one for Whip. I exhaled as slowly and silently as I could.

"No, Your Honor."

The nattily dressed district attorney flushed crimson and sat in his chair. He turned and glared at Assistant District Attorney Julie Hamada, who studied a spot six inches above her tidy stack of folders.

"Proceed, Mr. Bodine."

"Thank you, Your Honor. If it pleases the court, when we requested copies of the evidence, we received a list of documents the district attorney intends to use against my client, Mr. Pugh. I haven't been given all the documents and frankly question the relevance of some of them. May I approach the bench?"

When Judge Hamilton nodded, Vince walked forward and presented a single sheet of paper, yellow highlighter marks visible. He turned and returned to his place behind the defendant's table.

The judge raised an eyebrow. "Mr. Weed, why have you withheld these documents? Have you forgotten the rules of evidence, that the burden of proof is on you and that you're required by the law of this state to give copies of everything to the defendant's counsel?"

Weed rose to his feet, braced himself on his fingertips, and lifted his head. "I thank the court for the reminder of my duty, Your Honor. We have the documents and can turn them over later today."

"Mr. Weed, it's within my power to review the evidence. I want to see if you have a case you can prove beyond a reasonable doubt. Do you have such a case?"

"Of course we do, Your Honor."

"You'd better, or I'll send you back to your office for a further review of the law."

Had I retained a modicum of sympathy, I wouldn't have wasted it on the district attorney or Julie Hamada. Weed's jaw clenched so hard the muscle in his cheek jerked with a will of its own. I was almost embarrassed to witness a public dressing down, but my son-in-law's future was at stake. I relaxed and enjoyed it.

"Mr. Bodine, continue."

Vince rose and opened the first of his now-familiar color-coded folders.

"Your Honor, the district attorney indicates divorce papers filed between Mr. and Mrs. Pugh are germane to the case. I examined the various filings and conclude what Mr. Pugh was offering Mrs. Pugh, who admitted in her filing she was having an affair with one Dr. Randall Andrew Hunter and intended to leave the family home to live with said doctor, was more generous than required by law."

Vince handed the legal documents to Judge Hamilton. The judge put on a pair of half-glasses and scanned the documents. She raised an eyebrow at Weed.

"Continue, Mr. Bodine."

"Thank you. Next on the list is a temporary restraining order. I assume the district attorney plans to use this to show Mrs. Pugh was in danger from her husband."

Vince glanced at the district attorney, who nodded. "We do, Your Honor."

"I've highlighted two key points in the TRO. If it pleases Your Honor, would you look at those sections?"

Vince handed the second document to the judge, who glanced at it.

"Mr. Weed, I fail to see how this has any relevance on the case at hand. Can you explain it to the court?"

"Yes, Your Honor. We will use it to show Mrs. Pugh was worried enough about Mr. Pugh's violent temper to seek protection. We consider this important in light of the fact Mrs. Pugh was murdered."

"I see. Do you have anything else, Mr. Bodine?"

"Yes, Your Honor. Two more documents. One, a police report about a domestic violence call at Mr. Pugh's house and a hospital record of a visit to the emergency room."

Judge Hamilton took more time looking at the newest papers before setting them on the stack.

"Is this your last document, Mr. Bodine?"

"Yes, Your Honor, but we have a request. We'd like to see the glove."

"The glove?"

"Yes. Item number eighteen on the list. We'd like to see the glove."

Weed sprang to his feet. "Your Honor, I protest. We found a glove in the apartment where Mrs. Pugh was brutally murdered. This is our most important piece of evidence, Your Honor. We don't have to turn it over to the opposing counsel."

"You're right, Mr. Weed, but I will see it."

"Your Honor, I must protest."

"Protest away, Mr. Weed. Send someone to fetch it. The court will take a ten-minute recess."

The gavel banged the session to a close.

CHAPTER SIXTY

Whip turned to Vince, who held up his hand. "Why don't you talk with your children?"

Whip leaned toward the rail, asked Alex some questions, smiled at Emilie, and nodded at his folks. Johnny slipped into the courtroom and sat behind me. He made a circle of his thumb and forefinger, grinned like a Cheshire cat, and sat back with his arms folded across his barrel chest.

The rear door of the courtroom banged open. Nine minutes into the recess, a clerk raced down the center aisle and handed a sealed evidence bag to the district attorney before running out.

Precisely one minute later, the bailiff rose and called the court to order. Almost before he got the words out, Judge Hamilton entered and took her place behind the bench and banged the gavel.

"Mr. Weed, I assume you have the glove." It was a statement, not a question.

"Yes, Your Honor. Sealed in our evidence bag. I must request, however, we not have an O.J. moment here."

"Rest assured, I won't ask the defendant to put it on."

Weed walked to the bench and handed the bag to the judge. She laid it on the stack of papers.

It looked like a surgical glove. Whip glanced at Vince, who nodded. Whip was home free. It was all over but the whuppin'.

"Someone here is a village idiot. I assure each of you it's not me.

I've examined the documents given to me by Mr. Bodine. I assume they're the same ones you've already reviewed, Mr. Weed."

Weed nodded and leaned back in his wooden chair, hands relaxed on the arms. Only the muscle in his cheek, the one with a life of its own, danced a samba.

Judge Hamilton shuffled the papers. "I'll set aside the divorce filings to start with the TRO. This seems to form the core of your case against Mr. Pugh."

"That, the police report, and the glove, Your Honor."

"Have you read this report, Mr. Weed?"

"Well, Your Honor, as you know, I have a very heavy caseload. My assistant reviewed it."

"And that would be ...?"

"Hamada, Your Honor. Julie Hamada." The woman in the middle of the table rose and sat in one fluid motion.

"Miss Hamada, can you read?"

"Yes, Your Honor." Miss Hamada rose as she responded. Her face turned a sickly pale gray.

"Then you are aware, Miss Hamada, this TRO was taken out by Mr. Pugh against Mrs. Pugh." Again a statement. "How is that relevant to Mrs. Pugh's murder?"

"Your Honor, I don't understand." Weed sprang to his feet.

"I'm sure you don't. Mr. Pugh charged Mrs. Pugh with a physical attack and received a TRO to prevent his wife from visiting the house or seeing their children without supervision." The judge set aside the filing.

Weed glared at Hamada.

"Next, the domestic violence report. The police were called to the Pugh residence where they found Mr. and Mrs. Pugh involved in a loud altercation. According to the report, they found blood all over the porch and a knife on the concrete."

"That's right, Your Honor," Weed broke in.

"I'm glad you agree. The report further states Mrs. Pugh attacked Mr. Pugh with the knife. Officer Jerome Skelton arrested Mrs. Pugh for assault and took her to jail. Is there a reason for you to enter this into evidence?" The judge raised her expressive eyebrows and peered over her half-glasses once again at the now twitching district attorney.

"I was led to believe the police report would incriminate Mr.

Pugh."

"And that would be by Miss Hamada?"

"Yes, Your Honor." Miss Hamada again performed her fluid rise-and-sit motion.

"Please remain seated, Miss Hamada. We're not playing Whack-A-Mole."

"Yes, Your Honor." Julie Hamada started to rise but caught herself. Her butt remained Velcroed to her chair.

"Were Mr. Pugh the victim, we might be looking at Mrs. Pugh for murder. As it stands, this proves Mr. Pugh is guilty of marrying a woman who was unfaithful and violent."

"But, Your Honor ..."

The district attorney rose.

"Yes, you have something to add, Mr. Weed?"

"Not at this time, Your Honor."

"Then sit down and be quiet. I'm not through with you."

Weed glared at Assistant District Attorney Hamada. My ever-intuitive gut said she'd be out of a job by noon. Sundown at the latest. She was sloppy and could have cost Whip his life had this been a capital case. As it was, she cost him his freedom for far too many months.

Judge Hamilton next took up the evidence bag. This was the famous glove that could convict him.

"This looks like a surgical glove. Is that what you see, Mr. Weed?"

The district attorney nodded. He'd passed puzzled two minutes after the second session began and was approaching catatonia.

"Mr. Weed, I have to commend you and your team. Never in my thirty years on the bench have I seen a case as thoroughly mishandled as this. If you'd done your homework, you would have learned the truth about the TRO and the police report. If you'd followed up on the police report, you would have gone to the hospital and subpoenaed the report on Mr. Pugh's injuries. Then you'd know your key piece of evidence could never have been used by Mr. Pugh."

Weed slumped in his chair, no longer capable of sitting upright. So much for a shoo-in re-election. I clapped my hands, in my imagination, of course. In reality, my hands remained relaxed in my lap.

"Will you read the warning highlighted at the top of this emergency room report?"

Weed stumbled to the bench, took the paper in a trembling hand, and stared at the top of the page. His face went from red to purple.

"Read what it says out loud." Judge Hamilton's voice was calm.

Weed cleared his throat. "It says," he cleared his throat again, "latex allergy."

Vince turned toward Whip; his teeth showed in a grin.

The judge pushed harder. "Is the surgical glove you entered into evidence made of latex?"

"I believe so, Your Honor."

Although Weed's voice was barely above a whisper, the judge didn't demand he repeat his admission.

"Mr. Pugh, if you put this glove on, what would happen?"

"My throat would close up in a matter of seconds. I'd be unable to breathe. In a couple minutes, I'd be in anaphylactic shock or dead."

"What do you have to say, Mr. Weed?" The judge took off her glasses and folded her hands.

"It, um, it looks as if we may have made a mistake." Weed sat down, deflated.

"You don't have the murder weapon. You don't have DNA or even a fingerprint linking Mr. Pugh to his wife's murder." The judge ticked off the points on her fingers. "You don't have evidence. Period. Not only couldn't you convict Mr. Pugh, you didn't have enough to arrest him. I will deal with you later."

The judge turned toward Whip. We held our collective breaths. We had to hear it from her lips.

"It is so entered into the record that there is insufficient evidence to arrest, prosecute, or convict Mr. Pugh of the murder of his wife." Judge Hamilton looked Whip in the eye. "Mr. Pugh, all charges are dismissed with prejudice. You are free to go. You have the court's deepest apology."

"Thank you, Your Honor." Whip's voice was a croak.

The gavel banged one last time. Whip was free. He turned just in time to brace himself for Alex's launch over the railing. Emilie pushed through the swinging gate and threw herself into his arms as well. Behind both kids, Bette and the Colonel were hugging and crying, and Johnny and I hugged and cried.

Whip freed a hand and gripped Vince's. His attorney, his Vinnie, had gotten him off.

As Vince started up the aisle, Johnny and I flanked him, talking earnestly but quietly. Vince stopped, asked a couple of questions, and took a thick envelope from Johnny. He turned back toward Whip and mouthed, "I'll call you."

Waving the envelope, Vince left.

CHAPTER SIXTY-ONE

I heard a disturbance outside the courtroom. I had a sneaky suspicion I knew what it was. I glanced at Johnny, who opened his eyes wide, shrugged, and looked at the ceiling. For a second, I caught a glimpse of the impish little boy he once was.

The district attorney pushed through the door and into chaos.

"Mr. Weed! Mr. Weed!"

"How does it feel to lose your second high-profile murder case?"

"Was Mr. Pugh guilty like the murderer a few years back?"

"Or was your office sloppy this time too?"

"What's this going to do to your re-election campaign?"

Whip, with Emilie and Alex on either side, Bette and the Colonel right behind, followed Johnny and me through the doors just as Weed shoved the breaking news reporter from the NBC affiliate against the wall. Cameras captured everything. District Attorney George Weed's re-election campaign and his career were both in the dumpster. No more would he ruin the reputation of honest men.

Other reporters, both print and TV, turned toward Vince, who stood off to the side. "I have a brief statement. This hearing should have taken place two months ago. The district attorney's office delayed turning over copies of the evidence, which judicial rules of procedure mandate. As a result, we were forced to ask Judge Hamilton to review what the district attorney said would prove my client, Mr. Pugh, guilty of the murder of his wife."

"Is he innocent?" A reporter from the *Richmond Times-Dispatch* shouted.

Vince continued without missing a beat. "As it turned out, the judge ruled Mr. Pugh is innocent, and the evidence proved it. Judge Hamilton dismissed all charges and set Mr. Pugh free. Now, please, allow this family to leave and spend some time together."

As we walked through the crowd, the NBC reporter called out one last question. "If Mr. Pugh is innocent, doesn't that mean the murderer is still on the loose?"

Vince smiled a real smile. He let silence tell the rest of the story. He tucked a manila envelope under his arm.

We followed Whip to the jail where he signed papers, received an envelope containing his personal effects, and shook hands with the police officers, even Pete, his main jailer. It was just like Whip to be thanking his captors for humane treatment.

The Colonel and Bette drove to the house. Johnny tossed Whip the keys to his truck so he could take Emilie and Alex to lunch. I climbed into my Jag with Johnny and followed the Colonel and Bette. Bette talked with Emilie before court and knew she wanted to throw a welcome home party. The idea appealed to all of us.

"I don't have to get dressed up, do I?" While Johnny looked terrific in his court suit and tie, I knew he'd be much more comfortable in jeans and boots or sneakers.

"No, funny man. No tie. Go home and change. Be back by six for cocktails." I stood on tiptoe and kissed him, before pushing him toward the door.

"If you don't mind, Max, I'll just watch a little TV and catch a nap." The Colonel had taken his shoes off and put his feet on an ottoman. His head nodded as his chin sank toward his chest.

"You do that, Colonel."

Bette made her husband a sandwich and left it beside his chair. She stood before the fridge list for long moments. There was so much she didn't understand.

After stopping for a quick lunch at the same diner where Whip made his first to-do list, Bette and I shopped for food. I'd spent little time with Whip's parents, although I talked with them every few days before and after Whip's arrest. Bette was my polar opposite—

quiet, a homemaker, married to the Colonel since high school.

Whip's truck was in the drive when we rolled up with our groceries. Emilie ran out to help unload and asked if we had everything. Bette assured her Dad's favorites would be on the table.

"Yippee," Emilie whispered. "Let's make it a surprise, okay?"

"Won't that be hard with Dad in the house?"

"Oh, he's upstairs getting the full story of what Alex did to help. They could be there the rest of the afternoon. You know Alex. No story takes less time than the original event."

The Colonel snuffled in the family room, the TV tuned to an old movie, sandwich crumbs on the plate beside his chair.

We women retired to the kitchen. Emilie ironed a white linen tablecloth and napkins and set the dining room table with Merry's favorite china and crystal, which we only used at the holidays. *Why not use the good stuff all the time? If it breaks, it breaks.*

Around six, Whip and Alex came downstairs. Johnny arrived at the same time and gave me a huge hug and a kiss on the cheek. The Colonel mixed martinis and opened beers. We toasted Whip's return. Emilie put snacks and hors d'oeuvres on the poolside table. We drank, ate, and talked until we had the whole story exposed.

I thought about my latest middle-of-the-night chat with Emilie. Even though Whip was out of jail, he was always on the road. How could he keep that up without someone to care for the kids? I was here, but maybe he'd want someone else.

I never gave "after Whip was released" a single thought. Well, I was in "after" now.

"We have all your favorites, Dad," Emilie continued.

"Honey, anything not served on a tray with a plastic spork will be a favorite."

We laughed, but Whip's time in jail was the elephant in the kitchen. We had to talk about it, to acknowledge how much our family changed.

"Steaks on the grill, if the men will do the honors." I held up the starter.

Whip took the hint and the starter. With the grill heating and the potatoes nearly done, Emilie and Bette made a huge salad while I put a loaf of sourdough bread in the oven to warm.

The Colonel carried a tray of ribeyes out to the patio while the women attended to other tasks in the kitchen. Their laughter drifted in through the open window. Soon enough, word would spread through the neighborhood Whip was home, but I was grateful for a quiet evening with just the family. We would plan a welcome home party but with a different outcome from the one we had for Merry.

"Are we eating outside?" Whip called through the window.

"Not quite warm enough even with the patio heaters."

Whip flipped steaks onto the platter and carried them into the house, his posse following. After dinner, we sat around with various drinks, coffee, and strawberry shortcake. Bette was the first to talk about what brought us all together. "What's the significance of the list in the kitchen?"

"That's the 'fridge list,' Gramma," Alex said. "It's what we did to get Dad out of jail and prove Dracula killed Mom."

The kids had been so wrapped up in their roles, the whole process was routine.

I brought the list to the table. The Colonel hadn't seen it. He stared at it as I completed it. While I wrote, Alex and Johnny explained the Dracula nickname and the significance of Kiki.

"So why did he kill Merry?" the Colonel asked. "Was he playing God?"

"More like a rabid Henry Higgins trying and failing to turn Eliza Doolittle into a lady," I said. "When he realizes he hasn't reproduced Kiki, his first and most likely only love, he kills the women."

"Women? You mean he killed someone before Merry?"

"Yes, he did. Alex?"

Alex told everyone how he searched the Internet for all references to Hunter and how he followed his career as he moved westward from New York.

"Dad, don't get mad. After I hacked into his computer, it was easy."

"You did what you thought was necessary. Just don't make hacking a habit. Okay?" Whip tried to look stern, but I knew he was too proud of his son's ingenuity to be angry.

"Okay." Alex beamed from ear to ear.

"Do you remember, Whip, how Hunter bragged about being an artist?" I asked.

"Yes. It was the first time I met him."

"Well, most artists keep portfolios of their works." I prodded my grandson to continue. "Go on, Alex."

"Dracula kept pictures of all the Kiki-soon-to-bes in a password-protected file. It was easy to figure out the password."

"It was?" the Colonel asked.

"Like du-uh. 'Kiki.' How unoriginal. Anyway, I printed the file and searched the Internet. I found several victims." Alex stopped and stared out the window. I could tell something just clicked.

"What? What's the matter?"

"Um, nothing. Just some ice cream on a sore spot in my mouth."

I knew he was lying. So did Emilie, who turned the color of the whipped cream she piled on her strawberries. Beads of sweat popped out on her upper lip. She looked at me, or perhaps through me.

With one eye on Emilie, I explained how we put together packages of materials for the police departments all over the eastern half of the country with similar unsolved murders.

"Those police departments are now paying a lot of attention," Johnny said. "Believe me, they're very interested in Hunter. If we could find his gun, we could close out at least four more murders. Next, I visited the parents of the missing women and told them what we thought happened."

"They must have been happy to know their daughters hadn't been forgotten."

"Not Lydia-Marie's. They'd moved on and convinced themselves they'd never know the truth. My visit churned up raw memories."

"You're wrong, Johnny," Bette said. "Mothers always want to know, even if it causes pain. You did the right thing."

"Thanks, Bette."

"So, what do you think happened to Merry's missing stuff?"

"Who knows? Hunter probably tossed it in a dumpster," Johnny replied.

"Have you turned your evidence over to the local police too?" Bette looked at the fridge list again.

"That's the problem, Grandma. We don't have any real evidence against Dracula," Emilie said.

"The police have bullets that may match the one ..." Johnny stumbled to a halt and swallowed hard. "Well, if the gun ever turns up, they'll be able to close their cases."

"You mean that if and when Hunter kills again, there'll be another piece to the puzzle?" Whip asked.

"We gave Vince everything we found after the hearing. He's going to look into Hunter and see if he can't convince District Attorney Weed to reopen the investigation. This time Hunter will be under a magnifying glass." I topped off glasses for those still sipping wine.

The party broke up around ten, since the Colonel and Bette had a long drive to get home by eleven. As we waved goodbye, I overheard part of a conversation between Emilie and Alex.

"Do you have Mom's, um ...?"

"I'll get it." Alex headed for the stairs.

"He's coming." Emilie followed.

"Yeah. I know. Are you ready?"

"Yes."

I didn't know what they meant, but I didn't like what I heard.

CHAPTER SIXTY-TWO

I woke from a bad dream and glanced at the bedside clock. It was three forty-eight on the third morning after Whip was released from jail. Something felt different. The house held its breath.

Whip had reset the perimeter alarms again. If anyone broke in, the noise would wake the neighborhood, and the dead would walk the earth. I heard a more intimate sound, the squeak of the den door. *Gotta get Whip to oil those hinges.* Still, I was awake before the squeak.

I slipped out of bed, opened my closet, and reached up to the top shelf where I'd hidden a gun. I settled my thirty-two caliber revolver in a hand too small for a Glock, loaded it, and eased my bedroom door open.

Alex's door was ajar. His screensaver glowed. Emilie's door was shut tight. No light filtered down the hall, even though I knew I'd left a night-light burning. Now it was out. I peered into the blackness and looked for something blacker and denser than normal. Near the bottom of the stairs I saw movement. *Going up or down?*

I crept to the top of the stairs and watched the shadow move down the hall toward the back of the house. I didn't sense danger in the shadow and assumed Whip too had awakened when the atmosphere in the house changed. I couldn't be certain. I dodged the squeaky tread and followed the shadow.

The air conditioner was off for the year, yet a cold draft stirred along the floor. Up ahead, the sliding glass door in the family room must be open. I put one bare foot in front of the other and moved toward the back of the house. The door to the family room was ajar, and a light cast thin shadows into the hall. I left the shadow and ducked into the kitchen.

I eased an eye around the door frame from the kitchen until the family room came into view. The outline of a man was backlit by the pool lights. Why hadn't the alarms gone off?

I squinted at the man. Son of a bitch! Hunter! Invading our personal space, violating our house. This murderer of five women was in our family room. I was about to call him out when Hunter spoke.

"I've come for you."

Is he talking to me? No, he wasn't looking at the kitchen. Was he talking to the shadow in the hall?

"I told you I'm not going."

Dear God, Emilie! Sitting in the same chair where the Colonel napped earlier. I couldn't see her; the side of the chair was too tall.

"Yes, you are. You're young enough. The others were too old." Hunter took a few steps closer to the chair where Emilie sat. Light from the reading lamp illuminated his face.

"Young enough for what? To become Kiki? I know all about her. You tried to make Mom into Kiki. It didn't work."

The shadow edged closer to the hall doorway.

"I can make you into Kiki. You'll love being her. She was so perfect."

"I don't want to be perfect. I don't want to be Kiki. I want to be imperfect Emilie Pugh, the daughter of Merry, who you killed because you couldn't play God."

"Play God? I don't play God!" Hunter took a step forward, his face radiating rage.

If I'd been sleeping, I'd have been awake now. The hall shadow slipped into the family room and blended into the wall. Hunter was concentrating so hard on Emilie that the shadow could have been covered with neon lights and sirens and gone unnoticed.

I didn't dare flinch, because the shadow was in Hunter's line of sight. I gripped my gun and waited. I knew I'd shoot if he made a move toward Emilie.

Oh God, he's holding a gun on Emilie! I could hit him, but

Hunter might, just might, squeeze off a shot. At that moment, I couldn't take the risk.

"I know about Lydia-Marie. The police found her body. I know about the other women you shot. And you killed Kiki."

"I did not kill Kiki!" Hunter shrieked, spittle flying. "I loved her."

"You killed her as surely as you killed my mother. You killed Kiki on the operating table. You shot Mom. We talked to your mother. She told us everything."

"That bitch doesn't know shit. She can't know what I've gone through." Hunter waved his left hand. He'd graduated from a hard cast to a splint.

"She knows you're sick. She knows you're a serial killer."

"I am not a serial killer!" More spit droplets sprayed the air as Hunter became hysterical.

I held my breath and prayed Alex didn't come galloping downstairs. He was such a trouble magnet that he could cause Hunter to pull the trigger.

"What do you call killing those women? Didn't you shoot them? With that gun?"

"They were experiments that didn't work. They had to go. Like in a lab, when we euthanize animals after they're of no further use."

"If you kidnap me and I don't turn out to be Kiki, will you euthanize me too?"

Cold sweat trickled down my back. I was amazed at Emilie's composure. Raising my gun half an inch at a time, I took aim. I saw the slightest glint when Whip raised his gun. I probably had seconds before Whip went for the double tap.

"I won't fail. I have drugs to erase your memory. You'll be Kiki within a year and all mine." Hunter moved toward Emilie again.

"No."

There was a small rustle as Emilie shifted.

Hunter backed up and raised his gun.

Whip stepped through the door, sighted, and squeezed off two shots. I fired at the same instant. Hunter jerked down, then up, then sideways before he fell to the carpet. Blood flowed from his torso, neck, and head.

Whip ran into the room and dragged Emilie out of the chair.

"Daddy!" Emilie threw her arms around his neck and almost strangled him. She was shaking so hard she nearly fell down.

"It's over, baby. It's all over. He can't hurt you now."

"I knew he was coming. He's been following me since he killed Mom. I've been waiting every night since you got home."

Emilie backed away and turned toward the body. It was then Whip realized she had a gun.

"Did, did I kill him, Dad?"

Whip took the gun. Merry's little twenty-five-caliber Beretta.

"I don't think so, baby. I hit him twice."

"I hit him at least once." I walked into the pool of light and kicked Hunter's gun away.

"Look." I pointed. Hunter wore a double pair of latex gloves.

The smell of cordite filled the room.

"Oh wow! Is that Dracula? Is he dead? Who killed him?"

Alex ran toward the bloody body. I snatched him before he could get a closer look. Even though he was all boy, he didn't need to get close up and personal with brain matter on the walls.

"Who knows? Call it a family affair."

We had a dead man in the family room with at least three bullets in him and blood and bone fragments all over the glass door. I took the kids into the kitchen and closed the door. They'd already seen too much. Whip called nine-one-one.

EPILOGUE

Six weeks had passed since Hunter lay dead in our family room. Three of us hit him four times. Whip aimed the best. He got Hunter in the throat and head. I aimed at his chest, too, but shot him through his armpit into his heart.

Emilie's bullet went in his torso. I never knew who fired the killing shot because the autopsy results were inconclusive. I didn't care.

One major change. I no longer fainted at the sight of blood. Or brains on the wall, drapes, and glass door.

The night it happened, Alex thought a dead body was "way cool" and wanted to see it again, but Whip sent him across the street to the neighbors. The rest of us stayed until the police released us. Our old friend Jerry was one of the cops who answered the nine-one-one call. He kept the others from losing their heads. The crime lab came. This time we made sure it did a thorough job.

Not that there was any doubt about what happened. Hunter was in the house, a gun near his hand with his bullet lodged in Whip's chair where Emilie sat, latex gloves on his right hand. My teeth chattered from the adrenaline rush wearing off. Emilie held up better than I would have as she answered the questions.

"Why did you think Dr. Hunter was coming to kidnap you? How could you know?" Jerry asked.

Emilie excused herself, went up to her room and returned with an envelope. She handed it to Jerry. "Here."

"Jesus."

Whip looked over his shoulder. When Alex hacked into Hunter's computer, he found a file on Emilie. It contained pictures taken all over Riverbend, even in her bedroom.

"He's been stalking me." Emilie's voice shook.

I leafed through the pictures: long-range shots at school, in the backyard pool, when she was asleep in the house. There was a picture taken in his office and a variety of computer images with the changes he planned to make. Couple those with the information I got from "Joe the PI," and the police had no doubt about Hunter's intentions.

"That was one sick son of a bitch. Too bad he's dead. We have enough to send him to death row."

"We have more." I gave Jerry the *Cliff Notes* version about the other women we thought Hunter murdered.

"Christ on a motorcycle!" Jerry shook his head.

The piece de resistance was the recording Emilie made while she talked to Hunter. She caught his confession and his bragging about his future plans on her cell.

I felt certain there would be no repercussions from the shooting, but I was worried District Attorney Weed might see another open door. He filed no charges, however. The Richmond police sent ballistics reports and copies of other photos from Hunter's computer to out-of-state police to close their cold cases.

As soon as he could, Whip took Alex and Emilie to Peru to wrap up the project he started before Merry's death. We arranged for both kids to continue counseling with doctors Silberman and Schwartz through Internet and satellite phones. Tiny digital cameras gave the kids private sessions with their therapists. Emilie suffered recurring nightmares she killed Hunter. Alex showed no outward effect, but Dr. Silberman said he was very much overly stimulated and needed the diversion of being away from his house. Peru was the perfect place for him to begin healing.

And me? I promised Whip I'd get rid of the house, since he said he never wanted to set foot inside again. Jerry Skelton dropped by with a card for a company that cleaned up crime scenes. Who knew you could make a living cleaning up gore?

I hired a different crew to clean, repaint, and redecorate the house. It sold in two weeks in a hot market. Besides, there was a ghoulish curiosity about a place where someone was shot and killed. I packed up what we wanted to keep and donated what we no longer needed. All but Whip's favorite chair. It, and the bullet hole in the headrest, went out with the trash the day after Hunter's death. None of us wanted to see it again.

Emilie came to my room the night after we killed Hunter. I'd left my door ajar, expecting a midnight chat. She didn't disappoint me.

"Have you thought about how you're going to take care of us?"

"Only every minute since your mom died. What do you have in mind?"

"I was wondering if we could find a way to travel with Dad and still keep up with our schoolwork." Emilie put an orange and brown head on my shoulder.

"You mean, homeschooled on the road? Alex'd love 'on the road' but would hate 'homeschooled.'"

"Time for him to grow up, huh?"

We would have a very different lifestyle. I had to think about all the pros and cons, the logistics. That night it was too much to wrap my brain around.

"Just think about it, okay?" Emilie wiggled out of bed and closed my door behind her. There was a deep sigh. Wasn't mine. Or was it?

CPSIA information can be obtained at www.ICGtesting.com
Printed in the USA
LVOW12s1126170314

377731LV00002B/127/P